BLOOD OCEAN

D0584687

WWW.ABADDONBOOKS.COM

An Abaddon Books™ Publication
www.abaddonbooks.com
abaddon@rebellion.co.uk

This omnibus published in 2012 by Abaddon Books™,
Rebellion Intellectual Property Limited,
Riverside House, Osney Mead, Oxford, OX2 0ES, UK.

10 9 8 7 6 5 4 3 2 1

Editor-in Chief: Jonathan Oliver
Desk Editor: David Moore
Cover Art: Luke Preece
Design: Simon Parr & Luke Preece
Marketing and PR: Keith Richardson
Creative Director and CEO: Jason Kingsley
Chief Technical Officer: Chris Kingsley

ISBN (UK): 978-1-907992-86-5
ISBN (US): 978-1-907992-87-2

Printed in the US

THE AFTERBLIGHT CHRONICLES

BLOOD OCEAN

WESTON OCHSE

ABADDON
BOOKS

ACKNOWLEDGEMENTS

MAHALO TO PAUL Legerski for his first read and to Faeri and Kimo Kalanui for their lessons in the history and culture of Hawaii and its peoples. Thanks also goes out to Robert Heinlein and Edgar Rice Burroughs for showing me how action yarns are meant to be made. Double-handed shakas go out to Luke Preece, David Moore and Jonathan Oliver for letting me play in the Afterblight sandbox. You made me feel welcome. And Mahalo Nui Loa to my wife, Yvonne, for putting up with long hours of my Pali Boy shenanigans as I acted out many of the scenes before I wrote them. Aloha Au Ia'oe.

For
The Kalanui Family

In the first decade of the new millennium, a devastating plague, known as The Cull, swept the planet, killing all but those with the blood group 'O-negative.' Cities crumbled, countries ceased to exist, and entire populations lay dead and rotting. Civilization tumbled and in its place arose a world ruled by petty tyrants, sadistic fiends and religious zealots. Small, disparate communities of survivors sprang up, trying desperately to build a brave new world, fighting against all odds to survive.

This is the tale of such a group. This is the tale of *Blood Ocean*.

CHAPTER ONE

PALI BOY AKAMU hid in the shadows beneath the piping on the main deck of the old fishing boat. He'd been waiting until the fire guard passed before moving on. Nothing worse than fire aboard a ship, especially a floating city made of ships. In reality, the chances of a fire were so slim as to be non-existent, but the possible consequences of such a conflagration were so terrible that the tradition was maintained. So a fire guard dressed in all white and carrying a Cousteau tube to light his way made his rounds, then moved onto the next ship. Probably earning an extra ration of fish cakes for his family.

The Pali Boy could just make out the red-painted, flaking letters of the words *All Day Rental*. According to old Donnie Wu, who was a walking, talking encyclopedia of the time before, the boat had once taken tourists into the ocean to catch fish as a form of entertainment. When Akamu had asked what a tourist was, Wu had explained, 'It's like a refugee who only wants to have fun.' The concept was beyond Akamu's understanding, but he acknowledged that there had been such a thing when the world was different, before the plague, before everything changed and their life was lived on the water.

Now the former tourist fishing boat was home to a menagerie of Chinese, Filipinos and Indonesians. Like all of the other ships in the floating city, all were descendants of those who had worked aboard the boats, deciding a life on the water was far safer than one on land, where predators of all types, especially those of the two-legged variety, roamed freely. Also, on land, the ability to feed such a population would have been a challenge. On the ocean, it wasn't so hard.

Still, in order to eat, Akamu had to worry about how to either bypass the Water Dogs so he could get a free line in the water, or find enough to pay them so that he could feed his family. Although the Corpers aboard the Freedom Ship provided weekly fish cakes produced from fish cultivated and stored in their bins, most of it couldn't be trusted not to have mercury poisoning or disease, so the Water Dogs, who controlled everything below the waterline, were the only option.

But they cost, which was why he was skulking across the decks of the city rather than swinging through the rigging like he'd normally do. Although he could move easier if he traveled the way of a Pali Boy, the last thing he wanted was for Kaja and the others to find out what he was doing. Not that he was doing anything illegal—it was just frowned upon, and there would be no end to the crap they'd heap on him if they found out.

"Who goes there?"

Akamu halted. His left hand automatically went to the pouch on his side. He had to keep it safe. So who was challenging him? Nautical sunrise was just beginning. The sky was a lighter gray than the water, but barely provided any illumination. Try as he might, he couldn't see who was making the challenge. He dragged his foot heavily across the wooden deck to see if he could get the person to talk once more and determine where the voice was coming from.

"I can hear you," the voice warned.

Akamu finally made out a darker shadow near the rail,

about a dozen feet down the walkway and close to the deck.

"It's a Pali Boy." He took two steps closer.

"Can't be. Pali Boys are like the birds." The shadow put his thumbs together and waggled his fingers above his head. "They live in the air."

"Not this Pali Boy. I'm on an errand." Akamu took another step and was finally able to see the speaker's features. He was an elderly Chinese man, his eyes sewn shut. Probably lost to Minamata disease.

"You're not to rob us," the Chinese man warned. "My daughter has a gun on you."

Akamu glanced around but couldn't see her. It was probably an empty threat. He didn't have to worry about it anyway. He was just trying to make his way across the city to the Mga Taos for delivery. The longer he held the package, the heavier it became. He'd be glad to get rid of it.

"Don't worry, old man. I'm not here to rob anyone. I just need to pass."

The old man nodded. "Just so you know."

Akamu stepped carefully past him. "I know. I know," he said, then crossed onto another ship using a gang plank.

Los Tiburones could have transported their own drugs, but they'd have to pay. No captain or ship's mate allowed anyone else to transport commerce across their ships without getting a piece of the action. And when *Los Tiburones* moved, it was automatically believed that they were transporting drugs, which made Akamu a perfect alternative. They'd never question a Pali Boy. After all, Pali Boys were empty-headed, muscle-bound thrill-seekers, not drug runners.

He was carrying Waffle Dust. He'd watched Lopez-Larou weigh out three hundred grams of white powder, slide it into a paper bag, then fold it into a pouch. She'd tied the package in a special way which he couldn't replicate, then warned him against trying the product. She shouldn't have worried. Using the drug was the farthest thing from Akamu's mind.

"It's a mixture of MDMA and amphetamines. What they used to call X and Speed. Everyone wants life to be just a little better. This will make it better for awhile."

Then she gave him directions and made him repeat them back to her three times, and he went on his way. Once the delivery was made, he'd return for his fee. If it was as promised, it would be enough to keep his mother and little brother in Water Dog-supplied fish for a week. They could use the protein, and the nutrients.

The next ship was much like the one he'd left—some sort of fishing trawler. He'd never been on it, but had swung above it before. He remembered that there had been nothing to set it apart from any of the others.

A breeze stirred the air as the sky lightened, and Akamu wrinkled his nose. The stench of rotting plankton and raw sewage came from somewhere nearby, and he could smell a sharp chemical tinge which he recognized as decomposing jellyfish. The captain and mates of this ship should be keel-hauled for keeping it in such a state. He hurried across, eager to get to the next ship and away from the smell.

In the end it was his hurrying that got him killed.

The wind picked up and began to spin the turbines high above the bird nets and the rigging. They whined as they began to move. As on all the ships, the wind turbines powered cells in the holds that provided power for much of the day-to-day operations. Gone were the engines or any need for combustion. Refined fuel was as rare as an albino narwhal. Wind power was all they had now, augmented by the occasional biological solution, like the Cousteau tube lights, containing bioluminescent arrow worms harvested by the Water Dogs from the ocean depths.

He rushed past the old wheelhouse, which had been converted into a kitchen. A light was on, illuminating an ancient Filipina just beginning to boil water for tea. He made eye contact and smiled, and she stared at him with something just short of malice. This wasn't his ship and he wasn't welcome.

Chased by the stench and the hatred in the woman's eyes, Akamu didn't notice the trip line until he was falling face first onto the deck. He was barely able to bring his hands up to cushion his fall. When he hit, he rolled over and jerked his legs over the line.

Three members of the Fists of Righteous Harmony—known as Boxers—hovered over him, long-braided hair queues falling from the backs of their otherwise shaven heads. They wore black on black. Even their faces and foreheads were painted black.

"Sorry," he said, pushing himself to a sitting position. "Didn't know you had this territory marked. I must have missed it in the dark." He gave them his best *please don't fuck with me* smile.

"Your loss," the one in the middle said. He held a metal briefcase in his left hand. The thumb of his right hand was hooked in his belt.

Akamu wondered what was in the briefcase.

"What brings you through here?" the Boxer asked.

Akamu avoided the compulsion to reach around and check the package to make sure it hadn't become dislodged; the movement would be a dead giveaway. He smiled harder to cover his nervousness as he vowed that this was the last time he was going to do side work for *Los Tiburones*. His smile evaporated as a foot caught him in the side of the head, sending him rolling to his right. He gritted his teeth at the pain.

"He's talking to you, Poi Boy," the Boxer who kicked him said. "What are you carrying?"

Akamu fought the urge to fight. He had to keep a low profile, especially since he was amidst a Corper hunter-killer team. They must be. This couldn't be just some random gang protecting their territory. They were too well attired. They were casual, but too professional. They were definitely working for the Corpers. They might be after him, but he doubted it. He just needed to find out what they wanted, maybe point them in the right direction, and he could be on his way.

His heart pounded, and sweat beaded on his forehead. Still forcing a smile, he pulled himself to his knees, and in the process slid a media stick from his pocket. He kept it to record some of his more daring stunts; he felt the need to use it now. If nothing else, the other Pali Boys would enjoy seeing the panache he employed while avoiding these Boxers. He kept the stick in the hollow of his right hand, then rubbed his head where it had been kicked with the back of the same hand. The shadows hid the media stick as he pointed it towards his attackers. He pressed record and aimed the low-light camera in their direction.

"I'm not carrying anything," he finally said, as he got back to his feet. He wiped dirt from his bare chest, and casually straightened the pouch on his back hip. Maybe too casually, because the Boxer carrying the briefcase nodded towards it.

"Is that what you aren't carrying?"

Akamu shrugged. "Probably."

"Who's it for?"

The other two attackers had positioned themselves on either side of him. He glanced at them. They held no visible weapons, but by the way they held their arms they seemed like they wouldn't need them. Akamu calculated his odds and didn't like what he came up with.

Suddenly they fell on him with hammer fists into his chest and stomach, driving all the air out of him in an incredible timpani orchestration of pain. He lost control of his legs and fell to his knees. A final blow knocked him all the way over, and he landed on his side. He almost lost the media stick, but somehow managed to stuff it back into his pocket.

Pain thrummed through his torso, and he gasped for a breath that wouldn't come. In desperation, he kicked out with both legs, striking the man on his left just below the knee and driving him to the ground. Then he brought his right hand around in a haymaker and clocked the other attacker between the eyes. Akamu kept rolling in that direction, over his downed opponent until he came to a stop at the boat's side rail.

He glanced at the water below and saw a Water Dog staring at him. Akamu could slide in right now and escape, but then he'd owe them a ransom. It was hardly worth it. He had things under control. He'd made it out of worse situations.

He pulled himself to his feet and lashed out with his other leg. He tried to catch the remaining attacker in the groin, but his opponent managed to dance away.

Akamu decided to abandon any considerations of stealth now that he'd been discovered. He searched for the nearest line into the rigging; if he got high, there was no way the Boxers could follow. He saw what he was looking for atop the wheelhouse. Leaping over his fallen foes, he took six running steps before he felt a hand grasp at the pouch on his back. He had no choice but to slow down. Worse than a ransom would be to lose the delivery. *Los Tiburones* weren't known for their understanding.

Spinning, Akamu slammed a protective hand over the pouch. "What the fuck you want with me, brah? I'm just trying to mind my business. Why don't you mind yours?"

"You are our business," said the one holding the briefcase.

Akamu realized that he did not want to know what was in it. Whatever it was it couldn't be good.

"Listen, you don't know who you're messing with. This is not just *my* business. There are others involved."

"We don't care about your drugs. We want your blood."

"My blood?" Akamu gulped and backed away until the side of the wheelhouse halted him. He was in more serious trouble than he'd suspected. He spun and hooked a foot over the window ledge, and saw the old woman again. Her glare had been replaced by a face carved in terror; she looked away and covered her face with her hands. He was levering himself onto the roof, when he felt four hands grab him and hurl him to the deck. The impact stunned him.

One of them ripped the pouch free from his back, while the other tied his arms behind him. He came to his senses in time to see the third one step forward with the metal case.

"Please—leave me alone!"

"'*Please leave me alone,*'" one of the Boxers mimicked, in a high-pitched whine.

"We'll leave you when we're done," the one in the center said. "Hold him still." He kneeled and opened the box.

The lid hid his actions, so Akamu couldn't see what was in there until it was prepared and ready. He struggled against the Boxers, but couldn't do much with his hands tied. Still, he got in a kick, sending one doubling over, clutching his stomach.

The Boxer lifted a mechanism from the box, from which nine thick needles extended on glass tubes. He straddled

Akamu, sitting on his pelvis, and ripped Akamu's shirt away with his free hand.

"Hey, wait a minute, I—"

Akamu never finished. The Boxer shoved the nine-needled device into his chest.

Akamu opened his mouth to scream, but nothing came out. The pressure was too much. He gaped as the tubes turned red, his eyes rolling back into his head. He tried to focus on what was being done to him, but his body refused his command. The sounds of the floating city were replaced by a singular thumping that was soon the only thing he heard. After a moment, he recognized it as his heart beating. The sound took over his entire consciousness. He concentrated on it. He knew it for what it was—his life blood.

Then it began to slow.

And then he was gone.

CHAPTER TWO

DADDY, WHERE ARE the rest of the people?
  They're out there somewhere, wishing they were here.
  Why don't we invite them, if they want to come here?
  There's not enough room and not enough food.
  But the Corpers would help them, right? They'd figure out a way to help them, just like they've helped us, right?
  Corpers help themselves first.
  Then they'd help them?
  I wouldn't count on it.

KAVIKA KAMILANI STOOD high above the deck, staring far out to the horizon where he could see open water. Between him and the gray-blue of the Pacific Ocean were hundreds of ships of every type and size, welded, hammered, tied, chained or otherwise cobbled together. Grabbing the rigging for the bird nets with one hand and balancing on a support cable with his feet, the Pali Boy turned one hundred and eighty degrees to see more of the same—ship after ship after ship, until they were no longer individuals but a single floating city: *Nomi No Toshi*, or 'City on the Waves.' And there, blocking out the horizon like a black cloud, was the ten-story Freedom Ship, home to the Corpers, whose lifestyle was built upon the suffering of all others.

Akani swung in beside him. "Whatchu doing giving stinkeye at the haolies, brah? They gonna find out and come get you."

Akani and Kavika couldn't be more different. Akani was a head taller than Kavika. His arms were thick as anchor cables and covered with before-time tattoos, where Kavika's skin was smooth and unadorned and his muscles were just beginning to develop. Akani had his hair cut into a mohawk, but Kavika liked to keep his long. What they both shared were ready smiles, and now Akani flashed his at Kavika.

But the younger Hawaiian wore his ever-present worry on his face like a birthmark. "No stinkeye," he said. "Just wondering what it was like before."

Akani shrugged. "Why think about things you can't control? Might as well wonder why the fish swim in the ocean or the Sky Winkers stare at the sky."

The two of them wore shorts down to their knees. Cured sharkskin was lashed to their forearms and palms, providing protection against the burning of the ropes and cables as they used them to transit the heights of the city. On their feet were slips of rubber, cut to fit their soles and lashed across the top of their feet to provide better traction, especially on the wet decks and rigging.

Kaja joined them. Tall and lean, he was the leader of the Pali Boys. Kavika couldn't help but admire everything he did. Even the way he stood was cool, and made Kavika shift his position until he could match it. Kaja's skin was free of tattoos except for a single thick line that began at his hairline and ran down his face, neck and chest to disappear into his shorts. He'd Dived the Line and survived. The mark told everyone of his bravery.

"Whatchu two lolly-gagging for?"

Akani glanced at Kavika before he answered. "Little brah says he's waiting for the storm. Wants to become full-time Pali."

Kaja raised his eyebrows and apprised Kavika, who tried to stand straighter under the other's gaze. "You ready to make the leap? You wanna leave part-time and be full-time? Think you can do it, Kavika?"

The Pali Leap was the most dangerous stunt any Pali Boy could ever make, but to become a full-time Pali one had to do it. Like the leap from Nu'uanu Pali Pass on the old island of Oahu in the days of King Kamehameha, if the winds were right, a Pali Boy could jump out and be pushed right back. *If* the winds were right. More than one wannabe full-time Pali Boy had fallen to his death, or worse, been maimed when the winds shifted or suddenly died entirely, as they tried to change their fortunes and garner the respect of the Hawaiian people. When it happened it was considered Lono's will. Kavika wasn't so sure that luck didn't have a lot to do with it, too, and if there was one thing that he didn't have, it was luck.

Akani laughed. "Look at him. He looks sick."

Kavika tried to push the fear away, hide it behind a memory like the others told him to do, but he had nothing scarier than the idea of leaping into the air without a rope, cable or net to hang on to.

Kaja placed a hand on Kavika's shoulder. "Don't worry. Everyone's scared at first. Soon you'll be up here with the rest of us... like your father was, loving life and living large."

Akani leaned back, gripping a line with one hand and howled, "Living large!"

The cry was echoed in the rigging across several ships as other Pali Boys took up the cry. Kavika couldn't help but smile. If the Water Dogs ruled the water, the Pali Boys most certainly ruled the sky.

He watched as a Pali Boy named Oke dove from the top of a container two boats away towards the deck far below. The bungee line slowed him so that by the time he was a few feet from the deck, he came to a stop. He grabbed a line of fish from an unsuspecting haolie, then snapped back. The haolie, an elderly Filipino with gnarled legs and arms, screamed obscenities, Kaja and Akani exchanged grins and took off towards Oke, grabbing lines and netting as they went. They moved upwards so they could dive downwards, propelling themselves through the sky. The nets used by the residents of the city to harvest birds for meat served as the Pali Boy expressway.

Kavika remained. Part of him wanted to join the others, but he knew that if he did he'd be expected to do things he wasn't prepared to do. The Pali Boy motto was to *live large,* and they did so at every opportunity, but he seemed to be more aware of his own mortality than the others. He told himself that he'd love to *live large,* but he also had to find ways to feed his mother and sister. They'd never be able to eat if he became a crip, unable to climb into the heights again.

The wind shifted, bringing him the smell of cooking meat. He searched with his eyes and saw a group of haolies armed with handguns guarding a barrel hollowed out into a barbeque. Kavika's mouth watered. He could almost taste it. But as one of the smaller Pali Boys and with no other male in his family, meat was a very rare treat. He could count on one hand the number of times he'd been able to bring meat home to his mother and sister since his father died. Five Pali Boys hung on ropes above the cooking, just waiting for the haolies to let down their guard. The only thing better than stealing freshly-caught meat was stealing freshly-cooked meat.

Haolies were what the Pali Boys and the rest of the Hawaiian families called everyone else aboard the city, but in truth the city was divided into distinct ethnic lines. The Hawaiians called an old oil tanker home and were its sole occupants. Kavika and his mother lived in the bottom of the bottom. Hawaiian society was based on a meritocracy, so where you lived was based on your ability to contribute.

The Boxers lived aboard an old Chinese guided missile destroyer. They attempted to harvest their own fish and plankton, which put them in constant conflict with the Water Dogs. Water Dogs lived over the sides of the ships and called the water their home. They controlled everything outside of the Corper fish bins and fought constantly to keep anyone else from fishing. If you wanted to eat from the water and didn't want to go through the Corpers, you had to become friends with the Filipino Water Dogs. If you weren't their friends, you were their enemies.

A single ship far out on the edge of the city was occupied by a strange contingent of haolies. Once scientists and engineers, they were called Sky Winkers and spent their time staring at the winking lights in the sky. They said they communicated with the lights, but Kavika and the rest of the Pali Boys thought they were ten waves past crazy.

The Koreans, also known as the People of the Sun, held two ships on the other side of the Freedom Ship which the Japanese called home. The Koreans kept to themselves. Besides an affiliation with *Los Tiburones*, Kavika knew little about them.

Los Tiburones were multi-ethnic gangs. They owned the drug trade and did swift business in betel nut and marijuana. They had harder chemicals if one wanted, but Pali Boys laughed at the idea that something man-made could be better than a natural high.

The Mga Taos were perhaps the strangest of all the groups. They were monkey-worshipers, and allowed the creatures to roam their temple ship at will. Kavika shuddered. If anything was a sign of bad luck, it was the monkeys. No one really knew why, but the Corpers used them to filter blood, something to do with trying to find a cure for Minimata. One moment a haolie would be enjoying life and living as large as he or she could, the next they'd have a monkey surgically attached to their backs, tubes driving their blood through the monkey's organs to filter them for some strange experiment.

The Real People constituted the largest group of organized haolies. They were all white of some sort. They controlled a dozen ships and pretty much lived at peace with everyone.

The last major ethnic group was the Vitamin Vs. Their home comprised three former Russian nuclear submarines, interspersed around the city. The crews had mostly left ship and assimilated into the city, leaving only a core group who still maintained the submarines. Many of them had taken wives or husbands. They were the only contingent of whom the Corpers were afraid. Rumor had it that their missiles were armed and ready. They said that as spread out as the Vitamin

V subs were, all they had to do was begin firing inwards and the city would explode. Kavika didn't know if this was true or not. The only thing Kavika was certain about was if you wanted liquor, the Vs had the best hooch in the city.

A cry went up and was answered across the rigging.

Kavika echoed the call, turning to see where it originated. It took a few seconds, but he pinpointed it at about the time the others did. He climbed the netting, then dove across a gap, catching hold with both hands. Soon he was moving fast, using the nets and cables to propel himself just as he'd learned when he was seven and his father had first taken him into the heights.

They converged on one of the Real People ships. Several dozen haolies surrounded a body on the deck. Pali Boys from everywhere were converging.

Kavika felt a sour pit yaw open in his stomach. It looked like someone had fallen. "Oh, Lono," he murmured, invoking the God of wind and storms. "Let him not be a crip."

Kaja was the first one to get to the body. Akani and Oke were close behind. By the time Kavika arrived, there were twenty Pali Boys either hanging or standing nervously nearby. He slid down a line and joined Kaja on the deck. It was Akamu. He was a year older than Kavika. They'd played in the lower nets as kids and had crazy days leaping into the water, only to be fished out by the Water Dogs.

But Akamu's days of leaping and living large were over.

His skin had turned a light shade of gray. His eyes stared skyward; his mouth open in a scream. His legs were splayed but unbroken. The only signs of life were in his fingers; they slowly curled and uncurled, as if they were trying to clutch the air. His chest held the ghoulish evidence—nine puncture wounds, three by three—that he hadn't fallen.

Kavika brought his own hand to his chest, just as many of the other Pali Boys had already done.

Blood rape.

Someone had taken Akamu's blood.

Akami kneeled and held the Pali Boy's head in his lap. "I got no pulse."

"Then why is he still moving?" Kavika asked.

Akani shook his head. "Reflexes. I don't know."

They all watched as Akamu's hand uncurled, then stayed that way, a spider's legs dead on the ground.

Kaja was the first to act. He spun towards the haolies that had gathered around them. "Which one of you did this? Who did this? Was it you?" He pointed at a man who stood towards the front.

The man's eyes widened and he shook his head. Everyone shook their heads. Many of them stepped back.

Kaja balled his fists. "Who saw this happen?" He turned in all directions, trying to make eye contact with everyone in the crowd, but most looked away.

Kavika could see it if Kaja couldn't. No one here was involved. This was Corper madness. This was something they did. Everyone knew it, but it would be easier if it was a haolie. Pali Boys could get retribution from a haolie. Getting even with the Corpers was like trying to punch the ocean.

Akani waved for several Pali Boys to help him with Akamu. Soon they were carrying him back to the tanker. Kaja fell in line close behind, his head down, while Kavika walked after the Pali leader. Above them swung the others. They took up a mournful howl. And after a while, it seemed as if the wind itself had joined them.

CHAPTER THREE

"YOU NEED TO watch yourself, Kavika. Don't let what happened to Akamu happen to you."

Kavika nodded as he knelt beside his mother and sister. Their assigned living space was five feet wide by six feet deep and less than a hundred feet from the reservoir of oil still stored in the aft section of the hold. Although ventilation shafts had been punched through the sidewalls, the smell of oil permeated everything. That there were people who lived closer to the oil showed that their life wasn't as bad as it could be. But if it wasn't bad, it was close enough to be a first cousin. Kavika hated it. He hated more that he couldn't do anything about it.

"If he hadn't been doing his stunts, this never would have happened," his mother continued.

Kavika knew that he shouldn't argue, but he couldn't help it. "He wasn't stunting, mom. He'd been walking on the decks and was attacked." He dared to look up and saw the impatience in her eyes. He offered her a smile. "If he *had* been stunting, whoever it was would never have got him."

"You don't know that for sure." She frowned as she punched a needle through a stiff length of shark skin. She was making a dive suit for the Water Dogs. Once completed, it would allow her family unlimited fishing rights for a time. But completing it was difficult. Everyone wanted shark skin, and it was rare that the distribution made it to her on the lower levels. It seemed to Kavika that she'd been working on the same suit for years.

"They found the holes in his chest. It was a blood rape," he said.

"Ssst." She cut him off as his ten-year-old sister stirred. "Do you think she needs to hear such things? We know about the holes. Everyone on ship knows about the holes. No need to broadcast the fact."

Kavika watched his sister for a time. He remembered back when she was eight and how much energy she'd had. Who knew that a bad load of fish could so change her existence? Now when she walked it was as if she were a doll and her legs weren't her own. She still had convulsions, although they were becoming more and more infrequent.

"How is Nani?"

"She's getting better. The nurses think she'll come around. You know that she would love for you to spend more time with her."

"I'd love that too," he said.

"Then why don't you?"

How was he to explain something she didn't understand? He had to sleep on deck. He had to be part of the group of boys wanting to be full time Pali. How else was he going to have a chance to better their lives?

As if she could read his mind, she said, "You should try and work with the others up top. The Third Mate is always looking for good maintenance workers. You could learn how to weld and then you'd have a trade."

Kavika shook his head savagely. "I can't do that. I'm a Pali Boy. I can't be something I'm not."

"Your father said the same thing and now look at us."

"My father wouldn't want me to keep hidden in the dark."

"Your father would want you to take care of your sister."

He felt the blood boil inside him. "I am taking care of my sister." He stood. His hands were shaking. "I'm trying to move her and you to a better level."

His mother paused from her work and stared at him. He watched as her anger slid into something much worse... disappointment. "Your sister can't tell which level she is on. But she *can* tell whether you are here or not."

The guilt almost overwhelmed him. On one hand he knew that his sister needed special attention, but on the other he had a need to be with the others so he could have a chance of making their lives better. He felt stifled below decks. Even staying here for the few moments it took to talk to his mother felt like punishment.

He reached over and placed a hand on his sister's forehead. He held it there for a moment, then stood. "Listen, I got to go. Is there anything you need?"

She shook her head sharply and resumed sewing. "We'll make do."

The last time he'd been here they'd argued as well. When he'd left, he'd stooped to give her a kiss and she'd turned away, saying, "Only boys kiss their mothers. You want to be a man, act like one."

Still, he lingered, wanting to kiss her, wanting to hug her and tell her how much he loved her. But by the stern set of her jaw, this was not something she'd accept. The wanting of it wasn't enough, but it was all he'd ever have. After all, he was a descendant of an ancient warrior line and he should act as such.

So Kavika set his jaw, turned and made his way carefully through the families who lived on the lowest of levels. He tried not to make eye contact with anyone. He kept his gaze focused on the square of light filtering down the stairwell from the deck high above. He was so keen on thinking about his mother and sister that be bumped right into someone, knocking them to the ground. He mumbled an apology and continued on.

"Fucking piece of Tuna guts Pali Boy, why don't you watch—" Suddenly the speaker began laughing.

Kavika walked two more steps, but the laughing got even louder. He turned and saw that he'd knocked down a slip of a girl. Then the girl spoke again, and the voice was anything but a girl's.

"Go figure. I get knocked down by a wannabe Pali Boy who can't even stunt on his own."

Kavika stared hard at the figure on the ground for a moment, then turned and walked away.

The figure leaped up and followed. "Wait a minute, Kavika. I was coming to see you and your mother."

"She's back that way," he said, hooking a thumb back the way he'd come. "I'm going this way. See you later."

The figure paused to glance backward into the depths of the hold, then decided to follow Kavika anyway, not catching up until he was almost all the way up the stairs and out into the sea air.

"Kavika, wait!"

She grabbed Kavika's arm, and he stopped and turned. She was a scant Filipina who couldn't weigh more than eighty pounds. Her long hair and fingernails were perfect. Her pouty lips begged to be kissed. Her long, fake eyelashes accentuated her eyes. She went by the name Leilani. If her real name hadn't been Spike, he'd be sorely tempted to kiss her.

"What do you want, Spike?" He gently removed her hand from his arm.

"You hurl me to the ground and this is all you can say?" She wiped at her shimmering gray dress and found a microscopic piece of dirt. "And you got me filthy in the process."

Kavika smiled thinly, then turned and walked to the port rail. Spike hurried after him.

The old oil tanker towered over its closest neighbors, offering a bird's eye view. Immediately below them was a day tripper that had originally come from San Francisco. The words 'Alcatraz' were still edged in a glossy blue that had somehow withstood the elements. The wheelhouse ran from stem to stern, a hundred windowframes lining the walls, but the glass had long since been destroyed, and the windows were now covered by scraps of fabric and recycled trash. It was the morgue ship, the only above-ground enterprise run by the Water Dogs. Akamu's body was probably down there now.

His family would be repaid in shark skin and food for their donation.

When Spike slid next to him, he said, "Akamu was killed."

"I saw him inside. He was your friend, wasn't he?"

"Your brother and I used to swim with Akamu. We were kids together."

"And now that you're a Pali Boy?"

"He was full time. I'm just part time."

They remained silent for awhile. A northerly breeze promised rain. He could almost feel the moisture on his skin.

"They blood raped him."

She nodded. "I saw. My brother said that one of the needles pierced his heart. Sloppy."

"Who would do something like this?"

"Maybe this can explain it." She held out her hand. In it was a media stick.

"Where'd you get this?" he asked, snatching it and checking the display.

"It was lodged in the pocket of Akamu's pants. The area was drenched with blood, so whoever searched him must have missed it."

"Did you look at it?"

She shook her head. "We don't have that kind of old tech. Do you?"

"I don't, but I know who does. Come on."

The main deck of the tanker was composed of a six-storey bridge all the way aft, and a main deck that ran the other ninety per cent of the ship's length. The bridge was the home of the ship's captain, the mates, and Princess Kamala, and also housed all the community areas. The deck was covered in metal cargo containers spaced just far enough apart to allow people to pass between them. The containers were stacked three high. Those lucky enough to live above deck were the families of former ship workers and of full time Pali Boys. Kavika and his family should have lived here as well, but his father's death had knocked them all the way down the hierarchical ladder. He could still remember the morning after his father's death, when they were unceremoniously removed from their third floor container and taken down to the bottom of the hold.

"Kavika, Third Mate is looking for you. Says you need to join a maintenance crew." The speaker was a Pali Boy named Pakelo, sitting at the opening of his container, his feet dangling over the side.

"He knows I'm a Pali Boy. Why does he want me?"

Pakelo shrugged, but they both knew the answer. If Kavika wasn't willing to do every stunt, he wasn't going to get the luxury of living the life of a Pali Boy. Instead, he'd find himself sweeping, mopping, chipping and painting.

"Where is he?" Kavika asked.

"He was here about fifteen minutes ago, so watch out."

"Thanks, Pakelo." Kavika shot a worried glance at Spike; she smiled weakly in return but didn't offer any words of encouragement.

They picked their way through the containers. Most of the doors were either open or removed. Each container was roughly twenty feet deep by eight feet wide. Although they could comfortably hold a family, many were occupied by unmarried Pali Boys. There were even a few empty ones. Sometimes Kavika was greeted by the occupants. Other times they just watched him pass. He knew what they were thinking, especially the mothers and wives. They knew that they could get kicked down the ladder if their fathers or husbands died too. There but by the grace of Pele. Kavika was a reminder to them of all of the bad things that could happen.

They passed a first floor container where a Pali Boy he had once known lived, called Keoni. His father had taken him and the others away to work on the Freedom Ship, but it seemed as if they were back. Kavika started to say hello, then stopped in his tracks.

"What is it?" Spike peered around him, then brought a hand to her mouth. "Oh."

Kavika licked his suddenly dry lips. As Keoni turned his head slightly, the back of the head of the Rhesus monkey became visible. As the ex-Pali Boy continued to turn, he revealed the monkey that had been surgically attached to him. Tubes ran from the back of the monkey's head to the top of the boy's spine. Other tubes transferred fluids from the monkey's torso to his human torso. Kavika couldn't begin to guess what they did, but the connection served to make two into one and seemed irrevocable.

"Every time I see one of them it takes my breath away." Spike's fingernails dug into Kavika's arm.

One of them, she'd said. A monkey-backed.

Suddenly another person appeared at the entrance to the container. Looking haggard and drawn, clothes hanging like ill-fitting drapes from a once-plump frame, the boy's mother noticed the attention. She shook her head like she saw it all the time, then flicked her hand at them.

Kavika was turning to go when he saw the orange-robed figure of a Mga Tao. The hooded man or woman stood vigil over the monkey-backed Pali Boy from the side of a cargo container. Kavika shuddered. Partly he wished he knew what they wanted with the monkey-backed; mostly he hoped he'd never find out.

Kavika moved on. After a blood rape, his greatest fear was to be monkey-backed. The former he could fight, but the latter was Corper sanctioned. Part of the price of belonging to the floating city was to be available for monkey-backing if a match was found. To fight against it was to harm the community. After all, the monkey-backed were walking experiments into possible cures for Minimata. One day some unlucky monkey-backed would be the one from which a cure was developed. On that day his sister would be cured, and until then, Kavika knew that there was nothing he could do about it.

He reached the far end of the main deck. The last few rows of containers nearest the bow housed some of the most important Pali Boys. Kaja, several old leaders, and some of the legacy Pali Boys like Donnie Wu called these home. It was to Donnie's place that they were going. His third floor door was open and it didn't take but a moment for them to climb a knotted line and swing onto the landing.

Half-Chinese and half-Hawaiian, Donnie had never quite fit in. When Kavika's father had been the Pali Boy leader shortly after the plague struck, it was Donnie who'd been his best friend and had protected him. They'd been like brothers, and had helped consolidate the Hawaiian position aboard the tanker and the community that formed upon it. They had created the Pali Boys to help keep the warrior spirit alive, preserve many of the old ways, and stand ready to protect the Hawaiian people aboard the floating city. Since the death of Kavika's father, Donnie was even more of an uncle than he had been before. The only thing he couldn't do to help them was move them back to the main deck. Too much politics. His father had made too many enemies.

"Kavika, Leilani—how are you two?"

Donnie stood in the shadows at the back of the container. His legs were bowed with age. His left arm was twisted at a weird angle, the result of a long fall from a smokestack. He kept his head shaved and wore a Fu Manchu mustache. His arms, chest and thighs were covered with before-time tattoos of scenes of Hilo back before the plague. They were becoming blurred with age, but some could still be made out. Prominent amongst the indigo blur were women in grass skirts, warriors with fishing spears, palm trees, waves, and the Kilauea volcano, with lava rolling down its crusted slopes.

"How are your mother and sister?"

"They're fine, uncle."

"Do they have food?"

"Yes, uncle."

"You know if you need anything you can come to me, right?"

"Yes, uncle. I know. My mother thanks you."

Donnie laughed sadly. "No need to lie to me, boy. We all know your mother hates me. After all, she needs someone to blame. Might as well be me." He looked around for a place for his guests to sit. He found two chairs covered in clothes and junk. With a sweep of his arms he scooted the mess onto the floor "Here, sit."

They did as they were told. After a moment of respect, Kavika murmured, "Uncle, Akamu was blood raped."

Donnie stared at the floor and shook his head. "I heard. They say he didn't survive it. Bad business." He let a moment of silence lengthen, then asked, "So what brings you to Old Wu?"

"This," Kavika said, holding out the media stick. "Spike's brother found it on the body. Kaja missed it."

Donnie held out his hand. Kavika passed the media stick. The old man stared at it and picked a little dried blood away with a fingernail.

"I have something that I think will do the trick." He fumbled through the trash he'd put on the floor, worked a slim square of metal free with some trouble, found a wire, and then hooked it up to the square and the media stick. It took a few moments, but he eventually had a static-laced picture flipping across the square. He banged it twice on the edge of a table and the picture cleared.

"Okay. Here we go. Akamu probably kept this for stunting. I had one. So did your father, Kavika. They've fallen out of popularity, though. Coming up with the equipment to view them is hard."

This was the first Kavika had ever heard of it. "My father had one? What happened to his?"

"It was lost when he dived the line." Donnie shook his head. "Was never seen again. Anyway, my viewer hasn't been used in some time, but it's not like there's been any technology advancements since."

"Kavika thinks that he might have an image of his attackers," Spike pointed out.

"He just might." Donnie fiddled with the buttons. "Here we go. It was night and he had lowlight working. Hmm."

"Why *hmm*?" Kavika asked.

"Yeah. Why *hmm*?" asked Kaja, climbing into the container behind them. "What you doing talking to Uncle, Kavika?"

Kavika stared at Kaja for a moment, wondering how to answer. He didn't have any problems with the Pali Boy leader, but there was politics involved, some of which he understood and some of which he didn't. The worst times were when Kaja and the others sometimes just stopped talking when he joined them.

"Hello, Spike," Kaja said.

"*You* can call me Leilani," Spike said.

When Kaja raised his eyebrows, she stuck her tongue out at him.

"We found Akamu's media stick," said Kavika, before Spike could do anything worse to Kaja.

"Why didn't you bring it to me?"

Kavika glanced at Spike, then back to Kaja.

"Give it a rest, Kaja. You missed it," Donnie Wu said. "These two found it on the body in the morgue. Sloppy, if you ask me."

"I didn't ask you."

Donnie glanced around him, then at Kaja. "You're in my place, Kaja."

Anger flashed across the Pali Boy leader's face. Still, he apologized. "Sorry, uncle. Bad day."

"This might make it better. Look," he pointed at the square. They all watched as two figures coalesced in the low light. It took a moment for the autofocus to kick in, but when it did, there was a clear shot of a man dressed in all black. The queue on his head was unmistakable.

"Boxers," Kavika and Spike said simultaneously.

"What was Akamu doing to get *their* attention?" Donnie asked.

Kaja shook his head. "We'll never know."

"What do you mean?" Kavika asked, finally finding his voice. "We have a clue. Shouldn't we at least find out?"

"What are you going to do? Go to the Boxers and ask them? Think they won't try and kill you too?" Kaja scoffed. "Come on, Kavika. You won't even leap with us, what makes you so brave all of a sudden?"

"He'll do it," Spike said, "And he'll show you."

"What will he show us?" Kaja sneered.

"That he's braver than all the rest of you."

"That's right. Brave like his father, right?"

"Hey!" Donnie stood.

Kavika stared at the Pali leader's tattoo, the one proving that he'd dived the line. His father would have worn a tattoo just like it had he survived.

"Listen, you want to do something about this clue you found, then do it." Kaja took a step towards Kavika and pointed at his chest. "And when I say do it, it means you have to. If you don't, then you are no longer a Pali Boy. Not even a part time Pali. Get it? You and your mother and sister will find yourselves moving ship and working for the Corpers. Hear me? Am I clear, Kavika?"

Kavika nodded. Although Spike had put him in this position, it was an opportunity to show what he could do. Fear and excitement began to build inside him. Still, he had to gulp around his heart, which had found a home in his throat. "I hear."

"Good. Until then you're no Pali. Steer clear and we'll leave you be. Try and go skyward and we'll knock you down." Kaja laughed, then backed to the entrance and gripped the climb line. He shook his head and laughed again. "Ridiculous."

"What's ridiculous?" Spike demanded.

"That I'm even giving him a chance. He's never been able to prove himself. What makes him think he can do it this time?"

"What makes *you* think that you aren't really a woman in disguise?" Spike countered. "You're more of a woman than me. Now that's what I call ridiculous."

Kaja glared at her a moment, then shook his head and rolled his eyes. "Live large, Wu." Then he swung away.

Kavika sat down heavily, but Spike grabbed his arm and jerked him back to his feet. "There will be no sitting down. You'll have every Pali Boy eye watching you in less than five minutes. You need to start planning. You need to start *doing*."

Kavika knew she was right. He also knew that he felt sick to his stomach. He imagined the look on his mother's face as they were evicted, all because he couldn't come to terms with his fear. Bile rose in his throat as his face tried to turn green. It took a moment, but he managed to swallow it back down. When he finally had control of himself, he turned to Donnie and thanked him. Then he turned back to Spike.

"You ready?" she asked.

He nodded.

"Just to be sure, tell me what we are ready for," she said.

He licked his lips. His mouth had gone suddenly dry. "To find us a Boxer?"

"Seriously? Is that the best you can do?"

He tried again, with only the most minute of improvements.

"Your father would have been scared too, Kavika," said Donnie Wu. "Being a Pali Boy isn't just about being scared to do something. It's often about being scared *not* to do something. This might be your chance—your *only* chance."

Kavika stared out the door of the container to the open water far below.

Some chance.

CHAPTER FOUR

PIECE OF SHIT Puta!

Lopez-Larou seethed. It'd taken her weeks to scrape together three hundred grams of waffle dust. The others like Paco Braun and Sanchez Kelly produced that in a day, but they'd been around. They were established and had multilevel source networks to deliver their product. Sanchez Kelly had more than a dozen runners and could deliver whatever someone wanted to the farthest reaches of the ship. It was rumored that he even had customers aboard the Nip Ship, a tale that Paco Braun tried continuously to quash, reminding everyone that the Japanese were *his* customers and his alone.

How was a girl to get ahead?

Favor chits, that's how. Both Kelly and Braun had chests of favor chits, each one annotated with individual signs and sigils. They might as well be kings, for all the people of the floating city owed them. Lopez-Larou snorted at the thought of lard-ass Braun and sleek Kelly wearing robes and crowns like she'd seen in the picture films. But then she sobered as she realized that for all intents and purposes that was the reality. They had all the food and sex they wanted and lived without fear of Boxers, blood rape or the Neo-Clergy, and were as untouchable as the Nips.

She stared into the heights of the Japanese Freedom Ship at the center of her floating metropolis. She could just make out figures moving on the top deck beneath a high, hot sun in an almost cloudless sky. She wondered what favors Kelly was owed from the likes of those living on the freedom ship. She'd heard they had running water, electricity, and all the food they desired. For a moment she tried to imagine herself there, but it was just too impossible. She ripped her gaze away and focused once more on the task at hand. She had things to worry about that the high-living Nips could never realize. To get ahead, she had one choice and that was to steal from the dead.

She stood in the shadow of the prow of a small Chinese junk. Like her, it was out of place. Made of polished woods, it was a drop of beauty among the gray metal hulls and decking that made up the rest of the city. A reminder of a time when luxury was as important as functionality. Few knew that the owner, Joey Li, liked certain pictures and had a taste for old-school meth. What should have been obvious was hidden by the beauty. She understood this tactic of obfuscation, which was why she now wore a dress and more makeup than any self-respecting *Tiburón* would. For her kind, travel in the city on the waves cost. *Los Tiburones* owned the trade in making life livable. Their reality wasn't cheap, and everyone wanted a piece of it. Whenever they traveled it was assumed they were carrying, which was why she'd reached out to one of the aggravatingly acrobatic Pali Boys. No one would have ever confused one of those simpletons for a runner.

Which was why she'd thought her plan had been perfect—perfect, that is, until the Boxers had not only decided to blood rape her runner, but had botched it and killed him in the process. So here she was. Instead of harvesting scraps and combining her own chems, she was dressed like a transvestite and staring at the Morgue Ship, wondering how in a Cheech-and-Chong Hell she'd be able to get inside and retrieve her product.

"What you doing there? Hey!"

A Vitamin V staggered towards her. Bald. Old. Shriveled.

Please, God, no.

"What you hiding under that dress? Come on. Show me what you're made of."

Smiling on the outside, she shook her head slightly. What were the odds that she'd dress up as a man dressing up as a woman and actually be asked to prove it?

He stepped into the shadows next to her. His breath reeked of Vodka. His bloodshot eyes made it clear that he wanted to own her. Before she knew it, he groped her with his left hand, squeezing her breasts painfully.

She smacked his hand away and was about to shove her palm into the base of his nose, making quick work, but she wasn't ready to lose her disguise just yet.

"What's this?" He went cross-eyed. "Those are real?"

Lowering her head, she smiled and blinked her fake lashes. "I wish. Implants from the Corpers. You like?"

He stared at her a moment, then shook his head. He pushed her hard enough so she had to take two steps backwards to keep her balance on her three inch heels. "Ruined a good thing is what you did." He spat at her feet. "You took it too far."

She imagined piercing his left eye with one of her heels, but instead acted as if his words hurt and shoved out her lower lip. "You don't like me? You don't want me?"

The Vitamin V backed away and shook his head. He looked around, wild-eyed, for a moment as if he'd just discovered where he was, then staggered back the way he'd come.

The irony wasn't lost on her.

She straightened her dress and resumed her vigil. The Water Dogs owned the morgue. It was just about the only ship they owned. Otherwise, they slept in slings on the sides of other ships, divvying the wealth of the ocean to the ship owners for their own score of chits.

The thing about the sea was that everything eventually ended up there. Even the bodies. And when they found their way to the water, it was the Water Dogs who took them and recycled them. Everyone knew what happened to the bodies.

It wasn't something people talked about, but they knew. After all, the Water Dogs paid well for the bodies, providing fish futures to the families of the deceased for as long as the body lasted as bait. She'd heard that before the end time they'd planted bodies in the ground. The idea was too ridiculous. What would grow from them? Where was their use? She'd long ago realized that there'd once been a way of life based on waste. The idea of throwing anything away, even a body, was as alien to her as the idea of living on land.

The Water Dog she'd been watching left the hold of the ship and slipped over the side into the water. Now was her chance.

The Morgue Ship was little more than a low-slung pleasure yacht. About twenty meters from stem to stern, the main cabin stood less than a man's height. Clearly much of the ship was beneath the waterline. The deck was littered with stacks of old clothes and odd items of the deceased. Once every month the Water Dogs held a trade fair, offering what they had for what they needed. As Lopez-Larou approached, she saw a hip pack she'd love to get her hands on.

She glanced left and right, then peered into the rigging of the nearby ships. Seeing no one, she stepped onto the ship, removed both her shoes and tied them to her waist, and then hurried to the door to the cabin. She put her ear to it; hearing nothing, she opened it and slipped inside.

She took a moment to let her eyes adjust. Each side of the cabin had a bank of windows, but they were covered with a mish-mash of cloth that blocked most of the light. Holes in the fabric and inexpertly sewn seams allowed what light she needed. Boxes lined each wall, and a line of tables went down the center of the room. All were occupied except the one right in front of her.

She hurried to the first occupied table and pulled aside the fabric to check the identity. It wasn't Akamu, but an old Chinese woman. The wrinkles and creases in her sun-hardened face were smooth in death. A slight gray pallor colored her tanned skin. A faint odor emanated from her that was both sweet and awful.

She covered her again and went on to the next one. A young

boy, couldn't have been more than ten years old. Before she knew it, she'd cupped the dead boy's cheek. She pulled the fabric entirely free, searching for what killed him. His body appeared unmarked, except for bruising along the legs. She felt them and then knew. He'd fallen. The bones beneath the skin had shattered like a sheet of glass. His fall must have been from a great height.

She replaced the fabric, shaking her head. She was about to move to the next body when she heard voices. She stopped cold and spun toward the door. The voices grew louder.

Merde!

She searched frantically for a place to hide. Everything was too damned well-organized. Then she saw her only chance. She ran towards the door as the handle began to turn, and leaped atop the empty table as the door opened. She slammed her head back and pushed her dress down where it'd slid up, wiped sweat from her forehead with her left hand, and—as the door swung wide and washed the interior with light—turned her head, staring dull-eyed and holding her breath. It wasn't until two people were entering the room that she realized that all of the other bodies were covered in fabric and here she was laid out on the table in all of her wannabe transvestite glory.

Merde!

KAVIKA AND SPIKE entered the gloom of the morgue ship. The smell hit Kavika immediately; sweet and pungent, it wasn't altogether unpleasant until he reminded himself that it was the smell of death. Then suddenly it became intolerable. He glanced at Spike and saw that she was about as nonplussed as could be. Why shouldn't she be? After all, she'd grown up aboard this ship, her parents and brother working the morgue, feeding the fishes and paying back the families of the dead.

"You look green."

"I feel green. Where is he?"

A row of tables ran down the length of the ship's interior. All were occupied, and all but the first was covered with a length of fabric. The table nearest them held a Hispanic girl who couldn't have been more than twenty. Her sharp features were pleasant to look at, but he forced himself to turn away, unwilling to disrespect the dead.

"Farther down, I think." Spike took a step and then made a face. "This isn't right. She should be covered."

She turned to look for the fabric that must have fallen to the ground and as she did, the eyes of the dead girl shifted.

Kavika held his breath and stared. Had he really seen that or was it his nerves? He stepped closer to the body. Her dress lay rumpled against her lean body and her feet were bare. Spiked shoes had been tied to her waist. Her dark hair still held a luster as it splayed across the cold stainless steel. He stared at her eyes for a long moment, but they didn't shift again. Maybe it was her blood settling or something. Still...

"Hold on. Got to get a sheet. Not like my brother to forget something like this." Spike stepped to a long box on the floor, on the right side of the cabin.

Kavika nodded, but never took his eyes off the dead girl. It was almost imperceptible, but it really seemed as if her chest had moved. Was she breathing? Had someone put a living girl in here, thinking she was dead? He stepped closer to the edge of the table and leaned down until his face was inches from hers, close enough to count the freckles across her nose and see the birthmark at the corner of her left eye. Close enough to smell her. And she smelled good; like a girl.

Then her eyes moved and locked onto his. Anger burned in the dark brown orbs. She grinned, muttered *"Merde!"* and rolled off the table, coming to her feet on the left side of the cabin.

Kavika jerked back. "Spike!"

Spike spun, holding a length of fabric. "What the—?" Then she turned to look down the length of tables. "She's after something, Kavika. Hold her!"

Kavika stepped between the door and the young woman. "Who are you?"

"Get out of my way, *Maricone*."

"*Los Tiburones*?" Spike said softly, but loud enough to be heard.

The Spanish girl's eyes flashed.

"She's a Shark, Kavika. She's a drug runner."

The girl shook her head. "I don't run product. I distribute."

"Then who?" Her eyes went wide. "Akamu?"

"No way." Kavika straightened. "No Pali Boy would do such a thing."

The girl snorted. "You Pali Boys. You all think you're special. When it comes down to starving and feeding your family, you're no different than anyone else."

Kavika moved towards her. "That's not right. We're not like—"

Before he could explain, she feinted left, then dodged right, hitting the table and leaping over it. She slipped towards the door, but Spike moved faster than she anticipated. Long nails scraped the side of her neck, eliciting a scream.

"Chito! Where are you? Hurry! Come!"

The girl opened the door, but Kavika had managed to recover enough to reach out and grab a length of her dress. He jerked her back, the door slamming shut.

"Hold it," he snapped. "Who are you?"

She swung a fist and caught him in the side of his head. It stung, but he held on. She hit him two more times before she realized it wasn't going to do much good, then she reached to her front and tore the dress down the middle. Her small breasts swung free; sharks had been tattooed on her chest and stomach, but he barely noticed them.

"Kavika!"

His gaze snapped away just as her foot slammed into his midsection. He staggered back and gasped for air. He'd been trying to help until now, but the girl clearly didn't want any assistance from him. He growled and felt his blood rise like it rarely had before.

She saw the change in him and backed away, turning and confronting Spike, who had grabbed a length of wood. Spike swung it expertly, eviscerating the air in a complex geometry.

Just then the door opened.

Everyone turned for a moment to take in the surprised look on the face of the young Water Dog, still dripping from his recent swim in the sea. Spike's brother Chito took in the scene with narrowing eyes.

That moment was enough.

The girl pushed Spike hard, then rammed her head into the young man's midsection. His air left him with a *woof*, and she was out the door.

Kavika was the first to move and followed her. But as fast and agile as he was, she was faster. She was across and onto the nearest ship by the time he was out the door.

Chito and Spike cried out in their native Filipino. Suddenly, Water Dogs began to pull themselves from the water onto the ship. They gathered themselves, dripping, searching.

But the living dead girl was damned fast.

Kavika chased her for a moment, leaping across deck rails and running through living areas. He'd never been too good at traveling on the surface because of the sheer number of people and their closeness. He glanced at the rigging and noticed a few Pali Boys following him. He'd never get there in time. He could ask the Pali Boys to give him a hand, but he doubted they'd help him. After all, Kaja had given the task to him.

Kavika slowed and stared across the decks. There was no sign of her.

He trudged back to the Morgue Ship. Spike was chattering with Chito and half a dozen Water Dogs. When she saw him and realized he didn't have the girl with him, she shook her head and cursed. He watched as the Water Dogs looked at him. As one, they turned away and shook their heads.

Then a Water Dog leaped out of the sea and said something that got everyone excited.

Spike turned, all smiles. "They trapped her in a net on one of the subs. Come on, Romeo. Let's go."

"Romeo?" he asked, rushing after her and her brother. The rest of the Water Dogs dove into the ocean.

"I saw the way you were looking at her."

"I wasn't looking at her, I was..."

"Breasts. They were breasts. Everyone has them."

As Kavika ran, he grinned to himself. Sure everyone had them. But he kind of liked the ones the living dead girl had.

Spike saw his grin and tried to push him; he avoided her and ran ahead.

She cursed behind him, tore off her pumps, and was soon running beside him.

He kept his grin going as he leaped into the rigging. Soon he was soaring above the city, swinging from antenna mast to chimney.

CHAPTER FIVE

KAVIKA MOVED FAST, just on the edge of control, while the other Pali Boys held back. Most of them were faster than he was, but Kaja must have gotten the word out, so they let him have the lead. That was just fine with him. He didn't need anyone getting in his way.

A hundred feet below he saw Spike moving quickly over the decks, sliding over rails and avoiding the guards who'd been put in place to keep cross-boat traffic to a minimum. As a Water Dog, she probably could have moved faster beneath the water, but the state of her dress and make up were always a big deal to her; in fact, they were who she was.

They had to skirt the Freedom Ship. No lines and no rigging ran to or from it. The Jap Corpers wouldn't allow it. In fact, other than two gangways, no other ships were allowed to anchor to it. They claimed it was for everyone's safety, but the people of the city knew it was because the Corpers were afraid of their unwashed neighbors. They didn't want their corporate lifestyle sullied by the ghetto of the ships. But that was okay.

All the ships had been tied off at the anchor line, run there and constantly monitored by Water Dogs.

So what was left was a big lagoon. Donnie Wu called it a moat and had explained about castles and protection against attack. Kavika had initially laughed at his uncle's comment, but the older he became and the more he learned, the more he began to believe in its accuracy.

Kavika swung down the rigging and onto the deck of a Chinese fishing boat that floated on the edge of the lagoon. Fishing lines stitched the water from the rails of the sixty foot yacht. The water was sludgy and laced with iridescent whirlpools. A wizened crone pulled a shad from the water and slapped it against the deck, knocking it out. She added it to a pile of sickly-looking fish, probably bound for a pot or to be reduced to fish paste. She glanced at the Pali Boy and grinned a single-toothed smile. Kavika returned the greeting, but bit back a comment. These were the kind of people bringing Minimata Disease to the rest of the city, but where else were they to fish? How else would they get their food? It was ironic that in the shadow of opulence, they had to eat mercury-riddled fish and play the Minimata lottery. The same lottery his sister had played and lost.

A slim Chinese youth carrying a gaff blocked Kavika's way. He wore black pants and had a tattoo of a Chinese Earth Dragon curving around his torso. He wore his hair long and wild.

Kavika tried to dodge to the left.

The youth swung the gaff hard, in a short arc that just missed Kavika's ear.

Kavika's anger flared. The youth swung again, but this time Kavika caught the gaff on the descent, redirecting it into the deck. The hook sunk into the wood and caught. Before the youth could jerk it free, Kavika caught him in the elbow with a palm slap. The gaff fell free as the nerves in the boy's arm deadened, and Kavika kicked the side of the youth's left knee, sending him to the deck in a sickening crunch.

Kavika felt his nostrils flaring, but he allowed the fallen boy mercy. He stepped over him, leapt onto the rail, and went on his way. He almost slipped into the water when he hit a deck covered in fish scales, but at the last minute he was able to keep his balance by bending his knees and going into a slide. When he hit the opposite deck rail, he propelled himself up and over, with a half flip that left him able to continue running.

A few moments later he was running across the flat deck of a barge, dodging lines of clothes from those who used the wide open space as a fresh air laundry. On the other side rested the old Soviet Alpha-class submarine. It was there that Kavika drew himself to a stop.

Four Vitamin Vs stood on the deck of the submarine, each holding a corner of a net. Ivanov waved from atop the wide metal mast, pointing towards the undulating net on the deck. Beneath the net, caught like a fly beneath a swatter, was the living dead girl. She cursed and spat, more like a Freedom Ship bilge rat than a living dead girl.

Ivanov put his hands to the side of his mouth and yelled, "Is this what you were after?"

"I was chasing her," Kavika called back. He ran down an edge, then leaped aboard the submarine. The submarine's mast was a good four meters above the deck.

"Finders keepers," said Egor. Kavika knew him from the snake tattooed around his bald, tanned skull.

The way his eyes flashed, Kavika had no doubt what Egor would do to the girl once he and his companions got her belowdecks. Normally the Pali Boy wouldn't care, but he felt his own heat rise as he watched the undulations of the girl, her brown skin beneath the grid-patterned net.

"She's mine," he heard himself say.

"What? Little Pali shit," Egor growled.

"A little Pali Boy doesn't order us around," said one of the men, who had arms as big around as Wu. His skin was covered with tattoos of the before time. White hairs coiled like wire, against skin baked to a nut brown.

"She has something of mine," Kavika said. It wasn't exactly a lie. He didn't know if she'd taken anything or not... that is, if she had a hiding place he couldn't see. Considering he could see virtually every part of her body, he knew he was reaching, but what the hell.

"Scat, boy," said a third Russian. "You don't want to get hurt over this little shark." Hunched, thin and mean, the man strained at his section of rope, but kept a hungry leer working beneath a hooked nose.

Kavika leaned back to see if Ivanov was watching, but the old man was no longer at the mast. He'd probably gone below. Not that it mattered. What did matter was that Kavika had to talk to the girl first. She was one of their few leads, and if he was going to be able to get back with the Pali Boys, he had to solve the mystery of Akamu's death. And looking at this band of rapists and criminals, Kavika knew that if the girl was taken below, she'd never be seen again.

"Listen," he began, "I don't think this is a good idea."

"Whoa, Little Bird," came a fatherly voice. Ivanov had opened up a hatch in the decking and was stepping out. "That's a good way to get yourself killed. Don't you know that it's suicidal to take a catch away from a wild animal?"

Kavika felt relief wash through him. "Uncle Evil," he said, using the name for the man he first learned on his father's knee. "I wouldn't exactly call your men wild animals."

"First of all, realize that they are my men, which means I know them better than anyone. Second, never forget that an animal can walk on two legs as easily as four."

"I won't forget. Thanks, Uncle." He embraced the man who had been his father's best friend. "I thought you'd gone below."

"And miss this? Not for the world. It's not often my men are able to catch a shark with the net meant for birds. At least not with those—"

"Violation! You are violators, all of you! You'll be lucky if I don't turn you over to the Corpers!"

Ivanov turned and rested a tired gaze on Kavika before he addressed Spike.

"Water Dogs should stay in the water. What are you doing out here, sniffing in corners that aren't yours?"

Spike had lost her heels somewhere in her struggle to keep up. Strands of hair had fallen across her forehead, one covering her left eye. Her chest heaved, and she rested both hands on her hips. "It's my business that you have a net."

"We use it to catch birds." Ivanov winked at his men.

"Looks like you used it to catch a shark."

Ivanov shrugged. "If the shark is going to pretend to be a bird, how can I help this?"

Two Water Dogs swam to the edge of the sub and pulled themselves up to stand beside Spike. Each held hand gaffs with hooks long enough to rip out a lung. They were heeled, but looked ready to attack if Spike were to flex so much as a finger.

Ivanov saw this too and held up his hands. "Okay, okay. We don't really need any trouble, do we?"

"We are not giving her back," said the biggest Russian.

Ivanov spun and spat a long stream of Russian at the man. Kavika couldn't understand the words, but there was no doubt what they meant. Then Ivanov pointed. He had to do it twice, but Kavika gave the men credit. They didn't make the old man do it a third time. They left, grumbling and dragging their now-empty net with them.

Ivanov turned back, the world's greatest fake smile playing across his face. He held out his hands. "There. You see? No problem."

Kavika heard a foot slap against the metal deck. "Hey." The shark was on her feet. Bruised and battered, the fire still burning in her eyes.

He dove for her, but missed her ankle by an inch. He crashed hard to the deck, his elbow and chin taking his weight, pain singing from the dense metal of the submarine.

She glanced back once, a slight grin tugging at one corner of her lips. Then she was off and running, a brown-skinned shark with breasts swinging free.

Kavika leaped to his feet and shook his head. "Damn—see you later, Uncle Evil!"

Then he was on the chase again.

Far above, he heard Pali Boy laughter.

Kavika got as far as the old nudist charter when he gave up. There was no sign of the girl. Above him, several Pali Boys continued to laugh. He could always ask them. They knew. But to ask would be to acknowledge defeat, and he wasn't prepared to do that yet.

So he loped back to the submarine. Spike was still there, arguing with Ivanov not only about his ownership of a net, but about the propriety of having one. To the old man's credit, he stood and listened. He could have gone back aboard his sub and closed the hatch and there was nothing anyone could do. After all, the city's entire power came from the nuclear batteries aboard the submarine.

Kavika appreciated the old man's patience. He and Spike were his two favorite people in the world. To have them against each other would split his heart.

"Hey Uncle!" Kavika shouted as he approached. "Why don't you just admit you catch fish with that net and be done with it?"

"Where would be the fun in that, Little Bird?"

Spike gave both of them the stinkeye, then shook her head and cursed in Tagalog. She bent and strapped her heels back on.

Ivanov smelled of diesel and cigars; Kavika had always found it comforting. He'd broken his ankle the year after his father died, and blood poisoning ended up threatening his foot, making more than one midwife want to amputate. But it was Ivanov who had taken Kavika into the submarine's med unit and had sat with him, making sure the foot was elevated, arranging for medicine from *Los Tiburones*, and ensuring that his mother and sister were fed. Kavika never consciously remembered that time except in brief lightning-flashes, but the smell of diesel and cigars had made him feel safe and cared-for ever since then.

"So what gives, Uncle Evil?"

"Actually, the boys were out on the deck repairing the net." He pulled out a cigar and began preparing it. "We might occasionally use it for fish, but only out of sheer desperation when the Water Dogs fail to pay us for the energy they use."

"Hey!" Spike protested. "We're never late."

"Keep your wig on, sweetie. Your boys are always late. Everyone is late. They take the power for granted because it's always on." He paused to light the cigar and puff out several clouds of rich tobacco smoke. "Anyway, my boys were on the deck when the girl, bosoms flying everywhere, bounded onto my boat like it was a sidewalk in downtown Moscow and she was some escaped stripper from the Circ de Soleil. Didn't take much. One minute she was running, the next she was caught, twisted and held."

"Do you know her?" Kavika asked.

"Her? No. Do I know the Sharks? Sure. I deal with some of them occasionally, but never with her."

"Any chance of finding out who she is?"

"Why do you want to know? Looking for a date? I wouldn't trust a Shark if I were you."

Kavika told him about Akamu and the botched blood rape. He also told him about his conversation with old Donnie Wu and the proclamation made by Kaja, ending with the discovery of the young *Tiburón* skulking around the morgue ship.

"Knowing why she was there could help us figure out what Akamu was doing."

Ivanov stared at Kavika for a long minute. Occasionally he'd glance at Spike. When he spoke next, his mouth formed the words as if they tasted bad. "Listen. I can't help you there. I don't know her and I don't know what, if anything, she and your Pali Boy were involved in. Remember, there's still very little proof they were even tied together. For all you know she could have been stealing from the Water Dogs, or perhaps trying to collect a debt."

Spike rose on her toes to argue, but Ivanov wouldn't let her. "But be that as it may, I do have some ideas about the Boxers, probably the same ones who killed Akamu. You do want to get back at them, don't you?"

Kavika hesitated. The Boxers were part of the circle of possibility for a cure for Minimata Disease. They had always been a necessary evil. Still, it was their only chance, especially if Ivanov was right about the living dead girl knowing Akamu.

"Friend of mine had the same problem," continued Ivanov, "only his kids were monkey-backed."

"I don't know what's worse," Spike said. "Getting monkey-backed or getting dead."

"Dead is always worse, sweetie." To Kavika he said, "His name is Pak. He's one of the People of the Sun."

Both Kavika and Spike exchanged a worried look. But before they could say anything, Ivanov hastened to add, "Don't believe everything you hear. Pak's a good man. He's a father who loves his children. Everything else is in the wind."

CHAPTER SIX

"A BLIZZARD OF black" is what his father had called them. Birds.

So many of them.

Always circling.

Waiting.

Hungry.

Sometimes resting in the upper reaches of the rigging, but always waiting. Always there. Pali Boys avoided them. They carried disease. They marked their rookeries and protected them with their sharp claws and beaks. And the way they looked at you, with their heads cocked sideways, it was as if they were reading you from the inside out. The sky was only truly free of them when the wind was up.

What's a blizzard, papa?

When the rain turns so cold it's the color of a cloud.

How can it be that cold? Like an ice chest? Like the ice the Corpers *sometimes give us?*

Like the whole world is an ice chest. Like the look in the eyes of the birds if you get too close.

Kavika dragged his gaze away from the circle of birds and let the webs of his memory drift in the breeze. Ever-present, the birds were thicker above the ships the People of the Sun called home. The demarcation from general public to their territory was marked by red-painted railings. If he were a bird, he could probably see the shape of it.

They stood just on the other side of the *line*.

"Where'd you go?" Spike asked.

"Thinking about my father."

"I wish I could have met him."

Kavika lifted his chin. "He never liked birds. Said that they were bringers of everything bad."

"Do you think they brought the plague? That's what people are saying."

"Pele brought the plague. She was tired of the terrible things we were doing to the planet."

Spike regarded Kavika. "Do you really believe that?"

"No, not really. But it's as good a reason as any, I suppose. You can say it comes from the sea. Or the air. Or the rain. We'll never know where it came from. All the scientists are dead, or up there in that Corper ship. Ain't none of them gonna come down here and explain it."

"It's like wondering where the rain comes from when it's already raining."

"Exactly. If you're all wet, why do you care how you got wet? Just find a way to get dry."

Spike smiled affectionately. "You're stalling, aren't you?"

"Is it that obvious? I don't know what it is, but the birds bother me. It's like a... foreboding, I think is the word."

"You always have those words. We never talk much in my family."

"Maybe because you spend so much time underwater."

She smiled sadly. "Yeah. That's probably the reason." Kavika stepped past the red line and was immediately met by an old Korean woman. She was whispering something to the wind. Occasionally she'd jab a misshapen finger at something in the sky. Her back was hunched painfully beneath material made from an old tarp.

Kavika and Spike followed her crooked finger to where two orange-robed Mga Taos stood in the shadow of a ship. They faced the Korean ship and stood like statues. A monkey-backed was somewhere near. They were unwilling, or unable, to cast the sort of vigil they were used to. They were forced to stand outside the line, but still vigilant.

Kavika interrupted the old woman.

"I'm looking for Mr. Pak."

The deep wrinkles in the woman's cheeks pushed her eyes to the center of her face, dark seeds above a small nose. Instead of answering, she leaned in close and sniffed him.

Kavika stepped back.

"What is she, a watch dog?" Spike whispered. When the old woman started to step close to Spike, the Water Dog held out a long-nailed finger and waggled it. "No, you do not sniff at me."

The old woman paused, then stood straight. She grinned, the effort to push past her wrinkles barely won, and only for a moment.

Kavika cleared his throat. "Mr. Pak?"

The old woman nodded, turned and shuffled across the deck. Kavika and Spike exchanged glances then followed. They meandered across two more decks. They passed kids playing in the shadows, who seemed to be beating a stuffed animal with lengths of wood. As Kavika and Spike got closer, they saw it wasn't stuffed at all, but a dead bird. Here and there older Koreans sanded peeling paint and swept the decks. The People of the Sun had always been known for their industriousness and cleanliness. Kavika wished that some of the other groups could emulate this; even his own. Hawaiians were pack rats, and there seemed to be nothing that could dissuade them from keeping, stacking, and piling everything they've ever had, leaving the ships looking like the aftermath of a cyclone.

They climbed from a yacht to a cargo ship whose deck was much the same as the oil tanker Kavika called home, albeit about half the size with only single-story cargo containers. Tall cranes, which had once been used to offload containers, had rusted in place. Their way twisted and turned, like a deliberate maze. At length, they arrived at a container with a tattered green cloth draped over the entrance. The old woman rattled off something in Korean, then turned and left, leaning in and quickly sniffing at Spike as she did. Spike went to kick the woman, but the spry old Korean crabbed out of the way, cackling and smacking her lips together audibly.

A man's voice came from inside.

"Mr. Pak? I'm Kavika Kamilani. Ivanov sent me."

The man murmured something, then ducked out of the container, letting the cloth fall back to block any view of the interior.

Pak was a small, lean man. Wiry muscles told of hard labor. His lips were the kind that seemed quick to smile, but by the dull, worn look in his eyes, he perhaps hadn't worn a smile in a while.

"Ivanov... he's been helpful." Mr. Pak's voice was soft and tired and barely held the hint of an accent.

"How do you know him?" Spike asked.

"We work together. We have... enterprises... together." Pak looked at Spike for a moment, then his eyes narrowed as he noticed the truth of her. "This is a man," he said, matter-of-factly.

Kavika put his hands on Spike's shoulder. "This is a friend of mine and helping me," Kavika said. "She might be a man by birth, but she's a woman under the sun."

Pak screwed his eyes together. By his expression, he was clearly having a hard time trying to figure it out, only there was nothing to figure out. Kavika decided to just come out with it. "One of our Pali Boys was blood raped. He died because of it."

At the words *blood rape* Pak glanced back at the door covering, which had begun to flutter slightly in a breeze that had wound its way through the maze. "I'm sorry for your Pali friend. We see them sometimes flying over the ships. They look so happy." Pak looked down at his hands. They were gnarled. Two fingers were missing on his left hand. "I grow things. Tobacco for Ivanov. He helps me sometimes." A child's voice called out from inside the container. Pak called back. When next he spoke, his gaze was aimed at the floor. "What is it you think I can do?"

Kavika kept trying to glimpse what was inside the container whenever the wind shifted the cloth, but he could only get brief flashes of movement.

"Boxers are the ones who did this to my friend. Do you know which ones they could have been? Names maybe?" As he said it, Kavika felt the doltishness of his words. Embarrassed, he wished he'd practiced what he was going to say.

"I don't know any Boxers. Truly, I do not know why you are here."

"I'm aware that the same... the same thing happened to your daughters. I... I'm happy they didn't die."

"I am not so sure," Pak said, his voice barely audible. For a moment he seemed to wear the tragedy of the blood rapes like a second skin. "Listen, I am sorry for your friend. This blood raping"—he choked out the word—"is a terrible thing. But I cannot help you."

Then he turned and slipped back inside his home.

Kavika felt a growing sense of frustration. He glanced at Spike, who motioned for him to keep at it. But it was clear Kavika didn't know what he was doing. As it was, he was grabbing at cuttlefish in a desperate attempt to try and explain what happened to Akamu. Not that it mattered. The Pali Boy was still dead. Even if he was able to find the Boxers who killed him, then what? Boxers weren't like regular people. They were beyond any law.

Spike cursed and stepped in front of him, whipping the cloth aside. For the next ten seconds, it was as though the universe had stopped.

The interior was larger than they expected. A table and a stove took up the left corner, while a water closet with a fabric door was built in to the right corner. Chests ran the lengths of the side walls, doubling as benches and storage. Pak sat on the left side, and an older woman, who must have been his wife, sat on the right side. Each of them were spooning food into limp mouths. Twin girls sat back-to-back. Dull, sightless eyes, listless expressions and spittle-laced frowns owned each of their faces as their parents fed them.

This wasn't what ensnared Kavika's gaze. It was the monkeys attached to their backs. Beyond the horror of having another being attached to one's body by tubes and wires was the terrible recognition of its sentience. The monkeys' faces were less than a hand's-width apart; their eyes were open and their mouths moved as if they were whispering. By Pele herself, what did they have to say to each other?

It was the whispering that bothered Kavika the most, he realized. To whisper meant that they had something to hide. To whisper spoke of intent that no animal should rightly have, as if the tubes that ran from the back of the animal heads to the top of the girls' spines, along with all the others transferring blood and additional fluids, also carried consciousness.

"I see that you've discovered our tragedy," Pak said.

"I didn't know. I just thought—" Kavika became aware of a smell; animal musk combined with the acrid taint of antiseptic.

"Yes. First the blood rape, then this." Mr. Pak spooned another bite into his daughter's mouth. It looked like fish-paste and rice, but it smelled like meat.

The woman feeding the other twin said something that made Pak smile weakly. "My wife asked if there will ever be a cure for Minimata. I told her that with our daughters working on it, there just has to be." His eyes searched Kavika's and Spike's for some sort of agreement. "Don't you think so?"

Spike and Kavika nodded, but neither could find anything to say. Finally it was Kavika who spoke, uneasiness and embarrassment creeping through his curiosity and need to solve the puzzle of Akamu's death. "We're so very sorry to bother you and your family. Come on, Spike. Let's leave them alone."

They backed out of the doorway and let the fabric fall into place. They hadn't gone ten feet when Pak stuck his head out of his home. "Listen," Pak began, glancing back inside for a moment before stepping outside. "Abe knows. Abe wants to help. He's one of the Real People."

"I wasn't aware Real People wanted to help anyone," Spike said.

Kavika had to agree. He'd never interacted with them. He'd hardly ever seen them. They kept to themselves and didn't allow transit on or above any of their ships. And because skying above their boats was forbidden, the Pali Boys couldn't help but believe that the Real People were hiding something. And aboard a floating city, that couldn't be good.

"This one is different," Pak said, seeing the suspicion in Kavika's face. "Like your friend, the Boxers killed his son."

"Damn."

"He knows who the Boxers are who did this."

"If he knows, then why hasn't he done something?"

Pak stood with his hands out at his sides. "Look at me. Who am I to do anything? Who is he?" He gestured towards the Freedom Ship, which was a part of everyone's horizon, like it or not. "They are too powerful. They are too much for us."

"What about the rest of your people?" Kavika asked.

"They are too afraid. They don't want the Boxers coming to them, so they don't do anything."

"So who is going to stop them?"

A hopeful grin flashed across Pak's face. "Maybe you." Then he ducked back inside the container, hollow laughter chasing him behind the curtain.

After a moment Spike turned to Kavika and shuddered dramatically. "Ugh. I know I should be sympathetic," she whispered, "But God... ugh."

They began making their way back out.

"Why this maze, I wonder?" Spike asked suddenly.

The question got Kavika thinking. It fit his mood perfectly. Not knowing where he was going, not knowing the next step—it all gave him a feeling of powerlessness. He was led to Pak, and now a Real Person named Abe. What next? Why couldn't he see more of the solution rather than being led like a child through the process of discovery? He supposed that the thing about mazes was that one was never able to see the whole thing. If he could only see it, he could trace his route to the center. This was why he liked being a Pali Boy and living in the rigging. Up there, he was free. He could choose where to go and how to get there. Very much unlike living on the ground, where he could only see what was directly in front of him.

"Pssst—look," Spike whispered and poked him in the ribs.

He glanced left but saw nothing.

"Other way, stupid Pali Boy."

Kavika glanced right and saw a figure clambering over a cabin on a ship two away from the area demarked by the People of the Sun.

"Who is it?"

"Who do you think?"

"*Tiburón?*"

"Yeah."

"The living dead girl." He wanted to give chase, but she was too far away.

CHAPTER SEVEN

THE REAL PEOPLE was a confederation of white-skinned people comprising a large tanker, several dozen smaller boats and two perpendicular ships that had been fixed in place. Old Donnie Wu hated them, especially for the arrogance at selecting their name. *Real People.* As if everyone else wasn't real. But it was Kavika's mother who had taught him how the name came from a bad translation. Originally the ship's captains, they were referred to as the *Officials* in the early days of The Great Lash-up, when the city was forming. The Chinese word for *real* and *official* were the same. Once the People of the Sun, the Water Dogs, and the Mga Taos began to separate into their groups, the Officials were called the *Official People.* Somehow, whether it was self-generated or some sort of irony, that term changed to *Real People,* which found its way into the popular lexicon. Wu called them White People, because not a single one had skin darker than a tan.

Regardless of where they came from, if Mr. Pak was to be believed, the Real People had expressed their desire to help

Pak deal with the Boxers. But there was a logic problem with that, one which Kavika couldn't work his brain around.

"What is it?" Spike asked. "Stomach ache?"

"No. Just thinking." He glanced at Spike and saw her smiling. "Oh—you knew that."

"You always get that look on your face when you're thinking hard on something."

"Okay, then. Why would the Real People want to help Pak? They don't know him. They don't owe him anything."

Spike shook her head. "We don't know that. We don't know what their relationship really is. Look at me—what's on the surface isn't always what it is."

"Sure. I get that. But as much as we hate the Boxers, we can't argue their reasoning. After all, without them we'd be no closer to a cure for Minimata disease."

"Them? Do you think *they're* actually working for a cure?"

"No," Kavika acknowledged. "Not them. But the Corpers for sure. I mean"—he stopped to talk with his hands—"as bad as we hate blood rape, it's meant to help us find a cure. I mean, everyone who is blood raped has the possibility of curing my sister's disease... everyone's disease."

"Not that I'd want to be blood raped and then monkey-backed—no offense to you or your sister—but then I don't see the problem."

"You don't? If being monkey-backed is the way to find a cure for Minimata, then why is it the Real People want to help Pak?"

"You're right. Everyone should be looking forward to a cure. We've seen more and more deaths from the disease—the numbers are rising. But like I said, we don't know what their relationship is. Maybe Pak grows tobacco for them as well. Who knows?"

They'd crossed several ships and were heading back round the Freedom Ship to the area of the Real People. The lagoon created around the Freedom Ship had an aeration fountain. As they watched, a slender black boat with several men wearing full-body SCUBA gear exited a hole in the side of the ship. The hole slid shut and the boat rumbled towards the fountain. One of the men held out a long catch rod with a bucket. He let it fill a moment, then pulled it back to where one of the other men took it and placed it in a sealed metal jar.

"Corpers," whispered Spike.

"Has to be. Speaking of Minimata."

"Think that's what it is?"

Kavika grabbed her wrist. "Shh. Look."

The man who'd just retrieved the water now had something new on the end of his long catch pole, a slender black cylinder. They watched as he extended it over the fountaining water, then upended it. For a moment the water turned black, then returned to normal.

"Mother Pele, what is *that*?"

"Maybe a cure," Spike suggested. "Maybe they are close."

Thoughts of his sister running and laughing as she'd once done soared through Kavika's dark thoughts. "Could it be?"

"What else could it—"

Suddenly Spike shoved him out of the way, taking a club to the side of her head.

Kavika grabbed her as she slumped. He backed away, dragging her with him. When he saw who had attacked, his heart sunk.

Boxer!

As tall as Kavika, the Chinese man was double his age. Fine veins crawled around his slender muscles. His tonsured head held the long, telltale braid of his gang. A graying Fu Manchu mustache bounced above a mouth filled with filed and broken teeth, and he spat Chinese curses. He was shoeless and shirtless, with an old dragon tattoo on his chest; the only scrap of clothing he wore was a pair of faded black pants that frayed to nothing just above the ankles.

The Boxer lunged with the club, intent on catching Kavika in the head as well, but the Pali Boy was able to stay just outside the other's reach. The Boxer swung again and missed, but so close that Kavika could feel the rush of air. In one arm he held Spike; the other he used to reach behind him, searching for the nearest ship's rail.

The Boxer kicked out and followed the strike with a blow.

Unable to block both, Kavika took the wood on his shoulder and immediately knew he shouldn't have. The arm went limp and useless. Spike fell to the ground, still groggy from the blow she'd taken.

Fear lanced through him as he saw the blood seep from her wound, eagerly soaked up by the sun-bleached decking. If it was only him he might have fled, but he had to save Spike. So instead of retreating, Kavika did something that surprised both of them—he stepped into the Boxer's guard and kicked out at the Chinese man's knees. His opponent backpedalled, but Kavika kept up the attack, and the Boxer was barely able to keep from losing the use of a knee or splintering a shin. When he came to the edge of the lagoon, he planted his feet, blocked a kick and managed to swing his club wildly, and Kavika threw himself to the deck and swept with his foot, catching the Boxer at the left ankle. The Boxer twisted but managed to sink to one knee to keep from splashing into the lagoon; his wild eyes sought something to save him. He shouted something just before Spike's foot caught him in the face, then shot off the boat and crashed into the water.

When Kavika climbed to his feet, he noticed that the man's club had fallen, and was rolling towards the edge of the deck.

Kavika slid over and snatched it up, and then sprang to his feet and grabbed Spike with both arms just in time to keep her from falling again. Her eyes were still unfocused. He heard the Boxer thrashing, but didn't take the time to look. He propelled Spike before him and found the nearest ship. Kavika slung himself over the rail, then dragged Spike across after him. They'd gotten almost to the other side of the ship when he spied two more Boxers coming after them. One he recognized from Akamu's media stick.

The recognition must have shown on his face, because the other narrowed his eyes and shouted something to a third man.

Damn! Had they been following them intentionally or were they just in the wrong place at the wrong time? What were the odds?

"Spike—Spike!" He pinched her cheeks and shook her none too gently. "Come on!"

"Ungh."

She could barely keep her head upright. Kavika gauged his position on the deck by where the other three stood. He had a single chance. If he'd been alone, he would have climbed into the rigging and been gone. But he had the responsibility of Spike and he couldn't leave her, not after what they'd done to Akamu.

Against every iota of self-preservation he'd ever had in the fear factory of his soul, Kavika charged the nearest Boxer. A Hawaiian battle cry ringing, his newly acquired war club swinging madly above his head, he dragged Spike behind him by one arm.

The Boxer he'd targeted was leaning against the rail. For a moment he seemed ready to accept Kavika's onslaught, then his grin fell as he glanced behind him at the water far below between the ships.

But it was far too late for him to move. Kavika let go of Spike, launched himself into the air and hit the Boxer in the chest, bowling him over the edge. Kavika managed to grab the rail and wrap his arm around it before he, too, was propelled over the side by his own momentum. The Boxer scrambled for a grip, but there was none to be had. He fell the dozen meters to the water, hitting with a hollow clap.

Kavika pulled himself back over and ran to Spike. The other two Boxers were advancing. Instead of hurrying, having seen what had happened to the others, they crept across the deck in a defensible crouch. Kavika looked at first one, then the other, trying to decide which one would get to him first. He'd always hated the idea of waiting. Without further thought, Kavika threw the club at the nearest one, then dragged Spike to the rail. He glanced down, saw what he'd hoped to see, and with a quick apology, slipped her over the rail until her feet dangled and let her go.

He would have liked to have had time to see how she hit, but he couldn't spare the moment. Hesitation had proven to be the downfall of the others. No way was he going to make the same mistake. He leaped the rail and vaulted to the next ship, landing on an old icebreaker converted to a pleasure yacht. He sped to the cabin. Behind it was a smokestack one could see from many ships away.

The Boxers cursed behind him. Kavika risked a look; they were just pulling themselves over the railing. One fell and took a moment to gather himself, but the other came on strong.

It was time to do what Pali Boys were good at, regardless of what Kaja had told him. Three more strides and he leaped, catching hold of the vestiges of an old ladder on the side of the great smokestack. It was sizzling hot from the sun and never meant to be touched, much less transited. The cured sharkskin was as useless a protection for his palms as were the rubber soles on his feet. So like a lizard, he scrambled up the rough metal, careful to let his hands and feet make only the most fleeting contact. Still, the heat soon had him biting back tears and wincing.

Finally at the top, he pulled himself up the last few rungs and got his feet beneath him, staring down at the Boxers, who were unwilling or unable to follow him up the vertical shaft.

He gave them the double shaka, bit back the bile of his fear and laughed.

"You want me, you're going to have to do better than that." He felt the strain in his own laughter. He wasn't used to bravado of this sort, and he knew that he'd end up paying for those words.

The top of the smokestack was supported by two sets of wires. One ran down and connected to the center of a deck where children played. One of the Boxers ran towards it, cancelling the possibilities for that route. The other cable ran into an enclosed cylinder built aboard the flat deck of an old trawler, which was the home of the Sky Winkers. Since he couldn't ever remember them doing any harm to anyone, he chose that route and was soon sliding down the wire naked, using his shorts to protect his hands.

He gathered speed, dimly making out figures as he entered the darkness of the cylinder. Then he hit. He tried to tumble to dissipate the energy, but he only had a few feet before he slammed into the metal wall of the far side of the cylinder. He lay upside down, his vision blurry and jumbled, for a moment, until he was able to gather his bearings, then he let go of the shorts with his left hand and fell hard to the deck. He managed to stand on the second try, and wobbled as he pulled his pants on.

He began to hear whispering around the edges of the cylinder. Soon he understood the words.

Pali Boy.

He made a shaka and waggled his hand. "Aloha." He gave his best and brightest smile.

A hunchbacked old man approached him. He wore a T-shirt that said *I Grok Science*. What little hair he had on his balding pate was long and white. His eyes were covered with strange goggles that had a single pinpoint hole from which he could see.

"Sorry, Uncle. I did not mean to interrupt you. I was being chased."

"Chased is never a good state to be in. How is it you became the focus of such a thing?"

"Asking too many questions."

"Ah. Just as in science, sometimes good questions require answers that make people uncomfortable. Was your question a good one?"

The old man took Kavika by the elbow as he spoke and escorted him down a set of stairs.

"It was a very good question, Uncle."

"Good. Make people answer. Even when they don't like to. Here, we need to take care of your hands. You've burned them."

It was as if noticing caused his hands to begin throbbing. Pain surfaced and took over, causing him to grit his teeth.

They went down two flights into the hold of the ship. Kavika immediately felt the coolness. The lights were as low as they could go and the surrounding metal seemed to conduct the temperature of the ocean.

"You'll have to forgive us. We abhor the light. It keeps us from seeing what's in the sky, from communicating with those above."

Kavika didn't need an explanation. The eccentricities of the Sky Winkers was a common subject. Mostly it was because no one really knew what went on inside their ship. But also it was because of their constant vigil of the sky, their beliefs in something called a space station and the idea that it circled the earth with people inside of it.

They entered a large room with several families resting on scattered couches, many of them asleep.

Seeing his observation, the Sky Winker said, "We sleep during the day so we can be awake during the darkness." He tapped his eyeglasses, which he took off as he was speaking. "These help us protect our eyes from the light. I'm sure you understand."

"I wish I had something to protect me from the Boxers."

The Sky Winker sat back and exhaled. "Boxers... nothing good there."

"Name's Kavika Kamilani."

"Doctor Timothy Lebbon. Call me Leb. Here, let me see those hands now." Leb had grabbed a first aid box and now gently spread a cream onto Kavika's hands. It immediately began sucking out the heat.

Kavika relished the coldness of the medicine. "Ah." He couldn't help himself.

"This is only temporary. Be careful for the next few days. So what was the question?"

Kavika stared a moment, then grinned. "You mean the question that got me into trouble?"

Leb nodded.

"I was asking why a friend of mine was accidentally killed."

"And you're sure it was an accident?"

Kavika thought for a moment. He couldn't be sure, but then he'd never contemplated that possibility. "Leb, what is it that *you* know about the Boxers?"

The Sky Winker stared into Kavika's eyes as he began putting the medicine back in the box. "Knowledge is like pain. There's only so much that can be done to conceal it. Once you have it you have it."

"But I need to know. A friend of mine was blood raped, and he died because of it."

"Nothing good there."

"My sister has Minimata. If there's any hope, it is in the blood rapes, no matter how terrible they are."

"Nope. Nothing good there at all."

"What are you saying?"

"These are not connected issues."

"What does that mean? Are you saying that the blood rapes aren't to find a cure?" he asked, his eyes screwed around the question.

Leb shook his head. "Not connected. Sorry, Pali friend, but I can say no more."

Kavika sat back as the idea spread across what he knew of his own world like a fast moving cancer, covering it, devouring it, eating it whole. He'd always connected the two, because everyone else had. It was common knowledge. Blood rapes, monkey-backing and a cure for Minimata had all been intrinsically linked things, no matter how terrible they seemed. If this Sky Winker was to be believed, none of it was connected at all. And if the blood rapes didn't exist to find a cure, then what were they good for? *Who* were they good for?

Now that he'd begun thinking about it, Kavika couldn't get the thoughts of his mind. *Knowledge is like pain. There's only so much that can be done to conceal it. Once you have it you have it.*

And Kavika had it in spades.

If only he could get rid of it.

CHAPTER EIGHT

THERE'D BEEN A moment when Kaja had thought the boy lost. Then the youth had surprised everyone by dropping his best friend into the drink. The Boxers didn't know how to take that. Then again, they weren't used to dealing with too much outside the Freedom Ship. Neither were they familiar with the idea of someone, anyone, getting the best of them.

But as Donnie Wu often liked to say, the Boxers were a shadow of the people they'd once been. They'd named themselves 'the Society of Righteous and Harmonious Fists' after the Chinese who rebelled against English colonial rule in 1900, fighting for individuality and national identity. The old Pali Boy couldn't understand how representatives of the longest surviving culture on the planet could lay at the feet of the residue of a Japanese Empire that had peaked with Samurai movies and the Kawasaki motorcycle.

But then, Donnie Wu had always been a little too proud.

Kaja shadowed the remainder of the chase. It gave him pause when the boy slid into the hold of the Sky Winkers. An odd collection of nutcases who believed that the sky promised them salvation. Kaja gave the white-hot sun a wall-eyed look. On one level he was aware of his past; that his people worshiped the sun, water, wind and volcano, each taking on an Earth-given name. But that was superstition, not science. And in this modern age, it was science which had scoured the world. The Sky Winkers claimed to have a higher knowledge, but Kaja doubted it was any higher than his own relationship with Pele, or Ivanov's dedication to the old Roman god, Neptune.

A movement several ships over caught his attention—a man with a red bandana.

Kaja checked the package strapped to his waist, then took to the rigging, leaping and swinging until he leaned from a mast, staring down at the solitary man. He was definitely alone, as they'd arranged. About fifty and fat, his skin burned the color of a red snapper. As Kaja watched, he looked around, twitching like a bird, wiping his broad forehead. With the exception of the Sky Winkers, most people never looked up.

Kaja slid down the mast and alighted onto the deck.

The man gave an *eep* and backpedaled.

Kaja held up his hands. "It's only me."

His terrified expression faded, giving way to a sneer. "You could have warned me."

Kaja shrugged.

"Do you have it?" The man licked his lips.

"I do."

"Then let's do this."

Kaja removed the package he'd liberated from Akamu's body. He'd known what it was immediately. He handed it to the Mga Tao, who produced a small device with a LCD screen, attached to a water-filled glass vial. He sliced open a corner of the package, removed some of the white substance with a small metal spoon and added it to the vial, then stoppered the container, shook it for a moment, and pressed a button. It only took a few moments for the results to come through. When the machine beeped, the man let out a long low whistle.

"This is some intriguing stuff."

"So then we're good?" Kaja asked.

The man grinned greedily. "Yeah. We're good." He passed Kaja a bag full of chits.

SPIKE SPUTTERED LIKE a wet cat. She stood in the middle of the morgue ship, dripping. Her dress was ruined, she'd need *hours* to fix her hair, and she'd broken six nails. What had that ever-loving Pali Boy been thinking? One minute she was racing beside him, the next she was taking a club to the side of the head for him, and the next he was snatching her into the air and tossing her into the sea. She had had his back. *What the fuck?*

She stripped off her dress and tossed it into a corner. Nothing to do but make it into rags at this point. When she got her hands on that boy, she was going to turn him inside out.

"Take this," said her brother, tossing her a towel.

She snatched it out of mid-air, dried her hair and wrapped it up.

"He did the smart thing, you know."

She stripped down to her underwear, and in a fit of frustration, removed that too.

Her brother's eyes shifted away as her true form was revealed. He examined the floor for a moment, then turned around.

"The Dogs followed the action," her brother told her. "They watched what happened and said that he probably saved you."

"I can take care of myself."

"Of course you can. Those Boxers are usually pretty well trained, though."

"I'm trained, too. Weren't you the one who said I was the best student you ever had?"

"I did. And you are. It's just that I worry about you."

"Save it." But even as she said it, she felt her anger waning. Her brother had been both mother and father to her.

He was silent for a moment, then he cleared his throat. "Is there anything else you need?"

"No," she snapped.

He started to walk away.

"Brother," she whispered.

He stopped, but didn't turn around.

"Thank you."

Although the words were barely above a whisper, he nodded. Then he continued to the other end of the morgue, opened the door, stepped out and closed it behind him. After a moment, she heard a splash.

She shook her head. There was no way she could stay mad at her brother, not after everything he'd done to help her. But Kavika, on the other hand... *him* she could stay pissed off at for an age. Make him pay for it. She counted to ten as she itemized what she'd do to him if he ever returned. Several of her ideas gave her a moment's pause.

She headed towards the back of the long room, past the bodies laid out on the slabs, and came to a stop in front of one of the wall lockers. She opened it and began picking through the clothes on the hangers, her lips pursed, her left foot tapping impatiently, eventually selecting capris and a sky blue blouse. She dressed, and found a pair of flats that suited and slipped them on.

Now to get down to serious business. A small mirror had been affixed to the door long before the plague, back when these lockers were used by boat hands out for a week of fishing. A sticker in the shape of a peace sign took up the lower half of the mirror. The upper half was clear. By moving her head around she was normally able to apply the right amount of makeup so it didn't look like she'd escaped from the circus.

Spike began brushing at the tangles in her hair, urging her way through the knots. She'd just managed to subdue the left side of her head when she noticed something out of place in the view behind her. She should have been looking at a pair of wall lockers with a rack of shark skin hanging between them. But suddenly it looked as if the shark skin had grown a pair of legs... a woman's legs.

Appropriate for *Los Tiburones*, thought Spike.

She contemplated fighting and found herself smiling and grinding her teeth. Maybe this was just what the doctor ordered.

"You can come out now."

The other gave no response.

"Seriously. Unless sharks are able to grow human legs, you are definitely discovered, so you might as well show yourself."

The legs shifted.

Spike's left hand slid slowly to a length of rattan. She wrapped her hand around it and let it hang loosely against her leg.

"I don't know what you've been looking for, but it's not cool to mess with the dead."

"Isn't that what you Water Dogs do? Mess with the dead?" The voice came first, followed by the figure of the same girl they'd chased earlier. She wore shorts and enough material to cover her chest this time.

"We do it as a service. If you haven't noticed, the plague didn't leave us with much. We have to use everything we have, including the dead."

"How philanthropic of you to do all of this for free."

Spike wanted to scrape the smirk off the girl's face with the end of her rattan, but she held back. "Nothing's for free anymore. We all need to get paid."

"I'm glad you agree. I need to be paid as well."

"What do you need to be paid for? Someone running drugs for you?" Spike regarded the other girl's Spanish features, a small-boned face framed by sun-bleached brown hair, and something clicked into place. "Akamu?"

"He owes me."

"He's dead."

"Then someone owes me."

"That's not how it works."

The *Tiburón* girl paused. Spike saw the frustration in the other's eyes. Frustration, and something else.

Fear.

"You're in trouble, aren't you?" Spike asked, working it out as she said it. "Either the drugs weren't yours or you owe someone who you're afraid of. Is that right?"

"None of your business."

Spike laughed. "It *is* right."

The girl balled her hands into fists. She wore fingerless gloves with what looked like metal bands over the knuckles.

She took a step forward and held her hands ready, looking like she knew exactly how to use them.

"Easy now." Spike held up the length of rattan in her left hand and the hair brush in her right. "If that's what you want, we can go at it. In fact, I wish you would."

The girl stepped forward and swung lightly, testing the distance. Spike struck the tips of her fingers with the end of her brush. Just a gentle tap really, but hard enough to sting the other girl's fingers and make her put the tips into her mouth.

"Your hair..." the girl began.

"What about my hair?" Spike felt heat burn her face and was distracted just enough so that she was unable to block the lightning fast punch that sunk into her stomach and sent the air *woofing* from her lungs. As she turned away, she whipped the rattan against the outside of the girl's knee, and the girl went down. Spike has been struck in much the same way by her brother; it was like a jolt of electric bee stings. "Keep your comments to yourself."

The girl got back to her feet slowly, and her own hair fell over much of her face. She cracked a feral grin. "Why talk about your hair when I can talk about your face?"

Spike grunted like a struck animal and attacked.

Kavika swung across a gap between boats and hooked onto a mast line. Several boats ahead, a dozen Pali Boys played at flying. A broken antenna array made it possible for them to run along it as fast as they could and hurl themselves out, swan-diving in mid-air while they embraced the wind and left their fates to Pele, only to be yanked back by their feet as the bungees engaged. A needle buried deep in Kavika's chest jammed itself into his heart as each Pali Boy leapt free. He found himself holding his breath as he envisioned each of them crashing to their deaths, folding into broken bones and pools of body fluids.

The part of being a Pali Boy that allowed him to travel the skyways was no problem, but the part of being a Pali Boy that made it necessary for him test fate terrified him. How was it that he could battle the Boxers and overcome his fear, yet even watching the full-time Pali Boys getting their sport on sent shivers through his spine? He knew he wasn't a coward. He just couldn't come to terms with the dichotomy. Was it as simple as necessity? During the battle with the Boxers, he'd had little chance to feel his fear, much less dwell upon it. He'd been forced to act or die. But this other thing, the sport of being Pali, didn't seem as serious, accomplished as it was with hoopla and bravado to spare.

Donnie Wu had once told him that it was time that had become his enemy. The more time he had to think about it, the more terrified he became. Like the Pali Jump. They were in the middle of the summer gloom, but soon it would be swept aside and the rain would come, and with the rain, the wind. New Pali Boys would be made. No one had died or been injured in more than six years. One argument would be that the odds were in his favor because it hadn't happened in such a long time. But a more cynical dark argument begged the question, wasn't it about time for an accident?

And the next death?

Kavika shook his head. He hated himself for his hesitation, for the fear that grew unmanly inside of him.

"Hey, Brah. Whatchu doing up here on Pali Highway?"

Kavika snapped back to the present. While he'd been dowsing for impossible answers, the Pali Boys had come his way.

"Hey, Akani. What's up?"

"You up. You need go get down," said Kai, a stout Pali with arms like anchor cables.

Kavika smiled, but didn't see it reciprocated on any of the other's faces. Kai, Akani, Mikana, Mano, and Bane all stared back at him with a seriousness that stripped from it any semblance of brotherhood.

"Kaja told you. No Pali until you prove yourself."

"Ha. I know, but he'll be okay with it." Kavika tried to will the others to smile, to return the friendship he so eagerly wanted to share, but they were as implacable as a slate grey sky.

Kai and Bane swung around behind him.

Kavika held his hands out in front of him to show that he meant no disrespect, and that he wasn't going to try anything.

"The Boxers were after me. I was afraid they'd do the same thing to me that they did to Akamu. I had to use the highway."

Mano shouted, "Don't say that name, Wannabe."

"Yeah. Don't use his death as an excuse." Mikana stepped in close and smacked the back of Kavika's head. His skin burned, but he didn't make a move. Still, he wanted to make sure they knew he wasn't just making things up.

"No, really. I had to toss Spike into the water to save her."

"You threw someone over?" Kai asked. "Holy Pele, Kavika. What happened to you?"

"Nothing, Kai. I'm the same as I was."

"Then I was wrong to ever like you."

Kai kicked him behind the legs. Kavika fell to one knee, now balanced precariously on the cable. He looked imploringly at Akani and held out his hand, but he saw no love there. It was as if he were a hoalie transgressing on the skyward turf instead of a part-time Pali Boy on a mission. He'd once seen a young blond man swinging from one of the nets. He'd seemed so thrilled with the idea of being above the city; his face was cut from ear-to-ear by a crazy smile. Then the Pali Boys found him and kicked him back to earth.

The outrage on the Pali Boys' faces then was mimicked in the faces of his friends now. Kavika saw it coming and there was nothing he could do to stop them.

"Please—"

They fell on him, punching, kicking and gouging. Fists found his face, even as he tried to block them. A foot found his kidney and drove it into his spine. He felt a finger twist and snap. An elbow dug into his ear, rendering the world into a dull, hollow place.

Everywhere feet and fists and elbows found his soft places. The blows were too many to block. Soon he found himself swooning, the blows just too much for his body. He felt them strip him of his sharkskin forearm and palm guards. Then he felt the rubber removed from his feet.

"Only Palis need this. You're no Pali."

He never knew who said it. Nor did he care. He'd been transported to a universe of pain.

He felt himself lowered roughly, hand to hand, until he was on the deck. Someone kicked him between the legs, then he was alone. No longer Pali. No longer skyward. No longer a boy who could follow in the footsteps of his father.

Alone.

He curled into a ball and lay there until he was kicked awake by a passing fire guard.

Then he slunk off into the twilight.

He heard them chattering above him, but refused to look. He wouldn't give them the satisfaction. He limped and dragged himself from one boat to the other, inexorably heading towards the ships that made up his everyday life. The wind had come up with the falling sun. The coolness felt good against his skin, the only respite he'd had thus far. But where to go? He didn't want to go back to his mother and sister. He didn't need that sort of drama right now. He could go and see Donnie Wu, but that meant going past Pali Boy central. He could also go and see Ivanov. God knows he could use some vodka right now. What he needed first was some medical attention. His left little finger was pointed in the completely wrong direction. He couldn't see at all from his right eye. His left ear rang like he'd swallowed an alarm clock.

He managed to make it to the morgue ship. It looked deserted. The lights inside were off. He tried the handle twice before he managed to turn it. He slouched inside, then leaned against the door, using his weight to close it. As his eyes adjusted to the darkness, he saw that everything wasn't right. Boxes and plastic containers littered the floor, along with a body from one of the slabs. Farther down, another body lay half on, half off the slab, an elderly Chinese woman by the looks of it. Her head lolled, allowing her long gray hair to fall straight towards the floor. The knuckle of her left hand kissed the floor's surface. Across from her one of the wall lockers leaned drunkenly into another.

Then he heard the laughter. Low, from deep in a throat, someone was laughing down at the other end of the morgue.

"Hey."

He took a wobbly step into the room and had to reach out to the empty slab nearest him for balance. A pair of scissors large enough to cut a sail or an abdomen lay at his feet. He leaned down and grabbed them. When he stood, he swooned. Blood had shot to his head and didn't want to leave.

"I said, hey," he said, holding the scissors in front of him.

The laughter came again.

He edged forward.

Movement at the far end of the room. A foot scuffed, then came into view. A moment later it was joined by another as if someone were laying on the floor.

"Hey, yourself," came Spike's voice. "Come back here." Giggling. "Join us. Meet Lopez-Larou." More giggling.

He took two more steps and Spike came into view, sitting in the middle of the floor. Her wig lay across her knees like a small dead animal.

"You okay?"

"She's fine," came a voice he thought he recognized.

He took another painful step and the whole scene came into view. Spike sat back-to-back with the *Tiburón* girl, their legs spread out across the floor. The other girl held a bottle in her hand. She passed it back to Spike, who took it and drank, then held it towards Kavika.

"Looks like you need this."

"What happened to you?" Lopez-Larou asked. But then she giggled, so Kavika wasn't sure if she even wanted to hear him. Still, he answered.

"They kicked me out of the sky." The words came out easy, but the idea of it dammed up his insides. He felt his face turn red, and the edges of his eyes began to sting. He closed his eyelids to keep them from exploding. As sure as he was standing in the morgue ship, devoid of everything Pali, he knew that if he didn't do something he would cry, showering the universe with all his unfulfilled dreams and desires—the hatred he felt against his father for dying, the desperation he held and refined for his sister, and the bile taste of the hope he'd carried in the empty spaces between what he'd wanted to do and what he'd never be able to because of his fear of failing.

Spike laughed. "Is that all? I thought someone had died or something."

Lopez-Larou laughed with her. "Come join us."

Kavika was so tired. He sagged to his knees, then keeled over. His head landed in Spike's lap.

"There, there, silly boy. We'll get this figured out."

"I don't want to figure anything out."

"Then let us do the thinking for you."

"So what do I do?"

"Just lay here and pretend you love me."

"But I do love you."

"See?" Spike said to Lopez-Larou. "He knows just what to say."

"All you need now is for him to ask you to marry him."

"A girl knows when to stop. I'm happy just to be loved."

Then the cool comfortable darkness Kavika had been seeking found him, wrapped him in plastic, and dropped him in a universe where flowers grew from the sky, fish jumped from cloud to cloud, and Pali Boys were two inches tall.

CHAPTER NINE

Daddy? Why is there no land?

The land is where the plague lives.

Why doesn't it live in the ocean with the fishes?

Because it's man who made the plague and Mother Kapo who made the fishes. She won't let anything happen to her fishes.

Is that why we're in the ocean? Are we pretending to be fishes?

Yes.

And Daddy?

Yes.

What's at the bottom of the line?

The ocean floor.

Isn't that the same thing as land?

No. It's made up of the bones of a billion billion fishes.

So then we live above a graveyard?

Yes.

Does that make us ghosts?

No. We're headstones for a dead planet.

*   *   *

KAVIKA HAD AWOKEN lying on a slab, a plastic cover pulled over him. It had taken him a long time to figure out exactly what had happened. His wounds had been bandaged sometime during the night. He could barely remember anything from yesterday. The one thing that stood out was that he was no longer a Pali Boy. This he knew just as he knew his name was Kavika Kamilani.

Spike had come in later, looking none the worse for wear. She wore working clothes, with only a set of high heels and her wig as her signature. She'd cleaned him up and told him to get ready.

Evidently he'd been pretty badly concussed. They'd called Donnie in to help. Kavika had been in and out, talking about the Sky Winkers and Abe Lincoln and Akamu and his father, all in a mishmash of truth, supposition and dream-fueled lies. The one thing they had been able to parse was that Abe Lincoln was someone they needed to talk to, so Donnie had arranged it, setting the rendezvous for later in the morning.

Then Spike had dropped Lopez-Larou's bombshell. Sometime during their fight, between a left hook to the head and a spiked-heel kick to the gut, the *Tiburón* girl had revealed what she'd been seeking. The idea of a Pali Boy running drugs didn't sit well with Kavika, but what was worse was the fact that the drugs were missing. It could have only been the Boxers who'd taken it, which meant that the blood rape hadn't been a botched Corper attempt to get a blood sample, but a murder.

And now he waited.

They'd chosen an unaffiliated ship in the eastern section of the floating city: an old cargo container hauler, built to crate huge metal containers between the mega ships and the ports. It was about a hundred and fifty feet long, and a third of that wide. But the deck was devoid of cargo containers, and was instead covered with lines, for drying clothes, smoking birds, and airing out bed clothes. At noon, everyone was belowdecks, cleaning their morning's sky-catch of birds and doing whatever else they needed to survive. The deck was virtually empty, except for a few old men lounging in the shadows, watching with interest to see what Kavika had brought to their corner of the world.

Donnie ran sky watch, dangling from a lanyard on an old flag pole.

Lopez-Larou had returned to her people before he'd awoken.

Spike stood next to him, dressed in a simple white dress, fussing over her nails with an emery board.

Finally Donnie whistled.

Kavika glanced skyward and saw where the older man was pointing. Three men headed their way. Each was at least six feet tall, and all wore khaki pants with boat shoes and plaid shirts. They were all blonde. Their faces were free of hair, except for the one in the middle, who wore the signature whiskers of the long-dead president.

"Abe Lincoln?" Kavika asked, straightening as they arrived.

The man held out a beefy white hand and grinned, revealing impossibly white teeth. "One and the same." As they shook hands, he twisted Kavika's wrist so he could better see the Hawaiian's forearm, noting to his fellow Real People the missing sharkskin accoutrements. "I was told you were a Pali Boy."

"I am... or was. Will be again." He jerked his thumb above his head towards Donnie. "He'll vouch for me if necessary."

Abe released his hand and smiled sadly. "No need. It's not often that a Pali boy gets kicked down. We even heard about it in our spaces."

Kavika was taken aback. He'd planned what he was going to say, but this had totally thrown him off. He'd never anticipated the celebrity of his own misfortune.

Saving him from looking too stupid, Spike stuck out her hand. "Pleased to meet you. I'm Spike. And you are?"

The other two introduced themselves as James Madison and George Bush. George gallantly bent his head and kissed Spike's hand, which of course pleased her no end.

It gave Kavika enough time to regain his composure.

"I'm Kavika Kamilani. Thanks for meeting us like this."

"I knew your father," Abe said, then seeing Kavika's

narrowing eyes, added, "But we never formally met. I'm sorry for your loss."

Daddy, where did all the white people go?

There's some still around. You gotta watch them, though.

"It was a long time ago."

"Some things don't get any easier with time."

"Like your son. I heard and am very sorry."

Abe clasped his hands in front of him, but not before clenching his fists. He fixed a smile on his face. "I hear you're after some Boxers."

"Not just any; the ones who killed a friend of mine."

"I spoke with the Corpers after my son's death. They apologized. They even let me talk to a few of their pet Boxers. 'Unfortunate accident' is what they said."

"Too many unfortunate accidents speak to a different story," Kavika said.

"Why don't they just ask people for their blood? Why the need to blood rape?" Spike asked.

"They tried that," said Bush. "Didn't get enough. Their only choice was to take it by force. They used to take a lot more, but people resisted. Can you imagine what a war is like aboard this ship?"

"Devastating," said Madison.

"Devastating." Abe placed a hand on Bush's shoulder. "So they resorted to what they call 'Field Sampling.'"

"Blood rapes, you mean," Spike said.

"Yes. Blood rapes." Abe looked appraisingly at Spike. "You're a man, aren't you?"

Kavika held his breath as he watched Spike out of the corner of his eye.

Finally, she responded. "An unfortunate accident of birth, I'm afraid. One I've been trying to remedy for some time now."

Abe smiled. "We all seem to be trying to undo what was done by someone else." He wiped his brow with a handkerchief. "The plague put us all at a disadvantage."

"You more than most. My father told me that the world used to be dominated by Haolies. One thing I've been meaning to ask is, why Real People? Why that name?"

Abe shrugged. "It's a matter of translation. When Europeans moved into North America, they encountered many indigenous peoples. Most of their tribal names referred to themselves as the 'real people,' or the 'only people,' or something similar. They had a very introverted view of the universe, and until their interaction with outsiders, never considered that they weren't the center of their own universe."

"And you?"

"I suppose we had a very introverted view of our own dominance in the world culture. Some used to say 'White means Right.' Wars were fought over this."

"My mother told me that the white man was a plague," Spike said. "Wherever they came, people died."

That stopped everyone for a moment. Kavika didn't know what to say. Spike's curiosity had taken them to a place he didn't want to be, and his invocation of the word 'plague' in the same sentence as 'white man' could be tantamount to a slap in the face.

Abe cleared his throat. "Now that we've convened this meeting of the Real People Mutual Appreciation Society, let's get down to business." Kavika caught the twinkle in his eyes. "So what did this Boxer look like?"

Kavika described him as best he could, including all the details about Akamu's blood rape that he knew, but excluding the presence of drugs.

"I know this one. Calls himself Fang. He was involved in my son's death."

"This is bad business," Madison said softly. "Why are we even involved in it?"

"As bad as it is, we need to stick together if we're going to have any chance against them," Abe said.

"Why is it that you've never made a move against them?" Kavika asked.

"We're under constant surveillance. For some reason, our presence is threatening to them. No telling what's going through the Jap minds. You, on the other hand, are able to go places we can't." He pointed to the wires, cables and nets that made up the roof of the floating city.

"We're willing to do it if we know where to go," said Kavika. "That ship is larger than all the rest put together. We wouldn't get ten feet inside if we enter through the wrong window."

"That's your first mistake. You can't enter through the windows. They have them electrified."

"What?"

"Yeah. Kill you stone dead."

"Then how?"

"I'll tell you. Better yet, I'll show you." And with that, Abe held out a hand, in which Bush placed a rolled up map. Kneeling on the deck, he proceeded to show Kavika the best way into the lion's den, answering every question as best as he could and pointing out the dangers along the way.

CHAPTER TEN

WAITING UNTIL NIGHTFALL was one of the hardest things Kavika had ever done. It was too much time. Fear fingered its way through the plan to pinpoint every flaw and chance for failure. The more Kavika had to wait and listen to his own second thoughts, the more be began to believe them. Their initial plan had been pretty simple: Donnie Wu would create a diversion near one of the fountains. While the Boxers responded, and the Corpers' attention was drawn away, Spike and Kavika would enter surreptitiously through an access hatch where the screws had been loosened. Used for maintenance when the ship was still a pleasure palace for the rich and famous, the hatch was now used by scientists to gain direct access to the water for testing.

Dressed in black sharkskin, he and Spike hugged the deck of a nearby ship. The unaffiliated occupants had been ushered below and were too afraid to even ask for something in trade for their discomfort. Both Kavika and Spike wore skull caps made from reclaimed rubber tubing. They had the same material on their feet, thicker pieces of rubber for traction. The only parts open to the air were their faces and hands. Each carried a knife at the waist in a sharkskin sheath. Both of them also had back holsters holding two rattan Escrima sticks.

They were as ready as they'd ever be.

Of course, they almost hadn't gotten Donnie to help. He'd needed convincing.

"Tell me again why you want to go aboard the Freedom Ship?"

"Akamu's attackers are there. I need to find them."

"And then what? You think they'll automatically cooperate? They'll see this badass ex-Pali Boy and lay down their weapons and beg you not to hurt them?"

"I don't think that at all. But it won't be as hard as all that. The Real People gave us directions."

"And that's supposed to be a good thing?"

"They know exactly where these Boxers live."

"And the pair of you think it's going to be easier to go into the lion's den than to wait outside of it?"

"We don't think anything of the sort," protested Spike. "We know this is near-suicide. But what choice do we have? You saw what the Pali Boys did to Kavika. What's to stop them from doing it again?"

"They won't touch him as long as he stays out of the sky."

"You don't know that. You can't prove that. The only way we'll get this over with is to find the Boxer that killed Akamu."

"And when they catch you?"

Spike smiled. "There's catching us, and then there's catching us."

"So you *do* have a plan."

"Pali Boys own the sky. Water Dogs own the sea. And until someone stops them, Boxers own the decks."

"I'll buy that."

"We can't make them go to the sky, but we can get them in the sea. And if they're in the water then they become the property of the Water Dogs. They can be killed or ransomed. Whatever's easier and more profitable. And then there's nothing they can do."

"I have a feeling that there's always going to be something they can do, but I get it. I was just worried that you two were going off half-cocked, thinking you could infiltrate the Freedom Ship like a pair of plague ninjas to find the one Boxer you need among Pele knows how many are in there."

How many are in there?

Which was a question that Kavika was soon going to find the answer to. Ever since he was a child staring at the Freedom Ship, he and the others had daydreamed about how the Japs lived aboard. It looked so fresh and clean. All smooth lines and a fade-proof white hull. It was like a heaven they could never attain.

Ivanov had told him about the old Greek gods and how they lived on Mount Olympus. The Freedom Ship in all of its glory was like that. Those who lived aboard were gods, and the people of the city dreamed of the extravagances to be found aboard it. Showers. Movie theaters. Running water. Electricity to spare. Spreads of food fit for kings. Plush carpets and fabric. Cool metals. Soft beds. All these and more had become a mantra for generations of children growing up. On occasion a beautiful woman of the city would disappear; children would sometimes go missing. All these were blamed on the residents of the Freedom Ship. Most hoped that they'd been taken as a reward for something. But others, like Spike, scoffed at the idea that they'd been selected, or had 'risen' to the Freedom Ship, as people were known to say, delivering the pronouncement in soft, awe-filled whispers.

"More like gang-raped by a bunch of horny-ass Japs," Spike once told an elderly woman. "They're no different than we are. They're just the rich folk and we're the poor folk." She'd spat. "Doesn't make them gods."

Gods or not, Kavika was eager to see inside.

He heard the shrill whistle from the other side of the Freedom Ship. Donnie Wu was doing his thing.

He and Spike slipped over the edge of the rail and into the water, where a pair of Water Dogs were waiting. The Water Dogs grabbed them and, with their oversized flippers, quickly propelled them across the lagoon to the ship. They found the lip of the access panel, pulled it slightly to the left, then used a knife to free the three hasps on the inside. There used to be a rubber seal around the door, but that had long ago rotted away. It took maybe thirty seconds, and the door was slowly opening.

Kavika and Spike stared wide-eyed into the darkness. No one was waiting for them; a good start. Spike entered first and Kavika pulled himself up after her. They stood for a moment, attempting to acclimatize themselves to the pitch-black interior of the access tunnel. As they did, the last of the water fell away from the sharkskin. Finally it was Kavika who whispered, "I see a light. Let's go."

Kavika squeezed past Spike towards an almost impossibly dim strip of light. As he moved, one slow step after another, he heard Spike close the hatch behind them.

Kavika reached the interior hatch and placed his ear to it, but heard nothing except the thumping of his heart. Now all he had to do was open the door and hope for the best. For all he knew, it might lead them into a latrine or the main dining hall. The thought made him wish that Spike hadn't closed the hatch behind them.

They opened the door and found themselves in a closet. Except for several empty boxes, it was empty. They were as yet undetected, but they still had four floors to travel, and an unknown amount of people to get past.

The hallway was deserted and not at all what they'd expected. The Freedom Ship was universally thought of by the citizens of the floating city as a palace; a place with clear air, sharp corners, white walls and the antiseptic cleanliness of story-book royalty. Where everyone else lived in the ghetto, this was the shining beacon of civilization, just like the one he'd heard spoken about in the Bible.

But the Freedom Ship was nothing like that. In reality, it smelled terrible, with a distinct hint of feces. The floor was far dirtier than even the most slovenly third mate would allow. The walls had a coating of grime, like the lower holds of some of the older, unaffiliated ships, the ones without third mates at all.

Kavika and Spike glanced at each other. This was definitely not what they expected.

The hallway ran almost the length of the ship. It dead-ended at the engine compartment, which took up three levels of the rearmost section, but they wouldn't be going there. They had to get to the staircase in the middle of the ship. Once there, the plan was to travel directly to the floor they needed and find the Boxers they'd come to get.

They separated as they moved down the hallway. Kavika pressed his back against one wall, Spike the other, and as a pair they skulked down the hallway towards the center of the ship. They passed several sets of closed doors before they came to an open one on Kavika's side.

He gestured for Spike to edge forward so she could see into the room, which she did, moving inch by inch, leaning slightly forward to see in. Then she straightened and gave him a nod.

He approached the room, peered around the corner and found it empty. The only things inside were ropes and odd metal objects hanging from a wall: tools of some sorts, but he didn't know what they were for.

They waled on. By Kavika's count, they had thirty more doors to pass before they'd reach the first set of emergency stairs. At the next door, they heard shuffling from inside, and a pungent smell surrounded the opening. They tried to peer in, but all they saw was an empty floor. The wall to the next room had been removed. They exchanged looks with each other, but were unwilling to stick their heads into the room without knowing what was going on.

But the next room was the same way.

As was the next.

A whole series of rooms along the left hand side had been converted into something. They might never have found out what was in the room had they not heard voices emanating from farther down the hall and ducked into one of the open doors.

They plastered themselves on either side of the opening, facing into the room, and what they saw so shocked them that they stood there staring, even as a pair of Boxers walked past their door, talking jocularly about something or other in

Chinese. Only when the voices had been silenced by the closing of a door down the hallway did either of them say anything.

"What the hell *is* that?" Spike asked in a wondrous whisper.

"I think it's a cow," Kavika said. Then, after a moment, "But I'm not sure."

The cow stood in the middle of the room, amidst a mound of dried plankton and seaweed. It was black and white, just like the pictures Kavika had seen in books. In fact, it looked *just like* the cows from the pictures, except that this creature had been attached to some sort of machine. A metal cone was affixed to its mouth, at the end of a metal hose running from the ceiling above. A metal cone was also affixed to its rear, connected to a metal hose running into the floor. But the strangest sight of all was what appeared to be a set of metal fingers that reached under the stomach and was affixed to appendages there. These metal fingers pulsed in alternating beats, causing the metal hose to which they were attached to leap and shudder, as if something was inside.

"What are they doing to it?" Spike asked.

"I don't know. I just can't get over it." Kavika turned his head and realized that there wasn't just one cow. There were dozens, all lined up along the outside wall. The reason they hadn't seen them earlier was because they were centered on the walls of the rooms. Each had the same hoses attached to them, running into the ceilings and into the floors. "Cows... they have *cows* on this ship."

Kavika brought his hand up and rubbed his face. He was just plain amazed at the sight. He'd heard about these creatures. Donnie Wu had told him about entire businesses that sold nothing but beef to people driving by in cars. Cows had had a cult following in America, and had been a primary source of food, but that was on land. Not only was their presence strange, but it was damned insulting. That the Corpers had them aboard the ship, especially when there were ships where folks were starving, was an extravagance that seemed imperiously wrong.

Then he heard a sound that absolutely terrified him. Halfway between a whine and a cry, it came from all the way at the other end of the immense rectangular room, and soon it was joined by others just like it. The noises became more insistent and soon the large room was filled with their bleating.

Kavika and Spike drew their sticks from their backs and advanced carefully along the wall. When they reached a doorway, they hurried quickly past, but they were otherwise unimpeded in their journey to the source. They passed a dozen doors before they saw what appeared to be a small pen, holding smaller versions of the cows. These had yet to be assaulted by the metal hoses, and were staring hungrily at Kavika and Spike as they came into view.

They glanced at each other, then stared wide-eyed at the incomprehensible sight. Finally they just shook their heads. This was just too much. Nothing had prepared them for this sort of thing.

They checked left and right and moved out of the room, leaving the cries of the calves behind them. At length, they reached the stairs, which were covered with threadbare red material that muffled the sound of their feet.

Spike went first. Moving in a crouch, she held one stick in front of her and let the other one trail behind her.

Kavika came after her, moving the same way, his ears pricked for any sound.

They came to the landing on the next floor, and a hallway running parallel to the one below. They didn't know what was on that floor, but they didn't need to. They had to go up. The Real People had told them exactly where to go. Everything else was just getting in their way.

They were moving to the next level when they again heard voices coming towards them, ran back to the second level, and found an unlocked door. They dashed inside, closed the door and put their backs against it.

The room was someone's living space. Five times larger than a cargo container, it boasted more couches and chairs than any two Hawaiian families owned. To the left of the door was a kitchen area. A tall cabinet gave out a humming noise.

"Oh, dear God," Spike muttered. "It's a *refrigerator*." She opened the door and stuck her head inside.

Kavika heard her hollow giggle. He came up behind her and they basked in the chilled air blasting from the open door. Jars and containers rested on several shelves. An apple and three bright yellow onions sat on the bottom shelf. One of the jars was filled with white liquid. The other was filled with what looked like water.

Spike picked up one of the onions and inhaled deeply. She grinned in satisfaction. Then she grabbed the other two. She tried to stuff them in her suit, but it was almost skin-tight. She held them out to Kavika.

"Can you carry these for me?"

"I don't think so."

"But Kavika, do you know what I can do with these and some fish?"

He couldn't help but laugh. That she'd been born a boy was impossible to tell. To him, at least, she seemed girl through and through. "We can't, Spike. Look, if you must, you can carry them there and there," he said pointing at her chest.

She actually looked at them as if considering it for a moment.

"I was just joking," he said.

She blinked. "Oh... yeah." She smiled self-consciously. "Never mind."

Kavika chuckled softly. He grabbed the jar filled with clear liquid and opened it. A quick sniff and a taste told him it was water. He took a deep drink of the cold liquid. It was the best tasting water he'd ever had. He held some out to Spike. At first she took a small sip, but was soon gulping it down. Together they finished the water, and put the empty jar back in the refrigerator.

They didn't go any farther into the room to check out the sleeping area or the closets. Instead, they returned to the door. There they noticed a peephole that allowed them to look into the hall. Kavika checked and found it empty.

They stepped back into the hall and headed up the stairs. They made it halfway to the next level before they happened upon a man lighting a cigarette. He looked up at the same time they saw him.

Spike attacked with her sticks, catching him in the head and throat, and again in the head. He fell hard to the stairs, stunned, his eyes unfocused but still open, until Spike kicked him in the face, sending him to the place of happy Japanese dreams.

Kavika stepped forward and stubbed out the freshly lit cigarette.

This was their first encounter. Frankly, he'd expected more. The ship was easily the size of at least half of the ships in the floating city. It should have been able to hold thousands, but so far they'd only heard or seen a few. Sure, they'd only been in a small fraction of the space so far, but there still should have been more.

Spike beckoned for him to follow. They hit the next level and knew they were in trouble right away, when they saw dozens of Corpers wearing dark suits and white shirts. Some of the nearest stopped what they were doing and gaped at them, while, farther down, men and women came and went, busy at some task. Kavika glanced up the stairs toward the fourth level and saw a group of Boxers descending.

He had no choice. He grabbed Spike, turned right and sprinted down the hall.

An alarm went up behind them.

People screamed after them in Japanese, and a Klaxon sounded.

But all of those noises were drowned out by the sound of the roar they heard in front of them. They skidded to a stop as an immense space opened before them on the left, opening into an auditorium with stadium seating. On the floor-to-ceiling, wall-to-wall screen was an immense lizard creature attacking a city filled with skyscrapers. Fire leaped out of its mouth as it screamed again.

"Kavika!"

He dropped into a crouch, both sticks at the ready.

Spike had already engaged the first Boxer who'd caught up with them, taking out his knees.

Kavika stomped on the back of the man's neck, then attacked the Boxer coming up behind him. He twisted and reverse punched with the short end of the sticks into his opponent's sternum. The Boxer's face blanched white as he fell to his knees.

Then they were in the thick of it.

The Boxers didn't have any weapons, which evened the odds. Although they were outnumbered, Kavika and Spike had Escrima sticks, and they knew how to use them.

Kavika was kicked and punched several times in the face, but he gave better than he got, his sticks dancing in a fandango blur. Soon there was a gap in their opponents' defense as one fell unconscious. Both he and Spike saw it at the same time. They reversed their run back the way they'd come and burst through, running pell-mell towards the stairs.

They took the stairs two at a time until they ran into more opponents. Kavika had been wondering where everyone was; now, he'd clearly found them. It took them more than a minute of battering the Boxers' feet and ankles before they made the fourth level. At one point, they'd managed to tackle Spike and hold her down, one sitting on her back and another twisting her neck. Kavika managed to rap one of his sticks against the side of the first guy's head and snap his neck; while the other froze at the sight, Kavika did the same to him. Although he and Spike made it to the top, they didn't arrive unscathed.

They turned left into a narrow passage; the left wall was made of glass, beaded with moisture on the inside: a greenhouse, complete with plants, trees and grasses.

To the right was a room filled with six vats of cycling red liquid.

They limped past them and hit their target room at a run. Spike was battered and bleeding, but she kept right behind him. Dark shapes exploded from their beds, leaping to intercept them, but where the occupants were groggy, Kavika and Spike rode the leading edge of violence. They whipped their Escrima sticks in a modified Heaven Six, blocking with the broad edge and striking with the hard-knobbed ends.

Back to back, they were unstoppable. They were a machine of whirling pain.

Until a pair of dark figures took out their legs.

Kavika felt smothered for a moment as bodies surged over him, grabbing, slapping and punching. He kicked out and brought his arms across the bare skin of his opponents. Shark skin was as smooth as glass when felt one way, like a thousand tiny razor blades the other way... this was what he pulled across their flesh. They screamed, and with their cries came his own roars of outrage and fear and unspent energy.

For a moment, he was free.

Shouting came from outside the room; feet pounded along the hall. He and Spike only had a moment.

He stood as the lights came on and revealed a scene of chaos and murder. Two Boxers lay dead, one strangled with Spike's legs still locked around his neck.

Someone grabbed Kavika from behind. He raised his arm and spun, trapping the hand that had reached out for his shoulder. And there, as if a gift from Pele herself, was the Boxer whose image had been captured on Akamu's media stick.

Kavika shouted, "Come on!"

Spike released the dead man and fought her way to her feet.

Kavika pushed the Boxer hard and felt him lose his balance. Kavika kept up the pressure, angling them towards a window. He screamed, as if the sound could add fuel to his momentum. Face to face, the Boxer's eyes were wide with shock.

"Behind you!" screamed Spike.

Kavika felt a blow, but it did nothing to slow him. The Boxer hit the window at full speed, and it exploded outwards. As Kavika was pulled through with the falling man, he realized that Spike had grabbed onto his back. Together, the three of them fell four stories into the lagoon.

When he hit, all the air left him. He sank deep as he somersaulted through the water. Once he slowed, he wanted nothing more than to breathe, but he didn't know which way was up and which was down. The water was darker than any night, devoid of life and the light of the stars.

Just when he thought his chest was going to implode, Kavika felt hands grasp him, then movement as he was drawn to the surface. He surged into the night, sucking the cold air in with great gulps. Eyes open, he saw everything in a blink of an eye:

Boxers leaning out the broken window high above.

Spike surging free just as he was.

Water Dogs all around them, just as planned.

Donnie Wu hanging from the rigging of a nearby ship, a torch in his hand.

The Boxer floating face up in the water, a few feet away.

Kavika sank back into the water with the feeling one only gets at the end of the day when everything has gone to plan. Now to get the Boxer back to Ivanov, where he could be interrogated. No one would mess with the submarine, and the old Russian had hinted at being able to make anyone talk.

But when Kavika next surfaced, all wasn't as he'd thought it was.

Twenty windows had opened at the base of the Freedom Ship. Divers with flippers like the Water Dogs dove into the water. The Water Dogs around him backed away—they weren't prepared for a fight. Kavika grabbed the Boxer and yelled for help, and two Water Dogs returned for him, but just as they reached to grasp his outstretched hand, a great weight fell upon Kavika.

He sank down and down and down as something pressed all around him. The Boxer was still unconscious, his face inches from Kavika's. Then their descent was halted, and Kavika found himself violently jerked free of the water and flung into the sky.

A net!

Connected to a crane atop the Freedom Ship, a cable descended to the net that now held him and the Boxer. Spike was nowhere to be seen. Kavika tried to see below, but all he was able to catch was a furious fight in the water as it roiled and foamed with struggling Water Dogs and Boxers. Then, before he was pulled back into the ship, he saw the torch waving above Donnie Wu's head. Knowing that his old friend was there was a small speck of hope, dropped into a growing chasm of dread.

Hands reached to grab the net and it was soon pulled onto a high platform. The net dropped to the hard surface, making him shout in pain as his knee was wrenched by his own weight. They pulled the net off him and, while one man held a knife to his jugular, stripped Kavika of his sharkskin. When he was naked, they threw him on the floor.

Chests heaved. Eyes flashed. Angry mouths spat curses. He could see the Boxers' collective outrage in their stance— outrage that a disgraced Pali Boy would dare to breach their sanctum. Kavika knew that pain was coming. He knew he was going to be hurt terribly. And for one brief moment, he didn't even care.

Then he saw Spike as they carried her past him. They'd removed her sharkskin as well, revealing her for what she really was. He would have liked to catch her eye, but she was unconscious, a lump forming on the side of her face.

A minute passed, maybe more, as he listened to the Chinese talk amongst themselves, mingled with his thundering heartbeat.

Then a figure hove into view. His target. The Boxer. He rubbed his head, then replied to something said to him by one of the others. He stood imperiously above Kavika for a moment, looking down at him, before calling for something. There was a flurry of movement.

Two men grabbed Kavika's wrists and ankles and held them firm.

The Boxer knelt between Kavika's legs, pressing his knee painfully into his crotch. His other foot rested beside Kavika's hip. As the Boxer leaned over Kavika, his plait draped along the left side of Kavika's face.

"Fang," the Boxer said softly.

"What?"

"I am Fang."

"What? Fang?"

"Yes. I want you to know me." His English was fluid, with only a hint of Chinese. "I want you to know who it is that blood raped you."

The words sunk in like a stake through Kavika's heart. He surged against the restraining hands. He tried to kick out, but felt someone sit on his knees.

The Boxer pressed harder with his knee. He turned his face as if he were staring at a strange little bug.

"Who do you think you are to come to my home?"

Another face moved into view above the Boxer's shoulder.

This one had a rounder face and was hairless. He wore glasses. His short black hair was combed back. He held out a mechanism for Fang.

When he spoke, it was Japanese. Kavika realized he was seeing a Corper.

All he could see of the man was the upper part of his torso. He wore a dark suit with a white shirt and tie, and showed no emotion. Once he'd handed the device to Fang, he backed out of Kavika's vision and was gone.

Then Kavika's attention switched to the device.

Made of metal and elastic, the only thing he could focus on were the nine needles protruding from its center.

Kavika felt a scream coming from a million miles away. It rushed to him at light speed as the device descended. And only when his chest was pierced did it burst free, a scream of agony and anguish that came from a place in his soul that would never be the same again. Another scream came, but this one was from somewhere else and peeled away as his voice cracked, then silenced.

The last thing he saw was Fang's grin, wide behind the Fu Manchu.

The last thing he heard was a chuckle.

Then... nothing.

CHAPTER ELEVEN

"THEY TOSSED HIM into the lagoon."

"Water Dogs brought him."

"He's going to be okay."

"Why won't they let him in the sky?"

"Nothing many other people haven't experienced before."

"No sign of Leilani."

"Why'd he go on the ship?"

The voices came and went, and eventually Kavika regained consciousness. The first thing he noticed was the punctures in his chest. He'd stepped on a nail once and the metal had gone all the way through his foot; this was how his chest felt, but he had nine wounds instead of one. His hand went to the space but found nothing there, except a bandage.

Blood rape.

He'd hoped it had been a dream.

He cracked open his eyes and returned to the miserable universe he called home. He was lying on his side. His sister lay next to him, her sightless eyes staring at him. She lifted a trembling hand and touched his face.

"Brother." Her voice was soft and weak. "What have they done?"

The cloying smell of oil from the bottom of the hold wrapped around him like cheesecloth. "They got me, Nani." His voice was old sandpaper.

"You were crying in your sleep."

He tried to smile. "I'm too big to cry."

"You're never too big to cry. Sometimes I hear momma crying."

Kavika let the words sink in. The thought drew him deeper into the miasma.

"They took my blood," he said after awhile.

"It's not so bad. They're doing it for me, right?"

Kavika pressed his hand against her hair. "That's what keeps me going, Nani. That all this means something."

He shook his head and sat up. It was harder to accomplish than he'd anticipated; the paralytic they'd shot into him still had its sticky fingers wrapped around his spine and legs. He peeled the bandage away from his chest to see the thick central puncture, surrounded by eight smaller wounds.

"Old Wu brought you in last night."

Kavika looked up. His mother had been sitting there the entire time.

He met her gaze and saw in it everything he needed and so much more that he didn't. All her words about his father and about being a Pali and not taking care of the family slid beneath his love like a riptide.

"How long was I out?"

"Not too long. Maybe ten hours."

"Where's Spike?"

"No sign of Leilani."

He sat up straighter. No sign? "Are you sure?"

Her mother shook her head and poured him some water. He clambered painfully out of bed, took it and drank deeply. He saw that he was naked, rifled through his bag of clothes, and pulled out a clean set of shorts. He leaned over and kissed his sister on the forehead.

"Keep Mom in line, Nani."

His sister smiled.

He stood and gave his mother a nod. She nodded in return.

Then he was hurrying up the levels. His legs plodded against the deck, but the more he was able to work them, the easier walking became; by the time he reached the open air, his muscles felt like they were back to normal.

The first thing he did was lean back and inhale a lungful of fresh air to dispel the stench of the hold. He couldn't live there, no matter what happened. He was meant for the open air. For the sky.

A handful of the Pali Boys stared down at him from the heights as he emerged, and a call went out. Kavika wanted nothing more than to join them, but he still wore the bruises from his last attempt.

Kaja swung free and dropped to the deck beside him.

"How you doing, Brah?" he asked, eyeing the bandage.

Kavika couldn't help but touch the place where they'd taken his blood. "Fine, Kaja."

"We followed the action last night."

"We almost had them."

"Yeah. So... what was it like?"

Kavika turned and stared at Kaja, and a truth hit him so hard it startled him. Staring at Kaja's open and interested face, Kavika realized that he'd done something that no other Pali Boy had done. He'd gone into the Freedom Ship and returned. That was it, wasn't it? Kaja wanted to know what the inside of the Freedom Ship was like. Kavika glanced at the Pali Boys hanging out above him. Their number had tripled.

"It was different."

"Yeah? Different how?" Kaja, the leader of the Pali Boys who refused to let Kavika return to the sky, leaned in, eager to hear the rest.

"Just different, is all," said Kavika. Then he turned and headed away.

"Wait!"

The Pali Boys in the sky laughed at the exchange.

"Fucking wannabe Pali. You ain't ever gonna see the sky again."

As good as walking away from Kaja felt, the idea of never returning to the sky was something terrible. His smile wilted and slid into the hole in his chest.

Alone, he worked his way to the Morgue Ship, confident that the dead would give him less trouble than the living.

When he got there, the place was empty. Even the slabs were free of bodies. No one, living or dead. He was about to leave when the door was yanked open.

Chito, Spike's brother, stood in the doorway. "Where the hell is she?" he demanded. Water dripped from his sharkskin suit.

Kavika shook his head. "I thought she'd be here."

"Here?" He took several strides into the room. The door slammed shut behind him. "How can she be here? Do you see her anywhere?"

Kavika held out his hands. "Whoa, I want to find her as bad as you do."

"Then why'd you leave her on the ship?"

"What are you talking about?"

"We had it surrounded. When they took you up again it was only you who came out. We've been circling it ever since."

"How'd I get out?"

"They dumped you in the lagoon. We took you home."

"And she never came out?"

"Never." Chito stepped close to Kavika. He poked him above where he'd been blood raped, making him wince. "If anything happens to her..." He let the words die, but he didn't have to finish.

Kavika could only imagine what her brother would do to him. But no matter what that was, it wouldn't be worse than the loss of his only friend.

Now to figure out how to get back into the place...

DADDY, WHY CAN'T *we go on the big ship?*
  They don't want us there.
  Then how come we keep sending things to them?
  They give us help sometimes. They give us energy.

But why can't we go there? I bet when it storms, they stay dry.
I bet they do. Anyway, we're not invited.
You and Uncle Donnie could make them.
Might as well tilt at windmills, son. Might as well fight the
wind.

AN HOUR LATER found Kavika no closer to a solution. The immensity of his problem had begun to sink in. He'd managed to circle the Freedom Ship once, which wasn't easy to do. Some of the ships on the lagoon required chits for transit. Rather than pay, which no self respecting Pali Boy—even the grounded kind—would ever do, Kavika found ways that took him far from the direct path.

His father's words came back to him. "Might as well fight the wind." Sure, he could go back into the sky. Sure, he might even be able to defend himself. But he'd never really belong. Not as long as Kaja had grounded him. And it was the belonging that really made him a Pali Boy. Just as Spike being his friend gave him a certain sense of belonging. Sure, it wasn't a large group of high-flying stunt warriors, but his and Spike's group was a very exclusive crowd, one in which another person opened her heart and soul to him.

And he'd fucking left her behind.

If anything happened to her, he'd never forgive himself.

He watched two children, a boy and a girl who couldn't be more then ten years old, dangle a line over the side of their ship. They whispered to themselves for a moment, then jerked the line as it went taught. The girl who held the line struggled for a moment, then it came easily. As she stood, a Water Dog surfaced, holding the other end of her line. He waggled a finger. The kids shrieked and ran away, laughing.

The Water Dog, caught in the middle of a grin, turned to Kavika and his grin turned into a frown. He shook his finger again, a very different sentiment from that he'd given the kids. Then he sank back into the water.

Kavika had talked to Spike about Don Quixote one day, before she'd decided to live life as a woman. She'd loved the idea when she'd learned it during her lessons. That there'd been a man, fictional or otherwise, who'd daftly gone in the face of convention, regardless of what anyone had ever told him, caused her no end of appreciation.

Kavika had always thought of himself as smart, but the importance of Don Quixote was an idea that stretched his logic. He'd learned of the man from his father, and had then asked his Uncle to explain it to him. Don Quixote seemed more crazy than not and he'd told Spike that.

But she'd merely laughed. "You have everything, Kavika. You're Pali Boy. You own the sky."

"But I don't have my father."

"Is that something you can fight for?"

"No. He's dead."

"When I said you have everything, I meant that you don't have to fight for anything, so of course you don't understand Don Quixote."

"And you do?"

"Of course."

"And what do you have to fight for?"

"Myself. Or who I could be."

"You have to fight for that?"

Then he remembered how she'd told him that she really wanted to be a woman, and that from that day forward she'd be one, regardless of what anyone said. Their expectations would be the windmills at which she would tilt.

Don Quixote.

He was more an idea than a man. His father had talked about it. Spike had lived it. For one brief moment yesterday they'd both grabbed their lances and tilted at the great windmill of the Freedom Ship. And they'd almost won.

Except, Kavika realized in an electric moment of clarity, that you can never beat an idea, but only hold it at bay for a time.

"There you are. What are you doing in this place?"

"This place?" Kavika turned to see Donnie Wu slide down a rope, land on a wheel house, and lower himself to the deck. He turned and looked around; he'd somehow made it to the leper ship. In the lee of a crate sat a man with lesions on his face and twisted fingers on his ruined hands. They locked eyes for a moment, then nodded to each other. Windmills.

"I've been looking all over for you."

"Why?"

"I heard from one of my sources that they have her." He let the words sink in. There was no question who *they* were, or who he meant by *her*. "They're going to release her soon."

"What are we waiting for?"

"They want to release her to you and you alone."

Kavika took a step forward. "Where, Uncle?"

Wu shook his head. "I don't know. It doesn't seem right."

"Fuck right! We'll make it right when it's all over." He didn't have the sky. He didn't have the water. And he was alone on the decks. Damn, but he needed this.

Finally Wu gave a sad nod. "Okay, I'll tell you. But I'm going to be with you, just in case."

Kavika craned his neck skyward. Not a Pali Boy in sight.

"What about the others? I might not be a Pali Boy, but this is Hawaiian business. Are they coming with?"

Wu shook his head. "They're helping Ivanov set up new bird nets."

Kavika had arranged his share of nets in his time. Not only were they heavy, but wind—any wind—made stringing and lashing them difficult and dangerous. It would take all of the Pali Boys. He'd get no help from them. He hoped he wouldn't need it.

"So what's the plan?"

"Abe Lincoln proctored the deal. Said he felt bad about what happened. We're going to the ships belonging to People of the Sun. Mr. Pak is to be the go-between."

Kavika let the plan settle in his mind for a moment then asked, "What do you think they did to her, Uncle?"

"There's no telling. Let's hope they just roughed her up."

"Do you have any weapons for us?"

Wu tapped his forehead with a long finger. "Just these."

They headed past the wheelhouse and crossed several ships until they were oceanside. The sea outside of the floating city seemed to go on forever. Kavika intellectually understood that there was land somewhere across the water, but since he'd never seen it outside of a vid, or stepped on it himself, the concept was nothing more than someone else's memory. All he knew were the constantly shifting decks, or hanging from antenna masts, or clinging to nets.

Wu nodded to a handful of older men who were fishing oceanside. Since the Water Dogs owned the water in the city, it was the only way a person could legally fish. And the fishing was rarely good. Most of them blamed the Water Dogs, convinced that they were somewhere beneath the waves somehow sabotaging the fishing. But occasionally, someone would latch onto something immense. Giant Squid as long as a yacht weren't uncommon during those times. Kavika had once seen a Great White Shark caught here. He'd also seen a fisherman latch onto a humpback whale. The whale couldn't get away, but it began to pull the ship away from its moorings to the other ships. Even Water Dogs had reported strain on the anchor cable. In the end, the fishermen had to cut the line and let it go.

Kavika and Donnie Wu were forced to stop their progress when they reached a silver and black barge. The guards demanded a three chit toll. It was an unaffiliated ship; the mishmash of hungry-looking Chinese, Koreans, Filipinos and other Asians told of a melting pot of need and want. The ship itself was spotless, but the people were hungry. Even so, having no affiliation, they had no right to demand a toll, especially one as exorbitant as three chits.

Kavika was about to remark on it when he felt Donnie's elbow in his side. He watched as his Uncle passed the chits to the guard. Then, as they boarded the ship and began to transit the deck, his uncle leaned over and whispered in Kavika's ear. "Too many ears here. I'll explain later."

Kavika spied an older Hawaiian woman scrubbing the deck with a platoon of other women. They were on their knees, using buckets and sponges. Glancing at the rigging, he could see that he'd been here before, but he had been too high above to notice these details. In fact, until he'd been beaten down, he'd failed to notice pretty much anything at this level.

"But she's one of us."

"No family. She's working here."

His Uncle's response made no sense. The way the community worked was that one didn't have to work to be fed, clothed and housed. Sure it was expected, but the older you were, the less work was required. A woman of her age should never be scrubbing decks. That was left for people like Kavika. It was as if she were a... Kavika glanced around and saw the men lounging on the deck. They all had weapons of various kinds: clubs, mostly, but there was the occasional machete, the edge gleaming at their hips.

"Slavers?" he whispered.

"Shhhh." Wu shot him a look. "Not like what you think. This is different. Now hush until we get past."

Kavika noticed one of the men stand straight and angle towards them.

Wu began to hurry, and they were soon walking a plank to another ship. This one was an old garbage scow.

"Do you want to tell me what that was about?"

"Not particularly, and not now. Keep your head in the game, Kavika. Concentrate on what we're doing."

Kavika wanted to know what was going on and why one of their own had been sold to a slaver. The very thought of it contradicted everything he knew about his people. That this was going on raised the question of what else was going on that he didn't know about. Part of him desperately wanted to know, but he also recognized the importance of keeping his head clear. He made a mental note, however, to bring the subject up again.

He took inventory of his body. Overall and despite the recent beating and the blood rape, he was in pretty good shape, a testament to the lifestyle of a Pali Boy. He flexed his hands as he walked. The blood rape had bruised the muscles over his chest, which affected everything connected to them, especially the tendons in his shoulder area. But he found that the more he flexed his hands, the better the muscles felt.

What he couldn't fix were his feet. He wasn't used to using them so much. Since he'd been a kid of three, he'd been climbing and swinging. Other than for Princess processions, which happened three times a year, he hadn't walked from one place to another except for the time he'd broken his arm when he was twelve. And even then he was still trying to swing through the rigging one-handed.

As they reached the edge of People of the Sun territory, Wu held up a hand. Kavika stopped beside him.

"From here on out, listen to me."

"They're not going to let her go easy, are they?"

Wu stared hard at Kavika. "If you want, we can turn around right now and never look back."

"I couldn't do that. She's my friend. She's my family." *She's who I belong to.*

Wu placed a hand on Kavika's shoulder. "It's what your dad would have said. You're more like him than you know. But this is going to be for real, boy."

Kavika nodded. He took advantage of the moment. "About my dad," be began, not knowing what he wanted to know, but wanting to know so much about the man who'd never spoke unless spoken to and spent his life living rather than talking about it.

Wu shook his head. "Not here. Not now. Suffice to say that your father had a motto that he lived by: 'Never give up.'"

Kavika sighed and looked at the deck. He'd expected more.

"I want you to think about that," his Uncle said. "There's more to it than you think."

Kavika swallowed back his disappointment. "Let's go," he said.

Then they crossed the red line into People of the Sun territory. Like always, it was eerily deserted. No birds rested on any of the wires. A strange smell permeated the air.

They'd crossed two ships and were preparing to board a third when three men emerged from a cabin. Kavika recognized Pak, but he didn't know the other two. They were Korean, but they stood a full head taller than Pak, and were well-muscled.

"I brought him," Wu said sharply.

The three men bowed. Pak could barely meet their gaze. The other men stared at their feet.

"Sorry to be in the middle of this," Pak said. He shook his head. "I don't know why they asked me." His hands shook with worry.

"Let's get this over with."

"Fine. Come." Pak turned and beckoned for them to follow.

Wu started to go, then realized that the other two were going to bring up the rear. Wu stopped. "They can go first."

The two Korean men exchanged glances.

"Seriously," Wu said firmly. "They go first."

Pak said something harsh in Korean. The two men bowed, then ran ahead. Pak turned and smiled at Wu as if to ask permission to proceed.

Wu nodded and soon they were marching single file across the ship and onto another. This one had walls built upon the wide flat deck, to partition different spaces. Kavika remembered it from when he'd been here before. He also remembered Pak's twin daughters, both monkey-backed.

This time they traveled farther into the maze than before, turning left and right and left. A shack rested at each turn. Occupants peered at them from cloth-covered doorways as they passed.

They turned a final corner and into a space about ten by ten meters. Six Koreans, including the two they'd met earlier, stood in an arc around a figure tied to the wall.

Shock captured Kavika for a moment as he beheld Spike. Completely naked, her skin had been clean shaven from head to crotch to feet. Her face was a montage of black and blue. A dozen wounds bled from her chest and thighs. Several looked as if they could have been bite marks. Her manhood hung apologetically between her legs for the world to see.

"Pele fuck!"

He rushed to her and began trying to free her.

"Why the hell didn't you take her down?" Wu demanded.

"They made us keep her here. They wouldn't let us."

Her hands had been stapled to the wood with immense pieces of metal. Kavika tried to peel one free, but he was afraid of the damage he'd do. She barely moved, groaning softly when he touched her.

Kavika whirled. "For the love of Pele, someone help me."

Then he saw it for what it was. Instead of fear and loathing, the eyes of the Koreans sparkled with desire. Not the desire of a man for a woman, or even a man for a man. One of them had forgotten to wipe his mouth. Sharpened teeth dripped blood down his chin. These men had the desire a man had for a bird, or a fish, or any other sort of food.

"Uncle!"

"What? Oh—I see." Wu quickly snaked an arm around Pak's throat and spun the man around, pressing it deep beneath the man's chin. Pak's arms waved feebly.

"This is not going to go as planned," Wu told the six cannibals. "You can take your lunatic appetites somewhere else."

"She's ours. You are ours, too," said one of the Koreans, in barely intelligible English.

"I don't think so," Wu sneered. "One flex of my arm and Pak is dead." He released his hold enough for a pitiful scream to escape from Pak's mouth. "Haven't you all ever heard of tofu?"

It was a standoff. Everyone waited for someone else to make the first move. "Kavika," Wu said quietly. "You need to get her down. *Fast.*"

Kavika spun back to Spike, but he didn't know what to do. But he felt the urgency. Her left hand seemed less tightly pinned than her right. He placed a hand on either side of the bloody staple and tested the tightness. There was about an inch of give. It would have to do. With a great heave he jerked back as hard as he could on her hand. Her hand came free... almost. Her eyes shot open and she screamed raggedly. He jerked it again, pulling it out the rest of the way. Blood poured from the wound. It needed a tourniquet but he didn't have the time to tie it off.

"One down," he called over his shoulder.

He locked eyes with Spike. She stared into his for a moment with a totality of fear that saw through him, then she succumbed once more to unconsciousness. He had to get her other hand free. No telling what damage they'd done to her insides, to her mind.

"Kavika!"

He twisted and saw a dozen Boxers descending from bungees into their midst. He turned madly to Spike, then realized that he didn't have the time to free her. He spun back as Wu snapped Pak's neck, then engaged the first two Boxers. Wu was a whirlwind of low kicks and wrist locks.

Kavika waded in, swinging and connecting with the fucking cannibal who'd taken a bite out of Spike. He followed up a punch to his face with a kick to the crotch. When the man bent over, Kavika brought his knee up and lifted him off the ground. The cannibal hit the floor, his eyes open and unfocused.

Then Kavika was on the defense. Two Koreans and a Boxer had him trapped. Beyond him, Wu was in a similar situation. Just when things seemed desperate… they got worse. One of the Boxers produced a knife. One moment he held it, the next it was sheathed in Wu's chest ten feet away.

"Uncle!"

Wu turned to face him, his face pale. "Run!"

Kavika screamed with rage.

He was struck on the back, then the knee. He went down, but he never took his eyes off his Uncle.

The Boxer who'd thrown the knife stepped forward. Wu had fallen to his knees, held in place by two Boxers. The thrower placed a foot on Wu's chest and yanked his knife free, splattering those around them with blood, and stepped close to cut off Wu's head. More blood gushed down Wu's chest and covered the Boxer's fist as he cut. When he came to the spine, he had to bear down, grabbing Wu's hair with his other hand and yanking the head back and forth. The head eventually came free from the body with a wet sound.

Kavika cried out and tried to surge to his feet, but he was struck once, twice, then a dozen times.

He managed to crane his neck enough to look back at Spike once more, before he was bowled under by the blows. And for the third time in as many days, Kavika embraced the darkness.

CHAPTER TWELVE

HE WAS CRACKED.

He was broken.

He couldn't speak.

He could hardly think. Thoughts were born and died before they could coalesce into something intelligible.

Straps ran across his head, chest and abdomen.

A weight hung from his back, pulling him down, down, down.

Then the world exploded into a confetti cataclysm of white and dark, until finally only the dark remained.

THE WORLD WAS smeared and crooked.

He couldn't see it right.

Footsteps.

Feet came into view.

The smell of food.

Hungry.

Hungry.
Hungry.

SOMEONE PULLED BACK his eyelids.

A man in a suit. His hands smelled like fish.

Corper.

Kavika fought his aching lethargy with every ounce of energy he had. He wanted to ravage the man. He wanted to maim him. Images of Wu's head rolling on the deck flooded him. A murder for murder. He wanted to surge forward and eviscerate the man, but all he could muster was a sad cracked groan.

"LOOKS LIKE HE'S waking up."

"Keep monitoring him. I'll return tomorrow."

THE SULLIED EARTH *turned.*

He saw a sky made of black and white squares.

A smooth hand touched his face.

He wanted to scream.

He wanted to bite the finger.

Leavemealoneleavemealoneleavemealonegree-gree.

"THEY'RE BOTH DOING fine."

"Vitals?"

"As expected. Maybe a day or so, then they'll be ready for release."

"Keep monitoring."

DADDY?

Yes, son.

Why do the Corpers hate us so?

Because we know the secret to—

What secret daddy?
The secret to food fucking shit poke me in the eye scratch my
ear pick my hair dominate dominate dominate
You're not my daddy?
And you ain't my fucking son.

KAVIKA FINALLY AWOKE with some semblance of control. His dreams had left his mind fried. That, and whatever drugs he'd been on, made him a mute shadow of himself. He found it hard to concentrate. Sometimes his eyesight would fade out and be replaced by a crazy dream vision.

Lying in bed, he'd been able to do an inventory. It seemed as if he had both arms and legs. His chest had long since healed. But pain arched from his side in two places and from his back. Sometimes the pain was far in the background, but at others it was right up front, replacing every thought, smell and sight, as if his back had been ripped open and a weight had been placed on his spine.

The door opened. Corpers. They'd been coming in on a regular basis to check on him, which meant that he was somewhere on the Freedom Ship.

Two of them: a man and a woman. Black suits, with white shirts and black ties. The man wore round glasses, and the woman wore too much red lipstick.

"Good morning, Mr. Kamilani. I am Mr. Nakihama. I hope you're feeling okay."

Kavika stared blankly at them. They'd never really addressed him before. Sometimes he hadn't even thought they were real.

"You are ready for discharge," the man continued.

About fucking time, he wanted to say, but for some reason his voice had completely ceased to function.

"I want to make it clear to you that you are now responsible for the property of Ishihama International. Any modifications to your new existence are strictly prohibited and will result in immediate withdrawal of said property and therefore in your immediate death."

I'm not anyone's fucking property—

Death?

Seeing the light of understanding flash in Kavika's eyes, the man continued. "You are now officially part of the Minimata Project. It shows in our records that your sister has unfortunately been infected. With your help and sustainment, we'll be able to cure her."

His sister. With her came thoughts of love. How many times had he wished that she would receive a cure. And now to discover that he could be a part of it?

The woman helped him to a sitting position.

A tremendous weight pulled him backwards, making it impossible to sit straight. To manage, he had to lean forward at a forty-five degree angle. It was like carrying a pack, but more awkward.

"There's nothing specifically you need to do to the monkey. Just eat and drink when you are hungry. It will take its sustenance from you. Occasionally, one of our assistants will find you to gather blood for sampling. Nothing invasive; nothing to worry about. Do you have any questions?"

Kavika had a million, but because he was unable to speak, all he could do was open his mouth and make bleating noises.

"Fine, then. We are done here. Ms. Yamasaka will escort you out."

Then the Corper turned and left.

Ms. Yamasaka pursed her too red lips. She glared at him for a moment, then smacked him across the face with the flat of her hand. "No funny business with the monkey," she said.

A hollow place opened inside his soul. He let it take him and gloried in the loss of sight, sound, smell and touch as he fell, forever and a day, to a land where monkeys swung from trees and not people.

CHAPTER THIRTEEN

THEY LEFT HIM in front of the Freedom Ship's gangway, hunched over and broken-backed like a cripple. The metal bridge rattled back into the ship behind him as he stood there, blinking at a world that was no longer his. An old Chinese man was the only audience to his rebirth. Instead of applause, the man spit between two fingers and looked away.

Kavika took one step, then two. He wobbled under the weight of the monkey attached to his back. He wanted nothing more than to cast it into the lagoon, but it was too connected. The umbilicals might as well have been made of steel.

Hungry Hungry Hungry

He lurched forward another few steps. He felt so top heavy. He was forced to grab a nearby deck rail.

Kavika's mind was not entirely his own. He felt the monkey's thoughts insinuating hairy fingers of illogic into his. They tricked him into believing the thoughts were his own. With concentration, he could discern the difference, or at least he fooled himself into believing that he still managed that modicum of control. But if he relaxed his guard, his thoughts and those of the monkey were woven like an insane braid of wants, needs and desires.

Occasionally his vision would twist and he'd see something skewed, the colors all wrong. It took awhile to figure it out, but he soon realized that he was seeing through the eyes of the monkey—he was seeing behind him. With twists and colors like a kaleidoscope, the sudden jarring from his normal vision to that staggered him. He'd learned by falling down, then having to painfully climb back to his feet, that he needed to have constant support. He couldn't trust his legs alone, but with at least one arm, it seemed as if he might be able to navigate this new, monkey-backed universe.

So it was with three points of contact that he limped forward across the floating city. People skittered out of his way. They pointed at him, made signs against bad luck, and whispered amongst themselves—foremost, probably, in relief that it wasn't them.

It wasn't long before a Pali Boy spotted him. He swung down.

"Oh, shit, Brah! What the—"

Kavika tried to see who it was, but he couldn't raise his head enough. He was too exhausted by the constant pull of the monkey.

"Wait 'til Kaja hears about this," said the Pali Boy, before swinging up and away.

The pit of despair centered in the middle of his chest opened a little wider. The more people who knew about this, the more real it became, and the worse it seemed. Once Kaja knew, then all the Pali Boys would know. He'd inform Princess Kamala and everyone would know. Even his mother. And that was something he couldn't live with. It didn't take but a moment to determine that he was not going to go back to her. She had enough trouble trying to feed and deal with his sister, and she didn't need to take care of a monkey-backed boy as well. What a joke that would be on her. Husband dead. Daughter with Minimata. Son monkey-backed. Enjoy your life; thanks for playing.

He'd have to go to Ivanov—Uncle Evil. The old Russian had been a friend of his father's, and wouldn't think of turning him away. So it was that he limped and leaned and grabbed and pulled his way across the city towards the Russian submarine. He fell twice, each time a victim of the monkey's insinuation into his mind. Once he fell on the monkey. It lashed out, scratching and clawing at the back of his head. Screeching its outrage at him.

The voice of a Corper came to him. "*There will come a time when the theta waves merge with your own. This equalization will change you. You will no longer be merely Kavika Kamilani. The monkey will no longer be merely* Macaca Mulatta. *Instead you will be one. Your will and its will will merge until you are a new creature. A creature that will hopefully provide people like your sister with a cure for her disease.*"

When he finally arrived at the submarine, he didn't have the strength to climb aboard. He rang the bell, announcing his arrival. Soon a burly Russian climbed onto the deck. When he saw Kavika, he made the sign of the cross and covered his eyes.

"Be gone. We don't want you here."

"Ivanov, please."

"He doesn't want you here, either. Just go."

"But I need—"

"I said go!"

Kavika tottered away. He managed perhaps a dozen feet before he collapsed. He fell on his side and dreamed of flying. Whether he was a monkey or a Pali Boy, he didn't know, but he flew through trees and masts, alternately grabbing vines and cables, in and out of the jungle to the ships and back again.

A Filipina girl kicked him awake.

"Go, go, go. We no want you here." Her shrill voice sent blades through his aching head.

He'd pissed himself in his dreams. His back felt wet as well. The stench of the monkey's evacuation made him feel sick. When he reached back with his hands and realized that it covered his back, he couldn't help himself. He rose to one knee and retched on the deck.

Amidst the screams of the girl and her mother, who'd joined him when he'd fouled their ship, he managed to stand. He pulled himself away, using the rails and cables as an anchorage to keep himself steady.

He found a rhythm. He'd stagger for a moment, then sleep, leaning against whatever he ended up against. The sun fell and still he moved on, urged by boat owners and citizens of the city. They wanted a cure, but none of them wanted to see it in action. He wasn't sure how long he'd been traveling, but eventually he came to a ship he knew well. It was a super tanker, empty and ghettoized by the myriad peoples who lived within it.

Kavika knew this as an unaffiliated ship. It was free space. He could not be denied access. And the very bottom of the bottom was a place where he'd only been once, retrieving an old friend of Wu's who'd lost his battle with the velvety grip of the poppy. The place was called The Hole. He'd seen more monkey-backed there than he could count. At the time, he'd shuddered with the idea of anyone living amidst the offal and oil. But now, as he stood exhausted and devoid of friendship, it seemed the perfect place for him to rest his soul.

It took him another hour of falling and staggering before he made it to the bottom. He found a spot by two other monkey-backed, and lay on his side between them on the slanted floor. His feet slid into the oil pooling below. He didn't have the strength to pull them free and so left them there, his body resting against the shit-encrusted metal of the supertanker's hold, hands clasped together and placed between his legs as he'd done when he was a boy and scared of what might come next.

Sleep—or a version of waking that mimicked sleep—soon found him. The kaleidoscope of the monkey's vision twirled and cascaded through his mind, reliving the journey from the Freedom Ship to the hole, a lifetime of monkey memories, and the face of the snoring Korean girl behind him.

The last memory Kavika had for a long, long time was of Spike, her quick grin, her painted nails, and her lust for life. Then he dreamed of her flayed alive and hanging like a flag from the ship of Abraham Lincoln.

*   *   *

DADDY? WHY MONKEYS?
  What do you mean?
  Why not other animals?
  I suppose because they were more like us.
  But they're so dirty.
  So are we, Kavika. So are we.

SOMEONE FED HIM. Someone else came and cleaned him. He didn't have the strength or the inclination to move. The monkey's theta waves and his own were almost in synch. He knew this only because he knew nothing else. He lived and breathed the joining.

THE DARKNESS WAS complete. Kavika didn't know how many days had passed. He'd seen the light cycle, but had lost the ability to count. He passed his time by picking the fleas from the monkey in front of him. They slipped from his fingers unless he gripped them in a certain way. Once he had them, he slid them into his mouth. They tasted of oil and acid, but the crunch was satisfying. He felt his own hair being parted by something behind him. A joyful connectedness surged through him.

DADDY?
  What's Daddy?
  Daddy?
  Who you talking to?
  My Daddy.
  Your Daddy's dead.
  Then who are you?
  I am you.
  No you aren't.
  I am now.

* * *

GREE-GREE-GREE

HELLO?
  Who's there?
  Where are you taking me?
  Daddy?
  Gree-gree?
  Daddy?
  Gree?
  Daddy, where are you?
  Gree-gree-gree!

LOPEZ-LAROU HAD HER own troubles. She owed The Family for the loss. She'd fronted the Pali Boy three hundred grams, against her better judgment. But it was her avarice that had conspired against her. Her desire to be like Sanchez Kelly and Paco Braun had infused her every waking moment. If only she had her own company of runners, she could make some serious chits, and elevate herself within *Los Tiburones*. But that was a dream she'd never attain if she didn't get the grams back, or some equivalent value.

She'd determined that neither the Water Dog transvestite nor the strange Pali Boy knew about the drugs, which meant that it was either the Boxers or one of the other Pali Boys who'd taken them. She'd heard that they'd been first on the scene, gathering around their fallen brother as if their presence could bring him back to life.

She doubted it was one of the Boxers. They were like single-minded animals in their attention to their business. If the Nips had sent them to blood rape, then that's what they did. Their leashes were tight; she'd seen them pass up plenty of opportunities to cheat and steal, so eager were they to get back to their masters.

That left the Pali Boys. Most of the citizens of the city

thought of them as simple boys, or more commonly a nuisance. Their ability to stay high above everyone else afforded them a certain celebrity status. But the truth was that they were just like everyone else. They sinned. They lied. They desired things they couldn't have. Akamu wasn't the first Pali Boy to become a runner for *Los Tiburones*.

She'd heard from one of her sources that a Mga Tao had come into some Waffle Dust. The information was less than an hour old. She knew enough about Kelly and Braun to know that they didn't do business with the Monkey Worshippers. Plus, Waffle Dust was something in particular that she liked to make—it was her signature. Kelly specialized in opiates, which is why he was so popular with the Nips. Braun specialized in Benzodiazepine remodeling, which didn't give the same high as an opiate, but allowed the user to function while under the influence.

Like any good chemist, she could tell her own drugs from anyone else's. She added a little bit of thyme to each bag, giving it an herbal aftertaste that wasn't at all unpleasant. So unless someone had an incredible desire to replicate her own signature drugs, she'd be able to determine if the Mga Taos had gotten hold of her missing drugs or not.

Their ship was an old teaching ship. The name *University of the Waves* still held out against the weather, the raised black lettering stark against the white bow. Built like a cruise ship, the differences inside were unremarkable, except that the places where the cruise passengers had used to eat had been replaced by classrooms and auditoriums. It was an open ship, so she didn't have to pass a chit to board. She wore her standard black cotton pants and shirt, and had a knife at her waist, and another secreted on her calf if needed.

She made her way to the gangway and into the reception area, marking the two groups of people based here. The administrators were dressed in everyday garb, with silk orange bands across their foreheads, while the monks were dressed in full orange robes with flared sleeves and hoods.

An administrator approached her, speaking in Tagalog. Lopez-Larou introduced herself in Spanish, then English, and he frowned and held out an orange arm band. She took it. She'd be expected to wear it around her left arm during her time aboard ship.

One of the problems with the Taos was that they universally didn't speak English. They stuck to Tagalog as much as possible. Since Lopez-Larou only knew a few words of Tagalog, she was hoping that her target was willing to converse in Spanish; a few had been known to when pressed.

Her target's name was Bituin. She worked in the auditoriums, although Lopez-Larou didn't know what she did; she'd never been to the auditoriums, and her source worked in the engine room. He was a regular customer of Lopez-Larou's who did the night shift and found it hard to stay awake. With her help, he was now being considered for a promotion, which meant day shift. That meant he might not need her help anymore, but that didn't worry her. The word was out, now; his success story would drive more towards her and she'd be more than willing to help.

Lopez-Larou found an approachable young Tao and asked for Bituin. He gestured towards a hall. She followed it and found herself at the intersection of three hallways. There were signs on the walls, left over from when the ship had been a college. She was sure that Biology Wing, History Wing, and Sports Wing didn't mean the same things today as they had pre-plague.

She chose the middle hall, and walked down it like she belonged there. Each of the doors she passed bore name placards; she suspected that they were old dorm rooms, now used as living quarters. One thing that struck her was how clean everything was. Most ships weren't as large, nor were they as organized. Regardless of what she thought of their crazy religion, the Taos knew how to keep a clean ship.

She came to another intersection, but this one only went in two directions. She was about to take the one on the left, when a door opened and an older man stepped out. On seeing her, he raised his hand and spoke to her in rapid-fire Tagalog.

She responded with an innocent smile. "I'm lost," she said in Spanish. "Maybe you can help me."

He seemed flustered, but responded in accented Spanish. "You're not supposed to be here."

"I figured as much. Sorry, elder. Maybe you can direct me?"

"Go back the way you came. This area is private."

"I can't do that. I've come to see Bituin."

He shook his head. "She's busy. We're expecting an input and you can't be here."

Lopez-Larou saw her chance diminishing. She sighed and flapped her hands. She stammered, "I'm late for my appointment. I was supposed to be here an hour ago." She bowed and shook her head. "I'll be in so much trouble if I don't see her, elder. Please, if you can just show me, then I'll be on my way."

He appraised her, looking her up and down. She shuddered gently with implied fear and tried not to meet his gaze.

Finally he grinned. "Go back to the intersection and take the right hand hall that says 'Sports Wing.' It will take you to where she is. But be quick about it. She'll be busy very soon."

She bowed low and backed away, thanking him in his native language. She headed back the way she'd come. She'd noted the name on his door. *Joselito Senior*. She'd use that name if she came into contact with someone else who tried to get in her way.

When she got to the intersection, she followed the sign to the Sports Wing. She imagined the things she'd seen in magazines and on vids: tennis courts, basketball courts, gymnastic equipment, a boxing ring. The hall, when she arrived, was immense. The door opened onto a landing with a wide staircase descending along the wall and a platform overlooking the room. She imagined many things, but was totally unprepared for what she saw as she stepped to the railing.

Instead of sporting equipment, the entire room had been cleared, revealing a flat space the size of most ships. A raised round stage stood in the middle, atop which danced a naked fat man. He moved slowly to unseen music, his glacial gyrations sending him back and forth across the stage to the ebb and flow of the music. She tried to place the instrument but couldn't; some sort of mouth organ, perhaps.

Arrayed around the stage in ever-widening circles were plush red couches, the kind she would have imagined finding in one of the dining areas before the plague, when people spent money to travel and engorge themselves. Strange multi-limbed figures reclined on the couches.

No...

Now she saw it. Monkey-backs. Her hand went to her mouth. She'd never seen so many at one time; never in such numbers. She counted roughly sixty monkey-backs.

The orange-robed monks were going to each of them, massaging their muscles, wiping them clean. Some fed them, but it seemed only the monkeys were being fed. And here and there she saw a monk picking a flea from the chest of one of the monkeys eating it.

She realized she'd been holding her breath, and blew it out. "Jesus."

And there, in the far corner of the room, among a group of administrators, stood the only Tao woman in the room. It had to be her.

Lopez-Larou made her way down the stairs and across the room without bringing attention to herself. It wasn't hard. Everyone kept their eyes on the monkeys.

"Bituin?"

The woman turned. Her eyes flashed; she was unhappy to be disturbed.

"I need to speak with you," Lopez-Larou pressed.

The woman shook her head and glanced at her fellow administrators, who in turn were looking at her. "What are you doing here?" Lopez-Larou was a *Tiburón*; they could tell by looking at her. Her presence could only mean one thing.

"Please. In private." Lopez-Larou gestured to a space a few feet away.

The woman seemed ready to argue, then gritted her teeth and balled her fists. She shook her head as she made her way over. "What is it?"

"You bought something recently," Lopez-Larou said.

"I did nothing of the sort."

"Sure you did. We all know you did." The fat man drew her attention. She couldn't look away.

"Please—you have the wrong person."

Lopez-Larou wrenched her gaze away from the nude abomination. "Your name is Bituin. You purchased three hundred grams of Waffle Dust. And by the looks of it, I know who it was for."

She watched the woman closely, but she didn't bat an eye.

"I came because of the problem we have with that batch. Wrong chemistry. Just don't use it."

"What?" Bituin shook her head as if to clear it. "What?" she repeated.

"If you give it to someone, it will kill them."

The woman's gaze moved to the man on stage.

Just as Lopez-Larou expected.

The monk took a step towards him.

Lopez-Larou put a hand on her arm. "Who gave it to you?"

"I don't know his name." Tears formed in the corners of her eyes. She pointed at the fat man, "Will he be all right?"

Lopez-Larou pulled a pouch of white powder from her waist. She'd used the ruse a couple of times before, but it always worked. "He needs to have this within the hour to counteract the chemistry." She handed it to the woman. "What did he look like? The man who sold you this?"

She stared at the pouch in her hand. With her other hand she traced a line from her chin to her navel. "He had a tattoo along here," she said.

She seemed about to say something else, when a group of orange-robed Taos entered the room from the landing. Two by two they descended; between each duo they carried a monkey-backed. All in all three new monkey-backed were brought into the room and placed on couches.

When the third one was laid on the couch directly opposite her, Lopez-Larou was stunned to see it was the Pali Boy. Gone was the eager, dancing gaze of the young man she'd met, replaced by the dull stare of one forever connected to a monkey.

What a shame.

What a goddamn pitiful shame.

CHAPTER FOUTEEN

THEY WERE ONE.

Kavika didn't know where his thoughts ended and the other's began.

The smell was different. No longer were they inhaling the stench of The Hole. Gone was the cloying smell of oil. Their slick, greasy bodies had been washed, leaving his skin flowery, like memories of the jungle, and of the rooftops of Hindu temples.

Gree-gree-gree!

Music filled his mind. From somewhere it came, like the whisper of a desert wind, breezes slipping through a mountain pass, and the bending of trees after a summer monsoon. The notes lifted and carried him past his childhood, into a borrowed memory of buildings and temples and auburn skies, to a place where his new being swung free, serenaded by the sound as he pulled and swung forever in a breeze filled with love.

Gree-gree-gree!

Orange clouds of love touched them, running their hands and arms across their bodies. A touch here. A touch there. A long line of adoration slid down one arm, across their backs, ending at their chin; whose, he couldn't tell. The orange-clouded beings were everywhere, wrapping them in glorious devotion, billowing, billowing, billowing, like the breaths of a family of lovers, trapped in an orange-veiled universe.

And at the end of his milky vision undulated a great white being. Round and long and thick and strong, it moved with the grace of a heartbeat. From one side of heaven to the other, the being rode the unseen notes of the wordless lament.

They were fed through one mouth. Food entered one part of them, but both felt the surge of energy. Both moved their jaws. Both felt the satisfaction of sustenance course through cells new and old.

Gree-gree-gree!
Gree-gree-gree!
Gree-gree-gree!

They both murmured happy happys to the universe.

Content to be one.

Ready to be less.

Wanting to just be.

IVANOV BLEW SNOT out of his nose, wiped it with the back of his hand, and poured himself another glass of vodka. He watched the grue slide down the wall, then chased the outrage with the cool clean liquor. He grimaced, not from any effect from the Vitamin V but from the knowledge of a man who'd lived a life less than what he'd dreamed.

Once he'd been the captain of the *Stalingrad*, an Akulu Class Submarine from a Russia rising above the cesspool it had become after the collapse of the world's most powerful socialist union. He'd had the firepower to turn stern gazes into fearful ones. With a finger hovering over the launch button, he could convince third-world dictators and rulers of the free world to do anything he desired; the alternative being wrapped in a nuclear cloud-shaped bow.

He'd had power beyond power. Rasputin never held so much potential in his miserable dwarf fist. Not the sort of power Captain Victor Ivanov of the Imperial Russian Navy had once wielded.

And now?

Now?

Now he was the caretaker of a submarine attached to a floating city in the middle of nowhere. One at a time, the missiles had ceased to function until he had less than a handful with any chance at operational probability left. His reactor was at less than thirty per cent efficiency. His men had dispersed to fuck and suck the Asian men and women who called this extended scow home. And he was left with the ball of twine that was his friendships, partnerships, contracts, loves, likes, hatreds and responsibilities. He couldn't touch one without touching another. He couldn't unwind it without unveiling what he'd had to do to survive. What had began as a glorious appointment on the docks of Vladivostok, twenty-nine years ago had liquefied into the role of Japanese fuck-puppet as he prostrated himself for the Nip bastards to inject him with their desires and crazy machinations as they positioned themselves to be the next rulers of the universe in this sad, ruined world, which had once held the promise of unlimited caviar eaten from the velvet pudendums of Ukrainian virgins.

"Fuck!"

He swept the table clear; glass shattered and vodka dribbled down the walls.

A burly man with a snake tattooed on his bald head rushed to the doorway. "Okay, boss?"

"Egor, get me another bottle."

"Yes, boss. Want me to clean up?"

"*Nyet!* Leave it."

Victor stewed in his misery for five minutes as his bottle was replaced. He unscrewed the cap and took a deep swig. It burned, but not enough; it had been a decade since he'd been able to lose himself in the booze. One thing about vodka was that one could become adept at drinking it. You could become a professional. Just as the capitalist West had had professionals who played golf, badminton and lacrosse, and the East had had professionals who played ping pong and poker, Russia had experts in the consumption of vodka. Thankfully, the ability to make the vile substance was something learned by every young man and woman before they reached the age of maturity. In the old country, everyone drank it. Victor remembered sitting on his grandmother's lap in front of a roaring fire, his grandfather telling stories about wolves and snow, and deliveries made late or not at all. His grandmother would sip her glass and raise it to his lips. He still remembered the first acidic slide of the white liquor into his gut, and the nuclear explosion that consumed his inner core afterwards. In the deep cold of the old country, the fire did a little to warm the soul. That was one reason the old Soviet Union had made certain its people had bread and vodka, the two ingredients of a satisfied life.

A knock came at his doorway.

"Captain, it's Mr. Nakihama."

Victor started and turned to Valeri. He must have slipped into a half-sleep. "What? He's here?"

"No, in the coms center."

"Oh." His vision sharpened. "I'll be there. Tell him."

Valeri nodded and left.

Victor stood. His feet balanced themselves somewhere, a thousand feet below his head. He strangled the bottle in one hand, and dragged it with him as he ricocheted down the galley.

In the coms center he found a seat and fell into it. Valeri was there. He pressed a button and a small black and white screen filled with the wide face of a Japanese man.

The man began to speak. Like always, he had something to say, which meant that Victor had something to do.

God, how he hated to be alive.

He felt himself nodding as the Nip brought him to heel.

Then like a good dog, he smiled. If he'd had a tail, he'd have wagged it. If he'd had a pistol, he'd have stuck it in his mouth.

CHAPTER FIFTEEN

THE KNOWLEDGE BURNED in her head, catching everything it touched on fire. She hadn't many friends; she'd never had a mother; she'd never had any brothers and sisters. She'd scraped and clawed and begged until she'd gained the attention of La Jolla. The old kingpin had taken her under his wing and become more like her father than her real father. He'd called her *daughter*. He'd taught her the business. He'd taught her how to read people, how to survive. He'd also taught her to trust no one. She'd never thought to have any friends, happy to climb the ladder until one day she, too, would be kingpin and raise up a waif like he'd done, plucked from the gutter, her stomach so thin two hands could be wrapped around her waist.

That is, until the night she'd fought and befriended Spike. Kavika had come later, and although she'd always consider Spike to be a closer friend, the broken and beaten Pali Boy's sullen vision of the universe had made her wonder if that wasn't what her real brothers were like. It wasn't just him, but what he represented: a life not lived and a brother not known.

As she neared the Hawaiians' ship, the activity above her increased. She'd long ago stopped noticing the Pali Boys leaping from cable to cable. She might just as well watch the clouds, or the birds; what they did had nothing to do with her.

But she began to glance skyward now, because there was one she was searching for. A Pali Boy with a tattooed line running from chin to navel. She knew who it was. She probably wouldn't have to look far. Still, she kept her eyes open.

Her presence aboard affiliated ships normally caused some sort of disturbance. *Los Tiburones* were as universally known as Pali Boys or Water Dogs. Where she went, drugs followed. Her footsteps were filled with the full spectrum of emotions as she catered to the needs of the lives adrift in the floating city. Yet no matter how well she served, the affiliated saw the opportunity to tax her. Moving aboard or through one of their ships cost, which was why she used runners. The easier and cheaper she could get product to its destination, the higher her profit margin.

She'd had this crazy idea running through her head since she'd seen Kavika yesterday. She could end his miserable existence by slipping him something swift and powerful. She could end his misery and walk away and no one would be the wiser. Or she could do something else. She knew enough to do do just about anything with the right ingredients. She might even be able to save his sorry Pali Boy ass.

She was a ship's length from the *Hawaiian Legacy* when she spied him. Other Pali Boys orbited him like he was the center of a brown-skinned typhoon. He barely even moved. She saw him watching her. If he knew that she realized she'd been seen, he didn't make any indication. Then again, he probably didn't care. He was a Pali Boy. His version of the world was from the perspective of a child with an unbreakable toy.

So like them.

She made it perhaps ten meters closer before he swung down with one of his boys to intercept her.

She barely glanced at the tattoo, watching instead his hands and eyes. He was at ease. He didn't register his followers. Instead, all his attention was on her. She gave him points. La Jolla had had that ability as well.

"You circling, shark?"

"Always."

"Who you trying to bite?"

"Maybe it's you."

"You think you can bite me?"

"Maybe I already have."

He snorted and glanced at the other Pali Boy. That glance was enough to give him away, to show her his nervousness. She changed her mind. La Jolla never would have shown his unease.

"Serious, now. No selling on the *Legacy*."

"Why should I bother to sell when you got the market cornered?"

"What'd she say?" asked the other Pali Boy, confusion coloring his face.

"Talking out her ass. Scamper back up. I'll be there in a moment." The tattooed Pali Boy gave her a long look. He held his hands down at his side, but his fingers flexed and unflexed to bleed off energy. "Name's Kaja."

"Lopez-Larou." She didn't offer her hand. "You took something of mine."

He still smiled, and almost hid the tension behind it. "What if I was to say that I don't know what you're talking about?"

"Then I'd say you need to check yourself, because you're not fooling anyone."

He stared at her for a long moment, then nodded. He walked to the nearest rail with only the barest glance at the sky. When he stopped, he leaned against it and stared at the Water Dogs harvesting barnacles far below.

Lopez-Larou followed, and carefully slid in beside him. She placed her hands over the edge of the rail, aware of the stiletto she had hidden in the sleeve of her sharkskin top.

"How do I know it was yours?"

"It was. We both know."

"You arranged for one of my boys to take it across."

"That was between him and me."

"What'd you give him?"

"Enough chit to feed his family for a month."

Kaja nodded. "That'll do it."

"What'd you get for it?"

"An arrangement. The Taos promised not to come aboard our ship for awhile." He shrugged. "They make everyone nervous."

"Really? Is that all you got for the stash?"

"What? Don't you think it was worth it?"

"To keep the orange-robed monkey worshippers from your ship? Hardly. They're just a nuisance, is all."

"It is what it is."

Lopez-Larou snorted.

"What?"

"You're treating the symptoms, not the cause."

Kaja grinned at her. "You don't know what you're talking about."

"Okay, then tell me. What are people more afraid of; the orange robes, or the monkey that comes with them?"

"But you can't have one without the other."

"Spoken like someone who stares at the world through a hundred-foot lens."

"Mother Pele! Talking to you is like talking to a fortune cookie."

"You spend your days swinging away above the city and from that distance everything seems just fine. You can't see the misery. You can't see the fear. All you see is people moving far, far beneath you."

"I'm getting out of here." He put a foot on the rail and was ready to push off.

"You leave and I'll spread the word far and wide that the Pali Boys are running drugs for *Los Tiburones*. You won't ever be able to swing onto another ship again without paying chit."

Kaja stepped back down from the rail and glared at her.

Lopez-Larou grinned with delight. "I know. You hate me. I'm like an itch you can't scratch."

"Oh, I can scratch you."

Her grin remained behind sizzling eyes. "Try it."

Kaja stared at the Water Dogs for two minutes before he spoke again. He didn't look at her, but she knew she was so far under his skin that he didn't have to. "How can I make restitution?"

"Kavika."

That snapped his head around. "Him? What about him?"

"Do you know what happened?" she asked.

"I do. Unfortunate. He was never really very lucky."

"We need to see if we can free him from the monkey."

Kaja stared at her for a second, then laughed. "You can't be serious."

"I couldn't be more serious."

"Even if I could, why would I want to? He's been chosen because of his blood. He's working on a cure for Minimata."

"He's been chosen for his blood, all right. But listen to me closely when I say that Minimata has absolutely nothing to do with it."

"Now look who's crazy. Why else do you think the Japs strap monkeys to people's backs?"

"Here's what I know. I know what sells aboard the city. I know what different people want and need and would trade their nearest loved one for. I know and keep secrets like I'm a priest. And what I also know, based on the chemistry I've learned, is that in the post-plague world it's pretty rare for so many white-skinned people to be around without something keeping them alive."

"I—I don't understand. Are you saying that there's a cure for the plague?"

"Not a cure. But there is a treatment. A treatment in blood."

"This makes no sense at all. People wouldn't allow it."

"What people wouldn't allow it? Are you serious? Whose people are you talking about? Are there people strong enough to take on the Boxers or the Corper Nips aboard the Freedom Ship? I know that Spike and Kavika went there, but where were you when it happened?"

"Watching," Kaja said softly.

She couldn't help it. She smacked him across the face. He didn't flinch. "Maybe you should walk the decks sometime," she snarled. "See what's really going on. Maybe you should get close enough to see the misery. Maybe then you'd pay attention and *see*, and stop being a victim."

Kaja's eyes looked lost. His mouth hung open and his face sagged. It was too much to take in. Still, he somehow managed to ask, "What's your plan?"

"I don't have one. I was hoping that between you and Leilani, we could all figure something out."

Kaja looked at her.

"What is it?"

"You haven't heard, then."

"What?"

"Leilani. She's missing. Probably dead."

"What?" Lopez-Larou felt a fluttering in her heart. "*What?*"

AN HOUR LATER found them making their way on foot to Ivanov's. Kaja had filled her in about what he'd learned about Spike, and how the rumors had it that she was dead. Lopez-Larou wasn't taking it well. He didn't pretend to understand what had gone on between them, but he found himself wanting to understand. The *Tiburón* had gotten under his skin. She'd been more insightful than he'd given her credit. That she wanted to parlay the loss of drugs into helping that part-time wannabe Pali Boy, Kavika, was an equal mystery.

No, that wasn't fair. The boy had done something entirely unexpected. Kaja hadn't ever anticipated that Kavika and Spike would try and take on the Corpers. The very idea went so far beyond what anyone would do as to be unimaginable. Was it foolish? Yes. But was it a stunt equal to anything the other Pali Boys had done? Kaja felt himself nodding. Absolutely. The attack had been a badass move and something the boy's father would have been proud of.

But look where it had gotten them. The transvestite was reported dead. Donnie Wu was definitely dead, his headless body retrieved ten days ago. And Kavika was monkey-backed.

He glanced sideways at Lopez-Larou. The set of her jaw and the heat in her eyes spoke of a determination that would be hard to ignore. She claimed that the monkey-backing could be reversed, but how much of that was blather?

They made it to the old sub and asked to see Ivanov. They were made to wait for five minutes, and then escorted inside.

It smelled like sweat and piss. It always did. The smell took some getting used to. After they climbed down the ladder, they slid through several galleys until they came to an open room. Ivanov sat in an old-fashioned lounge chair that had been bolted to the floor. Made of some indistinguishable fabric, it was a motley color of stains and cigarette burns. He was watching a war movie on a television affixed to the wall. Men in gray uniforms shot at other men in green uniforms. Explosions colored the sky orange in the background. Without looking away from the screen, he gestured for them to take a seat on one of the benches along the wall.

They sat for another five minutes before he finally turned to them.

"Dirty Dozen," he explained. "Lee Marvin. He was a man's man." He smacked the arm of the chair. "I love that movie. What is it you want from Ivanov, now?"

After brief pleasantries, Lopez-Larou repeated her idea to him. His reaction was to laugh.

"Nothing chemistry can do for that. We've tried. I lost my first mate that way. Terrible way to go, to be attached to a fucking monkey."

"I don't try and tell you about submarines, so don't you tell me about chemicals. I have my own ideas of how to separate him from the monkey."

"And if it doesn't work?" Kaja asked.

"Then it doesn't work." She shook her head. "Please don't tell me you think living life like that is better than being dead."

"And your claim that it has nothing to do with Minimata?" pressed Ivanov.

"Don't insult me. I know that you know."

Kaja watched the pair stare at each other for several moments. Was it possible that Ivanov knew the secret as well? He'd been friends to the Pali Boys for as long as Kaja could remember. How could he have kept such a secret from them?

Finally Ivanov nodded. A slow sneer took over his puffy-cheeked face. "*Da*. We know."

"Holy Pele. When were you going to tell us?" Kaja demanded, rising from the bench.

Ivanov regarded him as a parent would a child. "You would want us to tell you everything?" he asked, shaking his head. "You Pali Boys have secrets. Water Dogs have secrets. *Los Tiburones* have secrets. Everyone has their fucking secrets. This is one of *my* secrets." He glanced at Lopez-Larou and gave her a vicious smile. "Although it seems that others know this secret. Tell me, how is it you know?"

"You want me to reveal my source?"

"I want you to do what you want to do."

She shrugged. "It was the Sky Winkers."

"Ah, the Night Men. Yes, they seem to know too much."

"Why'd they tell you?" Kaja asked.

"I don't know," she turned to him. "They just did. They also claim to talk to people in space too, so you have to take what they say with a grain of salt."

"Then how can you be sure?"

"I just am."

Kaja hesitated, but the more he thought about it, the more he was beginning to believe it, too. The Corpers had begun monkey-backing twenty years ago, and in all that time they'd never given any sign of having made progress on a cure for Minimata Disease. There should have been something. *Anything*.

"I've got to say that I never thought he'd get as far as he did." Seeing the looks on the others' faces, Kaja added, "Kavika—he pissed me off and I'm afraid that all of this was because I told him that he had to find out why Akamu had been killed."

"But you knew they left the drugs," Lopez-Larou said. "It was nothing more than an accident."

"I know, I know." He shook his head and closed his eyes. "I sent him on a wild goose chase. But you have to understand, Kavika had this problem he had to deal with. Something was always holding him back. Something inside him kept him from doing anything dangerous."

"Looks like he overcame that," snorted Ivanov.

"Yeah, and then some." Kaja shook his head. The other Pali

146

Boys wouldn't understand, but they'd just have to deal with it. He turned to the girl. "Listen, whatever it is, count us in. I'm not so sure that we can beat the Corpers, but we can definitely figure out a way to get Kavika back where he belongs."

"*A Bridge Too Far*," Ivanov murmured.

Kaja gave him a look. "Eh?"

"It's a movie, with Harrison Ford. Before he was in that damned space movie. Instead of doing what they can, they do too much."

"Ah." He turned to Lopez-Larou. "Look, not that I don't want to get revenge for Wu, but I need to go to Princess Kamala about this. It's just too big."

"I'd be surprised if she didn't already know," Lopez-Larou said, matter-of-factly.

CHAPTER SIXTEEN

IT TOOK TWO days to plan the mission. Two days of Ivanov talking about movies and strategies and World Wars from a time they could barely envision. Lopez-Larou pointed that out to the old drunk on several occasions, but he'd merely waved her off with the perplexing comment, "It's all Hollywood anyway. It was never as real as it really was."

Despite his incoherence, they were eventually ready. Their plan's success depended on their own boldness, and the Mga Tao's desire to protect their monkey-backed wards.

They waited until eleven bells before they put the plan in motion. It was important that whatever they did, didn't come back to haunt them. After consulting with Chito, who was eager to assist, they were ready.

So it was that Kaja, Lopez-Larou, and five of Ivanov's men walked up the gangway of *The University of the Waves*. At this time of night, most of those aboard the ship were sleeping. A pair of burley Taos stood at the entry, the orange silk headbands on their foreheads showing their affiliation. Lopez-

Larou ignored them. She marched by them and into the ship, her hood pulled forward until her face was hugged in shadow and her hands hidden in the sleeves. The others did the same, following two by two, heads down, pace moderated.

Ivanov's men were marking the pair; they'd most definitely attempt to bar their way when they left with their packages. She wondered how many Taos would die this night. Two, ten, twenty? It didn't bother her much. The Taos propagated an outrage. Whether or not they knew it mattered little. At the end of the day she'd trade all of them for someone she cared about.

She followed the path she'd taken earlier, down the halls, past the intersection and onto the landing of the *Sports Wing*. The room was lit with subdued lighting. Each couch had at least a pair of occupants. The stage was empty, which she privately appreciated. She didn't know if she could take seeing the naked fat man dance again.

They paused at the top of the stairs, and she searched for Kavika.

Kaja, who'd come to stand beside her, saw him first. He pointed. "There."

She followed his gesture and saw Kavika lying on a velvet red couch on the other side of the stage, two rows back. She turned and pointed him out to the others.

Then came the hard part.

In order to convince the Water Dogs to help them with more than just the robes from dead Taos, they'd had to promise to retrieve one more monkey-back, a twelve-year-old girl with a cleft lip. She and Kaja searched. Of all those they could see from their position in the room, they identified four girls that could match that description. But an equal number of monkey-backed were turned away from them, so there was no telling how many more there could be.

They left one of Ivanov's men on the landing, and the rest descended in a slow and stately manner. They'd already garnered the attention of an administrator, sitting at a desk in the far right corner of the room, but so far, she wasn't doing anything except watching. Lopez-Larou hoped to keep it that way, but knew that one false move, one un-monk-like act, would change that in a heartbeat. She had no idea what sort of response there might be for someone endangering the Mga Tao center of worship, but it was probably nasty.

Kaja turned left and Lopez-Larou turned right, searching for the girl. Moving slowly through the circular aisles, she approached the first girl. Hair had fallen to cover her face. She bent over and pushed it aside. The girl moaned. The monkey made a soft noise, *Gree*. It wasn't her. This girl was pure Chinese. Her lip was unmarred.

Lopez-Larou stood, and felt her hood begin to fall back. She grabbed it just in time, or at least she hoped she had. She felt the heat of the administrator's gaze on her back. When she turned along the arch of aisle, the administrator had gotten to her feet and was staring directly at her, hands on hips. If it had been Bituin, maybe she'd have some leverage, but it was someone else.

With her heart hammering in her chest, Lopez-Larou continued searching, purposely turning down an aisle that would bring her close to the administrator. She'd previously marked two possible candidates for the girl. With any luck it would be the nearest one. But luck wasn't to be had. The nearest girl had auburn hair. Not common in Filipino genetics. Sill, Lopez-Larou paused beside her to glimpse her face. Her lip was unblemished as well.

Which meant she had to get closer to the administrator.

KAJA'S FEET ACHED inside the boots, and his torso itched from the material. Sure, it felt soft to his fingers, but his skin wasn't used to being contained in any sort of fabric, much less the clingy orange robes of the monkey-worshippers. He much preferred the freedom of a Pali Boy.

They'd found Kavika, but they had to find the Water Dog girl as well. Looking at all the monkey-backed, it didn't matter to him. He'd take all of them with him if he could. After he'd learned what he'd learned, he wouldn't be happy until every one of the monkey-backed were freed from their enslavement.

That they were being used to filter blood for the white-skinned Real People was an outrage. The very idea of it surpassed every instance of slavery that had occurred anytime in his world's past. That it was a death warrant made the situation intolerable. If—he corrected himself—*when* Kavika was separated from his monkey and Wu was avenged, Kaja would set about creating a plan to halt the outrage permanently. Pele would be with him. Just as she'd held out her hand and pushed him back after he leaped into the face of the storm to become a Pali Boy, she'd do the same to protect the fate of her people.

Regardless of what Princess Kamala said.

He balled his fists as he once again played the conversation through his mind.

"You'll do nothing to stop them," she'd ordered.

"But they can't do this to our people!"

"They have more power than you can believe. We'll keep our eyes to the horizon and not see what we shouldn't see."

"But Princess, I—"

"You heard me, Kaja. Do nothing. Do absolutely nothing about it. As far as you are concerned, this is not happening. Now get skyward. The people need someone heroic. They need to remember who we once were. They need to see the warriors at play, and you'll go do exactly that. They need to forget who we've become."

It was that last bit that had stung him the hardest. The Pali Boys were puppets, she was saying; worthless, except as a symbol.

Yeah, Kaja had definitely experienced a change in philosophy these last two days, as he looked less and less at the horizon and more and more at what lay beneath it. He watched the people. He saw the hardships of living. He saw both misery and joy, sometimes equally directed at even the smallest things. Like the old man who worked laboriously, almost reverently, repairing the junctures of his bird net, bent under the sun. Or the Water Dogs sleeping in their hammocks on the sides of the ships. He had to admit, watching them was always a guilty pleasure. They seemed so at home, so at rest, and the peace they exuded in their slumber was something almost palpable.

He'd spoken at length with Lopez-Larou and learned things about the city he'd never known. She was right about so many things. She'd told him that he *stared at the world through a hundred-foot lens.* And he had; it was part of being a Pali Boy. And on some levels he knew that it was necessary. But he also knew that to be a citizen of this floating mess of ships they called a city required more than just playing at being a Pacific Ocean Tarzan.

Kaja heard a disturbance from the landing, and looked up to see one of Ivanov's men snap the neck of a young Tao in an orange robe. Then he turned to see if the administrator had noticed. Thankfully she hadn't. Her attention had been too focused on Lopez-Larou, who was now in the process of walking right at the old woman.

Kaja cursed under his breath.

The shit was about to hit the fan.

THE ADMINISTRATOR WHISPERED to her in unfathomable Tagalog. Lopez-Larou kept her head down as she walked towards the old woman. She hoped the shadow would be enough to keep her face hidden. The only way she could pass herself off as Filipina would be in the dark.

The girl was three couches away. To get there she had to pass directly by the administrator. She averted her gaze to stare at the monkey-backed.

This close, she could see the eyes of the monkeys staring at her. They'd always given her the creeps. Now, in a room filled with more than fifty of them, she felt sure that they knew what she was here to do. Even as she thought it, one of the monkey's eyes narrowed, as if it had just read her mind. Then it closed them and farted.

Gree, said the monkey.

Gree, said the child it was attached to.

The woman spoke to her again, more insistently, and reached out to tug her sleeve. Lopez-Larou ignored her.

She stopped beside the couch; the girl matched the description perfectly. So young. The scar bisecting her lip did nothing to take away from her youthful beauty. A beauty that had been stolen by a conspiracy to help the Real People, she reminded herself.

Suddenly she felt herself spun around. The administrator's face was right next to hers. She was saying something, but stopped once she saw Lopez-Larou's face. As the old woman opened her mouth to get enough air to scream, Lopez-Larou sunk her fist into her stomach. The administrator gasped, here eyes bulging, and Lopez-Larou clobbered her twice in the temple with a double right hook. The administrator fell to the ground, unconscious.

Lopez-Larou stood over her. "*Gree*," she said and kicked her in the stomach.

Then she reached down and scooped the child into her arms. She was heavy with the added weight of the monkey, but not so heavy that Lopez-Larou couldn't carry her to safety. She turned and found the nearest path to the stairs.

She spied Kaja staring at all the monkey-backed forms, a pained look in his eyes.

"Come on, you. Grab Kavika and let's go."

He snapped back from wherever he was and hurried over to Kavika, snatching the young man into his arms and following Lopez-Larou up the stairs.

They didn't encounter any trouble until they were at the first intersection. Three guards were waiting for them, all holding wickedly sharp-looking machetes. Everyone stopped for a moment, then two of Ivanov's men pulled out small pistols, pointed them at the heads of the men on either side, and fired. The shots echoed in the enclosed space. The man in the middle froze, and before he could bring his machete to bear, he was also shot in the face.

Lopez-Larou hadn't been expecting it, but after seeing the monkey-backed in the other room, she'd lost whatever fragile consideration she'd had for the Taos. Staring at the three blood splotches oozing down the wall, she realized that she didn't even care. Fuck 'em. Fuck 'em all. She didn't care if they were all shot dead.

She nodded to Ivanov's men, then stepped over the bodies.

Now they stepped up their pace. Their shots had to have garnered some attention. By the time they were down the hall and in the grand lobby, all five of Ivanov's men had pistols in both hands, brandishing them for all to see.

The seven guards and five administrators who were waiting for them with blades didn't stand a chance... and they knew it. They stepped aside as the party approached.

Then Lopez-Larou saw the holsters on each of the guard's hips. They had pistols; why not use them? And then she realized; they didn't want to accidentally shoot the monkeys. As they ran off the ship, Lopez-Larou laughed. Had she thought more about it, she would never have needed such an elaborate plan. She could have just walked into the ship, put a gun to a monkey's head, and walked out.

Finally, an alarm sounded. Lights all over the ship flashed on.

Kaja ran forward and handed Kavika's body to some of the Pali Boys; within moments, they'd taken him into the sky and were lost in the darkness.

Ivanov's men ran into the shadows, but not before they'd placed explosives on either side of the gangway.

Lopez-Larou walked to the edge of the ship, climbed aboard the rail, and stepped off. She plummeted twenty feet before her feet hit water. The cold stunned her. As she sank deeper, she found herself losing her grip on the girl.

Thankfully the Water Dogs had been waiting as planned. They took the girl from her, then gave her a mask to help her breathe. Soon, they were swimming under the ships. In the silence of the ocean and the smudges of lights from the surface, they traveled peacefully. As she was pulled to their destination, Lopez-Larou allowed herself to relax.

CHAPTER SEVENTEEN

THE FIRST THING they did when everyone was back at the Morgue Ship was to argue. The fact that they'd freed two monkey-backs from the Taos and were on the verge of possibly liberating them entirely from their simian umbilicals was totally ignored. Instead, they were more concerned about who would be freed first.

"They wouldn't even be here if it wasn't for us." Chito glared back and forth at the others. "Amy is going to be first."

Ivanov and Lopez-Larou squared off against him, but Kaja stood back. It didn't bother him either way; soon, both of them would be free, or at least that was the plan. The method they were going to use was another thing up for debate.

"It was our plan," said Ivanov, who for once appeared sober. "Without it and my men, you would have never seen Amy."

"Look around. Do you know where you are?"

"What? You think that this is the right place to do the procedure?" Kaja couldn't help but interject.

"Yes," Chito said matter-of-factly. "This is the perfect place."

"A place for dead people?" Lopez-Larou smirked.

"We have a state-of-the-art med unit aboard the sub. We should be there."

"She will have the procedure done here!" Chito insisted.

"Do you have an EEG? Do you have a heart monitor?" Ivanov shook his head. "This is ridiculous. All you have here are a bunch of slabs where you recycle dead people for the fish to eat."

"We need to keep her with us." Chito spoke evenly, but more softly.

"Listen," Lopez-Larou said. She put a hand on Chito's forearm and he didn't pull away. "Do you really think, after all the efforts we've made to bring her here, that we're going to do anything that would harm her? If you want her to go first, then fine, she can go first."

Ivanov moved to say something, but Lopez-Larou's eyes made him pause. Instead, he made a disgusted look and shook his head.

"It doesn't matter who goes first or second," she continued. "This whole thing is a work in progress."

Shortly after that, they had both monkey-backed in the submarine's medical unit. Chito brought two Water Dogs who'd been trained as nurses by an old woman before she died. They didn't understand the machines, but in an odd way, Lopez-Larou did.

"We use the EEG and EKG when we're testing new product," she told them. "Different chemicals affect different parts of the brain. They're the perfect tools to inform us about what's happening between someone's ears.

"In this case we're concerned with the theta waves." She pointed to a green line on the monitor. On close examination, there were actually two lines so close they nearly overlapped. "This shows the merging of the mind of the human and the mind of the monkey. This is what we believe keeps them alive together and links them in death."

This was the crux of the plan. The different drugs *Los Tiburones* made affected different parts of the brain. It was widely believed that the death of a monkey-backed arose from the shared theta waves, so if they were to have any success, they'd have to separate the waves before they separated the bodies, and Lopez-Larou had what she thought was just the right combination of chemicals to do that job.

As she brought out the small vial of chemicals to inject into the conjoined blood streams, she told Ivanov to prepare for the separation.

Half an hour later the monkey was dead and the girl was alive.

Amy's eyes were a deep ocean blue as they stared wide at the walls of the surgical unit.

Chito spoke to her softly in Tagalog. They were clearly sweet words, even if Kaja couldn't understand them.

The monkey lay dead in the corner. It had twitched at first, but soon stilled. The tubes that had run blood from Amy still hung from it.

The girl tried to speak. She opened her mouth and felt her face. Her eyes opened wider, almost painfully so, and her voice cracked as a tiny whine slid free. She shot to a sitting position and searched frantically for something.

Then she saw it—the monkey in the corner.

Her scream was sudden and piercing.

Chito pulled her to him and embraced her, whispering into her ear, but he didn't do anything to block her view of the dead animal.

Kaja stepped into her line of sight, blocking her view. She tried to peer around him, but he stepped in her way again.

She stared at him, and in those eyes he saw nothing but sheer terror. No, there was one more thing swimming behind those beautiful ocean blue irises: sheer insanity, exploding within her.

She struggled against Chito's grip as he held her tight. She shrieked, pounded his back, and scratched his face, but he held her tighter. Then she spasmed. Bile shot from her mouth, gushing over his shoulder. Her blue irises were gone, rolling up into her skull. Her whole body quivered, as she gasped and dry heaved, over and over and over.

Then she died.

Kaja felt his own breath disappear as he stared at the bleak, dead eyes of the girl. He stepped out of the way. It seemed more respectful that way. At least in death she could see what she'd lost, what she'd missed more than her own humanity.

Finally he drew breath, turned and stalked out of the room. He needed to punch someone in the face.

THEY'D NEVER HAD to bury a monkey before. It seemed wrong. On the slab, resting beneath a cover, it took on the form of a child. Although Lopez-Larou knew what it really was, a part of her heart went out to it. So helpless. So small. So dead.

Chito and several other Water Dogs, who'd been standing numbly around the bodies, made room for the girl's mother and father. They slumped to the slab, dripping water like tears. They knelt and began to pray. The other Water Dogs joined in.

It had been so close. Lopez-Larou had taken everything she knew about the brain and drug interaction and had actually thought she'd known the answer. The best technology available had been at her disposal and at the end of the day she was nothing more than a two-bit drug dealer with grand illusions about her medical ability.

Bottom line was that she'd killed the girl *and* the fucking monkey.

And now Kavika was lying in the submarine's medical suite waiting for her to do the same to him.

Come on, girl. Kill me, why don't you? Life isn't bad enough being attached to this fucking monkey. I need you to kill me, too.

Not that Kavika could actually talk, but she was sure this was what he'd say if given the chance.

She could still remember the girl's eyes, and how they'd bulged when she'd realized the monkey was no longer part of her. It was as if she couldn't live without it. Her death had nothing to do with the drugs. The drugs couldn't kill anyone in the dosage she'd been provided.

Lopez-Larou felt her grief pressing against her anger as she watched Amy's mother and father weeping, their arms around each other and resting on their daughter. Water from their bodies had pooled beneath them and the other Water Dogs, rippling with their sobs, and as she watched the rippling water Lopez-Larou finally cried, too.

Then, after a time, the Water Dogs took the wrapped body of the girl with them into the sea, and Chito took the monkey elsewhere. She'd heard him talking with the others; he had something planned, but she didn't know what.

They left her alone with the empty slabs and the pools of water. She wiped her cheeks with her palms. What was she going to do with Kavika? This entire endeavor had been about freeing him from his enslavement. She had neither the knowledge nor the fortitude to go about trying once more. She couldn't do it. She *wouldn't* do it.

Thankfully, she was saved from making a decision by Kaja, who entered the Morgue Ship with fire in his eyes.

"Come on," he said. "Now it's Kavika's turn."

"What? We can't. He'll turn out just like the girl."

Kaja shook his head sharply. "Not this way. I have a plan."

She pressed her hand against Kaja's chest. "But he'll die."

"That's the plan." He turned to go and marched for the door. "You are coming, aren't you?"

CHAPTER EIGHTEEN

"GET UP, YOU old drunk."

Kaja swept into the medical suite with Lopez-Larou following closely behind. Ivanov sat sprawled in a chair in the corner of the room, a bottle of vodka perched on his lap. He stared at Kavika, and at the monkey attached to him; his face was so long his chin seemed to be melting into his stained, grimy shirt. His eyes were red-rimmed and bright.

Kaja grabbed the bottle and set it on a nearby table. Ivanov swiped for it, but was a shade too late. "I said get up. We have to kill Kavika."

Ivanov grunted, his attempt at a laugh. "You do it too happily. Why not try and make it seem like an accident?"

Kaja grabbed the Russian under his arms and lifted him to his feet. The movement brought Ivanov's face inches from Kaja's, who turned his head as a gust of vodka fumes hit his face.

"I let his father down, too, you know."

"Enough of that. You want a priest, I can find you one."

"Bah. Fucking priests. We had one on the ship. I torpedoed him into the deep when he told me one too many times that the plague was God's will." Ivanov hiccupped. "Fucking God's will, my Soviet ass."

Kaja glanced back at Lopez-Larou. As much as he didn't mind the old man's stories, now wasn't the time. "Would you mind taking him?"

He passed the Russian to the diminutive but solid Mexican girl, who wedged her right shoulder beneath Ivanov's left, then wrapped her arm around his waist. "Where are we going?" she asked.

"Torpedo room."

"Ha ha!" chortled Ivanov. "Same as the priest."

Kaja went to the table and lifted Kavika and the monkey into his arms. He had to be sure to support them both, otherwise the umbilicals would rip free.

He shouldered past the Russian and the Mexican and out the hatch, then into the hall. He'd been to the torpedo room several times and knew the way.

Glancing down at the figure of the young man in his arms, he couldn't help but smile. Kaja had been hard on the boy. He'd let him get beat down. He'd even ignored a chance to help him take on the Corpers. None of that had stopped him.

Part of Kaja had hoped that any of the things he'd said or done would have convinced the boy to find another life. He could join Princess Kamala's shipwrights or deckhands with no loss of dignity. It would make Kaja's life easier as well; every time he saw the boy, he saw the boy's father in miniature. Kapono's shadow was long enough to stretch across the years.

But another part of Kaja, one that had grown over the last few weeks, felt pride. Pride as a leader of men; pride as an older man; pride as a father himself. He'd put hurdles and walls before the boy and the boy had found ways to bypass them. Instead of quitting, he'd tried harder. Thinking of the many Pali Boys now winging their way across the city, Kaja was hard-pressed to find one who had showed half the determination of the boy he now had in his arms. The same boy who in his search to overcome his fear and become a man had lost his best friend and his uncle, and had had his life taken away from him so that some old white men could profit off his blood.

Kaja would be damned if he'd let that happen. He'd already been talking with Chito and several other leaders of the Water Dogs; their command of the water and the Pali Boys' command of the air created a perfect partnership, especially when presented with a mutual enemy.

He took a set of stairs down a level, leaning heavily against the rail. The last thing he wanted was to slip and fall. The pipes and walls of the submarine were already too close for comfort. The thought of living aboard such a thing beneath the waves for so long made Kaja a little sick in his stomach. He could barely take sleeping inside his cargo container with the doors open.

They finally made it to the engine room where Purin was already waiting. The ceiling was a few feet higher here, but the walls, floor and ceiling were still painted the same immutable, claustrophobic gray. Pipes still hugged the ceiling, but the floor was cleared, with the exception of a central control panel like a raised dais. A wheeled rack of missiles stood in one corner, ready to be loaded into the two forward tubes, which were accessed by a door opened and closed from using the control panel.

"Is everything ready?" Kaja asked.

"I don't take orders from you." Purin turned to Ivanov, who was limping in with the help of Lopez-Larou. "Captain, what are your orders?"

Ivanov pushed away from Lopez-Larou and stood in the middle of the room. He swayed and for a moment, Kaja thought he'd fall. But the old drunk managed to find his balance. He pointed to Kavika. "Now what is it you're going to do with the boy?"

"Long or short version?" Kaja adjusted the weight in his arms.

"Short version," Ivanov said.

"Okay." Kaja pointed to a torpedo tube with his chin. "We're going to shove Kavika and the monkey into that tube. You are going to fire it and Kavika is going to die."

Everyone in the room stared at Kaja for a moment. Ivanov rubbed his face with his hand to get blood flowing into it.

"Okay. Better give me the long version."

Kaja nodded. "I thought so. First we're going to wake the boy. Lopez-Larou has some stimulants that will wake both him and the monkey. Then we're going to tie them together so that they can't pull each other apart when they're struggling."

"Struggling?" Ivanov looked to Lopez-Larou for clarification. She merely nodded.

"Then we're going to shove them in a tube and fire them into the water. The Water Dogs are waiting below and will attach them to the line and pull them to the bottom."

"That will kill them," Purin said.

"I'm counting on it."

"And you think this is a good thing?" Ivanov asked.

"I think that as long as these two are alive, one of them is in control of the other. Get rid of brain activity and you get rid of brain waves; I hope that we can pull Kavika back to the surface and give him CPR, and by then the monkey will be dead and he'll be free of it."

"It sounds too simple," Purin said.

"Sometimes simple is good," Lopez-Larou offered. "I had all the same questions when he told me. But the more I think about it, the more I think that this is a solution that could work." She shrugged. "It has to. We have nothing else."

"I'll be right back," Ivanov said after digesting the information.

Kaja closed his eyes and adjusted the weight. The muscles in his arms burned. He needed to relieve the pain somehow, but he'd be damned if he'd allow his Pali Boy to lie on the floor. *His* Pali Boy. Not part-time Pali, but full-time. The boy hadn't leaped into the wind like tradition, but he'd done so much more. He'd gone against the Corpers, and if he survived this, it meant that he was a favorite of Pele.

Kaja remembered so many times he and the older men had talked long into the nights. Rice wine or weed hooch stinging their brains, remembering how much space they had on the islands, and the challenges to their very survival. The symbol of Don Quixote was important to Pali Boys. Fighting against something bigger than one's self had been a founding principle, and one that elders like Kavika's father, Old Wu and Kaja had tried to instill in the younger Pali Boys. Most often they didn't understand, but it was this struggle for the unattainable that had kept the floating city alive. It ruled their lives and helped them to survive in the face of seemingly impossible odds. It had transfixed his ancestors and allowed them to leap into the trade winds, only to be pushed back into the mountain. Being a Pali Boy meant that you embraced faith, optimism, confidence, and courage, all wrapped into the memories and traditions of warriors who'd fought for King Kamehameha back before everything turned to shit.

Ivanov returned. His captain's cap rode his head, gold oak leaves of his rank stitched into a black background. He'd cleaned his face and changed his shirt.

"This had better work," he growled.

Kaja shifted the weight once more. "Can we get started?"

"Right." The old captain nodded. "Purin, open tube one."

The immense Russian pressed a button on the keyboard. With a rush of air and the *snap* of a metal hinge, the door to the tube clicked open. He opened it the rest of the way and pulled out the torpedo rack. About ten feet long and three feet wide, the curved cradle was more than adequate to hold Kavika and the monkey.

Kaja sighed with relief as he gently lay his Pali Boy down, adjusting first Kavika's head and then the monkey's. They were head-first into the tube. He straightened their legs and arms, adjusting here and there to ensure that they wouldn't get hung up in the tube when it fired.

When he backed away, he looked at Lopez-Larou. "Ready?"

She nodded and stepped forward. From the pouch at her waist she produced a slender box. She opened it and removed a long syringe. Then she removed a needle, which she attached to the syringe. Together it was as long as her forearm.

"What's in it?" Ivanov asked.

"Atropine." She prepared the syringe for use. "It'll kick start the dead." Seeing the look on Ivanov's face, she added, "It's a figure of speech."

"Keep it to yourself." The Russian looked to Kaja. "The Water Dogs are ready?"

Kaja nodded, unwrapping several lengths of scrounged electrical wire from his waist. He tied Kavika and his monkey together at the knees, waist and torso. He barely had enough wire to tie both sets of arms, and had to press them together to get the space he needed to tie off. When he was done, he tested the knots and stood back.

"Ready whenever you are."

THE UNIVERSE WAS ruled by his heartbeat.

Ker-thump.

Ker-thump.

Ker-thump.

He ran through a world made of trees. Rooted to the sky, the branches hung everywhere beneath a rain of leaves. Sometimes he'd jump, leaping impossibly far, his entire body extended so that it was one synchronized piece, taut from toe to fingertip, prepared for the grasp, rotation and swing of the next branch that would propel him high into space.

He was *gree*.

Suddenly a great pain coursed through him. The greens, browns and yellows of his tree-filled universe evaporated in an explosion of white so bright that it seared his senses.

There was *gree* but it was not his.

He was not what he was.

He was something different.

His eyes snapped open. Blinding light greeted him.

"Kavika? Can you hear me, Kavika?"

Strange nonsensical warbling noises assaulted him along with the light. But the light was dimming. His vision was clearing. He could make out shadows within the light, strange warbling shadows.

"Kavika?"

"*Gree*," he replied, searching in vain for the universe of trees and the feeling of freedom.

"Kavika!"

"*Gree.*" White hot pain and warbling. Had he fallen from the trees? Was he on the ground?

"Oh, God," came a different voice. "His mind is gone. What if...?"

"Don't say it."

He felt himself being shaken. Strong hands gripped his shoulder.

"Kavika!"

"What?"

Hands held his face as his vision cleared. The white universe had faded to a smear of grays. A man stood before him, a man who he'd known from before the pairing. It was someone who he'd swung through the air with... not trees, but something else, something...

"Pali," he murmured.

"Yes. Yes!" The face glowed. "He's going to be all right."

"How's the monkey?"

"Alert."

"So now it's time."

"*Gree.*" The word was said, but it was outside of his head. And it saddened him. The *gree* was gone.

"Hurry now," came a rough warble.

Then he was pressed into a dark tunnel. A number of loud *clicks* was followed by a *clang* as darkness sprang around him. Memories were coming to him: of people he knew, of things he did. They came in a jumble and made little sense, but he did know that they were his... and not the *gree*'s.

The he was propelled violently forward. His head sliced hard into water as bubbles soared around him. He almost took a breath, but something inside of him warned against it. He bit down on his lip to keep it from opening. But the *gree* struggled behind him. It hadn't done the same. It struggled and roared into the water, but bindings tying them together kept it from lashing out.

Then hands grabbed him. He and the *gree* were propelled deeper and deeper. His head began to hurt with the pressure, but still they went. He had to breathe, but if he did he'd die and he didn't want to die. He wanted to return to the land of... was it trees? Or was it nets? His mind spun with the idea of swinging from net to net above a sea of ships, the dull gray horizon never-changing.

They came to a cable as thick as a tree trunk. Using that as the anchor, he and the *gree* were pulled down and down and down. Handholds on the cable were used to propel them. Deeper. Deeper. The pressure in his head was intolerable.

His face scraped the cable as he bounced lower and lower. A block of orange paint momentarily captured his eye. In it was a number—169.

Then in a flash he knew that the *gree* was dead. He was overwhelmed by emotion. His eyes flooded with tears and without knowing it, he sobbed and in the sobbing, he let the water in. He coughed violently. His body convulsed. Fear and grief surged through him in a violent riptide of emotion. His vision turned black, and everything became dull. He coughed and inhaled the ocean, and his eyes shot wide as he realized that he'd ceased to move. A face in the water hung close to his own but it dissolved as his mind succumbed to the reality of death.

He fell into nothing.

CHAPTER NINETEEN

He came to slowly.

Everything hurt.

His chest felt as if a cargo container had fallen on it. His arms and legs ached. His head pounded so badly he had trouble keeping his eyes open. Even when he could, the world was nothing more than a silvery smear. Twin spikes of pain lived somewhere on his back. But the worst of it was inside. Emptiness. A space where something had been was now void.

Then he remembered everything.

The attack on the Corper ship.

The battle for revenge.

The escape.

The search for Spike.

The battle with the Boxers and the death of Donnie Wu.

Then his capture.

His pairing with the monkey.

Monkey-backing.

Gree.

He remained silent for awhile as visions of tree-filled skies and monkeys hanging from the moon captivated him, filling him with the idea of what he'd had, what he could have been, what they could have been had they just been left alone. The ennui was debilitating. A heaviness settled on his chest and stayed there for a long while.

But like the way his muscles sometimes tingled with numbness after sleeping awkwardly, the heaviness and the longing faded, until the monkey was nothing more than a memory of what he once had—like the memory of a string of islands where his people once roamed, or the memory of his father, someone who still managed to touch him from the darkest corners of his mind when he least expected it.

Kavika tried to get up to a sitting position, but the effort defeated him. He tried again and again, until exhaustion finally took over, and he fell back and turned to his left. And there, on the table next to him, lay his *gree*, his monkey. Kavika smiled and stared at his dream, eventually falling into a deep, deep sleep.

"*PUTITA!* WHAT HAVE you been doing?"

Lopez-Larou skidded to a stop. Now back in the *Los Tiburones* section of the city, she'd been free and easy with herself. They had guards posted surreptitiously watching for Boxers, Pali Boys and any other citizen who might interlope. It was the one place she could let her guard down.

"Paco." She used to call the fat old Mexican *sir*. Not just because he'd been a lieutenant of her father's back in Sonora, but because he was someone she used to respect.

"Putita, Putita... why?"

Used to respect. Calling her *Little Whore* did little to endear her. In fact, each time he said it was like loading a bullet into a gun. When the clip was full, she knew she was going to turn it back on him.

She gritted her teeth. "*Tio,* I've done nothing. Just a girl trying to be like her *padre*."

"What you want to be like him for? Old and fat and..."

He let the last word drift, but she knew what he'd left off. They both did. *Dead*. It was a veiled threat. Check that. It was a bald threat.

"*Tio,* my father wasn't fat. He couldn't have been. I remember him being so much smaller than you."

She watched the knuckles of his left fist whiten around the end of his armrest. Paco Braun sat on a cargo container, in the shade of an immense red and white umbrella. Like always, he wore a flower-patterned mumu. His bare feet were sunburned, and his naked torso bore what used to be a series of tattoos telling the story of a matador, his lust for love, and his demise on the horns of a bull, but now the images were nothing but blue blotches, stretched beyond recognition. She was reminded of the fat Mga Tao dancing on the stage. Paco's face was lost in the shadow of the umbrella, but she didn't need to look at it to know that he was puckered and frowning.

She reminded herself to dial it down. After all, even if they hated each other, he commanded and deserved respect.

"I'm sorry I haven't been around, *Tio*. I know you must have been worried. I should have told you where I was." She bowed her head and kept her face neutral.

After a moment he said, "Your friends caused quite a stir with the monkey lovers. The Corps and Boxers have no love for them either. What are you trying to do, alienate everyone so that you'll only have the fish for customers?"

"It was unfortunate what happened with the monkey lovers. I heard they were distraught."

"Distraught!" Braun snorted. "They were insane about it. Like if someone stole Jesus from the Pope."

"If there was a Pope," she said.

"Yeah, that. But you weren't involved in any of this, were you?"

"Was I seen?"

"Not that I hear, but some of the other *Tiburones* think you were there."

"Tell you what, *Tio*. They can think in one hand and shit in the other, then ask them to tell you which one is holding something."

Braun chuckled. "Your father used to say that. Maybe you are a little like him."

"Maybe I am." She looked around for his concubines, but didn't see any. "Where are the Marys? Have they left you?"

"No. Mary See decided to taste too much of my wares. She's on the outs. The other three Marys are helping her pack."

Braun named all of his consorts Mary, after a girl he'd known before the plague, when he'd been young and had dreams of being an architect of the big buildings in Los Angeles.

"Can I get you something, *Tio*? I mean until they come back."

She felt his eyes raking her skin, but took it without blinking. Finally, "No. I'll be fine."

"Call me if I can help." Before he could answer, she'd broken into a jog. Her place was two cargo ships over, far enough that he couldn't get to her without making a big ruckus. Which suited her just fine. She opened the lock on her container, passed all the chems and equipment, then tossed herself onto her bed. She hadn't slept much in the last few days. Kavika's life-and-death struggles had kept her awake. Now that he showed every chance of surviving, she had to take a moment for herself. Plus, she needed more chits, which meant she needed more product. That Braun hadn't asked her for what she owed was a godsend, and one that she didn't imagine would happen again.

WHEN KAVIKA NEXT awoke, the monkey was gone from his thoughts. It had been there for so long, the loss of it was stark. Even so, it was only a monkey. The importance of it not being there was lost on him, but that was the first thing he'd thought about. Strange, for him to think about a monkey when there was so much else to worry about.

Then the totality of what had happened to him took over. He began to shake. It started first in his hands, and as he held them out, he watched it move to his arms.

He'd been blood raped. At the time, that had been the worst thing that he could think of. The very act was an assault on his liberty, his expression as a free citizen of the city, and a Pali Boy. To be blood raped was a reminder of how weak he was, how dispensable he was, and how capricious life had become.

But blood rape, for all of its evil, was nothing compared to monkey-backing. The forced pairing had been an assault on his very humanity, an affront to his ancestors. Forced pairing had made him into something completely different from whom he'd been. He'd tried to stop it, to chase after his sense of self. But try as he might, he'd been completely unable to find a way to retain it.

The monkey's mind had taken control. A flash of him picking the fleas from the back of another monkey surged through him like an electric jolt. And the worst of it... the very worst of it was that he'd loved it.

Kavika bit his lip.

The new combined creation he'd become was something stronger, better. Not human and not monkey, but something other. Something—he bit his lip until it bled—*better*. And it was in that epiphany that his rage was born.

He tried to banish the memories, but the more he tried, the more the memories of the world of trees returned. Soon he found himself speaking the names of his friends; "*Pali Boy,*" he said, and "*Live Large.*" At first he spoke slowly, softly. But his voice grew in strength and confidence. With each repetition, his true self returned a little more.

He slid from his bed. His legs could barely hold him. They buckled twice, but each time he was able to catch himself against the side of the bed. Concentrating on keeping his legs under him, Kavika staggered, one foot in front of the other, towards the opposite bed, where the dead monkey lay. By the time he reached it, he was screaming his mantra.

Its eyes had turned milky. Its hair lay flat and smelled like sweet rotting death. Before he might have felt sorry for it, but not now—not fucking now. Now he only felt hatred and rage. Rage, all day long. Fucking, fucking rage, all fucking day long.

He raised his fists, then brought them down.

Thump—smacking into the dead monkey's flesh.

He screamed the name of Donnie Wu.

Thump!

He screamed the name of Spike.

Thump!

He screamed the name of his father. He screamed the name of every Pali Boy he knew, and then he screamed his own name. And having finally remembered his own name, he latched onto it and screamed it over the over, all the while hammering his fists into the monkey's corpse.

And that's how he was found.

Kaja and Mano didn't stop him, and it was only when he finally slumped to the floor, exhausted and human, that Kaja approached him, lifted him from the floor and held him like a long lost friend who'd finally found his way home.

CHAPTER TWENTY

THREE DAYS LATER, Ivanov let him out. Kavika had been ready after the first day, but the old Russian wanted to make sure he was fit enough to go, to protect himself should he desire to continue antagonizing the Boxers. Kavika had little desire to do so; all he wanted was to make sure his family was okay and find out what had happened to Spike.

Kaja had come by earlier in the morning. He'd brought clean shorts and had returned the hand and feet grips that marked him as a Pali Boy.

"You're Pali," he said. "You've more than proven yourself. I'm proud of you. Your father would have been proud of you."

"But I let them take me."

"You fought them and were overpowered. Look at Akamu. He was older and stronger than you and they got him. What's important is that you survived it."

Kavika then asked about Donnie Wu and discovered that his Uncle's body had been recovered. The Water Dogs had counted more than a hundred and thirty injuries before they'd recycled him.

"They're cannibals, you know," he said grimly.

Kavika stared. "What—who?"

"The People of the Sun. Mr. Pak, the Korean we were talking with and who gave us the false lead, he chewed a piece of Spike away." Even as Kavika said it, he felt bile creep into this throat.

It had taken some convincing, but finally Kaja left to send some of the Pali Boys to check and see. Although the People of the Sun forbade transit, they could still get close.

Kavika changed into clean shorts and went to the hold. His mother and sister weren't there. For a moment he felt a tinge of worry, until Ms. Kwan, his mother's neighbor in the hold, mentioned that they'd moved her up top.

Kaja had indeed moved her. His mother cried when she saw him. He told her that he'd been hurt, but didn't tell her about the monkey-backing. After all, she still held out hope that his sister could be healed; Kavika didn't have the heart to break it to her that the blood rapes and monkey-backing were nothing more than bullshit designed to keep white men alive who should be dead.

He stayed with them for an hour before he felt the pull to leave. Spike had been lurking in the back of his mind since he'd come to his senses. What had happened to her after they'd been attacked by the Boxers on bungees? The Water Dogs hadn't heard from her, and neither had Kaja or the Pali Boys. Which left Lopez-Larou. He was told that she'd been instrumental in helping him escape, but she hadn't hung around once he'd been safely delivered to the Russian. He needed to find her, to talk to her.

When he left, he headed towards the far side of the city. He tested his arms and legs, but didn't trust them to carry him through the sky, so he walked. He didn't particularly like it, but he had no choice. For the first few boat lengths, Pali Boys descended to greet him, welcoming him back to the fold, asking him how he was. He returned the camaraderie, offering embarrassed smiles when they asked why he was walking. They understood; they were just giving him a hard time. It felt good to be teased by them. They were like brothers, and that sort of abuse was always backed by love.

Then he was left alone, walking across the decks of the mad city. It began to drizzle, covering everything in a slick sheen. He stared into the glittering drops, opened his mouth and laughed.

Pele, it was good to be alive.

By the time he reached the ships belonging to *Los Tiburones*, there was a spring in his step. He felt better than he had in an age. A fat Mexican wearing a wife beater and clutching a machete stopped him and asked Kavika his business, and he told him. The guard disappeared for a few moments, then came back and let Kavika pass, with directions on where to find Lopez-Larou.

She saw him first. By the time he registered that it was her, she was running at him. She launched herself the last few feet, her arms entangled his neck and they almost went down. They stayed upright more through her strength than his.

"I was wondering if you were going to come by and see me!" She beamed at him.

Kavika grinned. "They told me what you did. They said you punched one of the women watching over me in the face."

She let go of him. "I did much worse than that. Did you see the ship?"

He shook his head.

She looked positively excited as she said, "The bombs the Vitamin Vs planted went off and damaged the ship worse than anyone could have anticipated. It's threatening to sink. They got Corpers with special hoses and foam trying to keep it afloat. Something about the structural integrity of the city, or some such bullshit."

His mouth dropped open.

"We should get us a bottle of rice wine and go watch it."

He shook his head. "We should, but I need to find Spike. You haven't seen her, have you?"

She stopped smiling and got serious. "Not at all. You weren't hoping I had, were you?" His face fell. "Oh, hell."

Kavika turned around and stared out at the sea of masts and antennae.

"I saw her nailed to the wall. They'd beaten her, hurt her, bit her. I was hoping that maybe someone had found her." A tear leaked from the corner of his eye.

"I want to find her, too. I was hoping you knew something. That maybe we could go together. Kavika, do you think she's still alive? Where'd you see her last?"

"She was hurt—bad. The People of the Sun used her to set a trap."

"The Koreans? Don't you know that they're... Oh, crap. You didn't know."

"I know. They're fucking cannibals."

"You don't think that they'd..." She trailed off.

"I don't know. But Pele help them if they did." He punched his palm. "I can't just assume she's dead."

"You have to see for yourself."

"Yeah." He paused. "We need reinforcements if we're going there," Kavika said as he rubbed his arm muscles. "I'm not as strong as I should be. I don't want to hold you back."

"Nonsense. Let me send out people to check and see if they can determine where she is. I have sources that can go anywhere on the city. If she's still here, they'll find her."

"And if they don't?"

She looked away. "Then she's probably dead."

"And it might be a good thing," he said, looking pained.

"It just might."

She took him to her place. He sat and stared at all the odd equipment while she pressed pills into hands and spoke to various runners in rapid-fire Spanish. Sometime during these exchanges, he leaned back and fell asleep.

He didn't wake until it was dark. At first he didn't know where he was; he sat up and looked around, but nothing looked familiar. There were lots of pillows across the floor, and the walls were covered with shelves, each filled with an assortment of containers.

A sound drew him. He saw a dim orange glow, then a curl of smoke. As his eyes adjusted, the room came more into focus. Behind the glow were a set of eyes, regarding him in a cool manner.

"You sleep deeply, Pali Boy."

At the sound of Lopez-Larou's voice, it all came back to him. He was in what the Pali Boys referred to as the Shark Tank, the home of *Los Tiburones*. More specifically, he was in Lopez-Larou's container.

He wiped his eyes and stretched. "I didn't mean to fall asleep."

"You've been through a lot." The orange glow flared with a sizzle and a pop, and then faded again. "Want some?"

"What is it?"

"A little something to calm you."

Kavika shook his head. "I'm calm enough."

"Suit yourself." They sat for awhile, and then she said, "You talk to your father a lot when you sleep."

Kavika didn't know how to answer that. He polled his mind and remembered scraps of a dream where he and his father were sailing across the sea in a small dingy. "What'd I say?"

"It's not so much what you said, it's how you said it."

"What do you mean?"

"You sounded... well, you sounded like a child."

Kavika smiled with embarrassment. "That's funny, because in my dreams I'm always a child."

The orange glow, a sizzle, a pop. "What happened to him?"

"Died. He was diving the line and didn't make it."

"You mean the anchor line? That line?"

Kavika nodded.

"You guys are *crazy*," she said, drawing the last word out. "Is there anything you won't do?

"Lots." And after a moment, "But I can't think of anything right now."

"How old were you?"

"Nine."

"Ahh. My dad died when I was young, too."

"Was he important?" Realizing how stupid that sounded, he hastened to add, "I mean, did a lot of people count on him?"

"I knew what you meant."

Somehow he could tell she was smiling.

"He ran the drugs from Sonora all the way south to Mexico City and east to the Sea of Cortez."

"Is that a big area?" he asked.

He watched her regard him for a moment, then she laughed softly. "Big enough to hold more than a million people."

Kavika thought about that number. It seemed astronomical, but he had no frame of reference. "Is that a lot?"

"More than a thousand times the amount of people in the city."

Kavika tried to imagine a thousand Kajas or a thousand Donnie Wus and couldn't make it work. "It sounds like he was important." She nodded and puffed again. "My own dad wasn't anything special before the plague, before the Cull."

"What'd he do?"

"He ran tours to the *Arizona*. That was a sunken ship in Honolulu Harbor. He once told me that that ship meant more to him than almost anything else in the world."

"Did he tell you why?"

"It went down in World War II in a place called Pearl Harbor. Do you know what that is?" Seeing her nod, he continued. "It was sunk by the Japanese, who'd surprised everyone by attacking. One thousand, one hundred and eighty-seven men went down into the sea, and none came back. He said that the ship weeps for them. Oil from the hold still seeps up to the surface of the water, even after fifty years."

"Nice story, Pali Boy, but what does that have to do with it being your father's favorite place in the world? I mean, it's a sunken ship, for God's sake."

"I'm not sure. He never told me, you know?" After a moment, "But sometimes I think that he thought of the *Arizona* like our world."

"And all the people gone from our world, do they weep too?"

"My mother told me once that we weren't really in the ocean. She said this was a sea of tears, and we were all that's left."

"Your parents were both romantics."

"What does that mean?"

"That they saw the world for what it could be, or maybe should be, instead of what it really is."

"And what is that?" he asked, rankling a little at her comment. "Not that I really think the ocean is made of tears."

"Easy, Pali Boy." She made the glow one more time, then snuffed it into a bowl. After a moment of arranging her clothes, she stood and came over to sit beside him. "You take things too seriously, you know?" She put her hands on his shoulders and turned him slightly so she could massage the knots out of his neck and shoulders. "What the world really is, is a place where only a stubborn few are left to live. What the world really is, is a place where the dreams of generations were squashed by an invisible disease. What the world really is, is a place where a boy like you can get blood raped and monkey-backed and still survive because people love you. It's a place still run by white men who don't know when it's time to just lay down and fucking die."

Kavika closed his eyes as she massaged his neck. He enjoyed the silence for awhile. Finally he asked, "What happened to your father?"

"He was shot in the back."

His eyes widened. "Do you know who did it?"

"Paco Braun."

He jerked his head back. "*What?*"

"He runs most of the drugs now in the city. I spoke to him this morning."

Kavika took one of her hands and turned towards her. Their eyes met. They were less than a foot apart. "How can you talk to him? Doesn't it make you angry?"

She shook her head. "My father was a bastard. Both of them."

"You had two fathers?" He shook his head in confusion.

"One that made me strong. One that made me smart."

"Which one did Paco Braun kill?"

"He killed the one who made me smart. I killed the other one myself."

"Who is the one that made you strong? The one you killed?"

"He was my real father. He left me in the desert when I was five just to see if God wanted to take me. I was out there for a day and a half before he came back and got me. He acted surprised to see me still alive. But no hugs, no kisses. He just told me to get in the back of our truck and he took me home."

"Really?"

"I never knew my mother," she said, her dull eyes staring at the light coming through the skylight. "Some said he killed her for having me, because I wasn't a boy. Others said that she ran away because he raped her and she couldn't stand for him to touch her. Or that she killed herself."

"Did he never do anything at all for you?"

"He called me Lupita—Little Wolf—and he made me strong."

He stroked her hair. She smelled sweet with a strange musk. "He made you strong so you'd survive. For as big a bastard as he was, he gave that to you."

She buried her face in his shoulder. He felt her tears; a trickle at first, then faster until it was like a summer rain. "Then when he tried to touch me I found a way to kill him. I became the wolf. That's when La Jolla found me."

"My father was a bastard for dying," Kavika offered. "But that's the only thing about him I could ever fault him with. I told you he was a tour guide, right? That's someone who shows other people things that have gone on before or what others have done. After the Cull, he never really stopped. When the Great Lash-up began, he was the one who got all the Hawaiians together. He taught them the old ways. He lifted them up from the decks, not all of them, but a few. He did this to remind them that they'd once been warriors. He did this to give them hope."

"Hope for what?" she asked, her voice hoarse.

"Hope that we'd all somehow survive, because as long as we were defying death every day, then we'd be afraid of nothing when the time came."

"Your father was smart. That sounds like a good plan."

"Except I used to be afraid."

"And you aren't now?"

"I was afraid of what would happen to my family if I died. I was afraid of what everyone would say."

"And now?" she asked again.

"Now I know it doesn't matter. I was monkey-backed and blood raped and I'm here to talk about it. Nothing happened to my family while I was down. Nothing anyone can say to me can equal what that monkey took from me. There's nothing anyone can do to me anymore."

She whispered in his ear. "What the world really is, is a place where a Pali Boy evolved from a boy to a monkey to a man."

Then she kissed him, softly, her lips lingering along his jaw.

"What the world really is," he replied, "is a place where a shark and a Pali Boy can find a little peace before it all turns to shit."

"Is it all going to turn to shit?" she asked, moving down to his neck and kissing it where it joined at his chest.

"Probably." He kissed her forehead. "But we'll find a way to survive it."

"Are you that confident?" she asked, looking into his face. "Or that crazy?"

He smiled. "There really is no difference between the two. Donnie Wu told me it was all a matter of point of view. My confident is your crazy.

He finally kissed her upturned lips. "If you're confident enough, you can get crazy with a shark and survive."

"You sure about that?"

"Watch me."

And he pulled her to him.

CHAPTER TWENTY-ONE

DADDY, WHAT DID you do before the Cull?

I showed tourists the consequences of history.

What's a tourist?

A person who pays to go somewhere so that they can feel bad about their ancestors.

Why would anyone want to do that?

They think they have to. It's a sort of punishment for living life too well.

KAVIKA WOKE QUICKLY. He felt better than he could remember feeling in months. The weight against his left shoulder and ribs told him that Lopez-Larou was still there. The sun had risen. They'd thrown off the covers. He could feel the sweat sheeting his body.

He lay there for as long as he could before his bladder demanded release. Easing her head to the mattress, he got to his feet, went outside, and found a communal bucket.

Turning to go back inside, he found a mountain now blocked his way.

"You're the one who had the monkey." Skin as white as the foam on the waves, chest bare, with an orange and purple mumu around his waist. The man reached out and touched one of the wounds on his side where an umbilical had been attached.

Kavika took a step backwards. "I don't mean any harm."

The vast man shook his head. "You did enough harm with that stunt to cause us trouble for years."

"I don't want to fight."

"You should have thought about that before, but then you were monkey-backed and didn't have a choice." He chuckled dryly. "There's a price on your head, you know."

Kavika glanced around. He could escape if he needed. He just had to make sure that the man's immense hands didn't get hold of him. He squared his shoulders and lifted his chin. "I don't want to fight, but I will if I need to, fat man."

The man's chuckle rumbled through his cavernous torso. "I'll give you this, boy. You got spunk."

"Leave him alone, *Tio*," Lopez-Larou said, leaning against the doorframe of her container and stifling a yawn. "What are you doing here, anyway? Isn't this a little ghetto for you?"

The man smiled. "I just wanted to see who it was that got my niece into bed."

"It could be half the Taos and half the Winkers, and it still wouldn't be any of your business."

"Maybe not, but it would be a notable achievement if that happened. Certainly one way to drum up business. Speaking of, we still need to talk about what you owe me."

"I'm working it out."

"It wasn't your product. I get to decide how you work it out."

Lopez-Larou immediately changed her attitude. "*Tio*, please. Give me until tomorrow."

"What's going to happen between now and then?"

"Anything. Everything." She shrugged and smiled like a niece who knew how to work her favorite uncle. "Just until tomorrow, okay?"

The moment stretched until it seemed as if *Tio* wouldn't agree. Then finally he nodded and lumbered away. When he was gone, Kavika asked, "Was that about the drugs Akamu was carrying? Are you in trouble with this man?"

She nodded. "That was Paco Braun."

Kavika frowned. "He's the one who killed—"

She nodded again. "I tracked the drugs to the Taos. Your friend Kaja sold my product to them."

"Then we'll get the chits or whatever he got for them and give it to Braun."

She shook her head. "That won't do it. He wants the product."

"Why? You were going to sell it anyway, right?"

"Yes, but he *wants* me to fail. He's got... plans for how I repay him."

"Can you still get it?"

"Not in a million years."

"Then what are you going to do?"

"I have no idea," she said, looking at the sky and shaking her head.

An hour later found them on Ivanov's sub. He had a table and chairs arranged on the deck. Breakfast was coffee, biscuits made from seaweed, and pickled fish. Kaja sat in a chair next to him. Oke, Mano and Akani swung idly overhead.

Ivanov beckoned for them to join him. He poured an acrid cup of coffee and sipped the hot liquid.

"Any news about Spike?"

Kaja shook his head. "I've had the boys out looking for signs. Nothing so far."

Ivanov gave Kavika a haunted look.

"What?" Kavika asked.

"Nothing. I just think that if it's been this long, nothing good can come of this."

"I can't *not* look for her." Kavika kept his head down and his voice low to control his emotions. "She'd look for me."

Kaja put a hand on Kavika's shoulder. "We'll figure this out. Don't worry." He wiped his mouth with the back of his other hand and looked around the table. "We haven't found

Kavika's friend, but the boys have discovered a few things."

They all turned toward the zeppelin anchored to the top of the Freedom Ship. It had arrived sometime in the night. It had come and gone perhaps a dozen times in Kavika's life. As a child, he'd thought it was an immense bug, and it scared him. Now it was a mere curiosity. The rumor was that it went out to hunt whales.

Kaja turned to Lopez-Larou. "You told me I should walk the decks sometimes, remember?"

She glanced at Kavika self-consciously, then back at Kaja. "I remember."

"It's amazing what you can see if you only look," Kaja said. "It should have been obvious all along."

"What are you talking about?" Ivanov grumbled.

"Girly here told me I was looking at the world through a hundred-foot lens. She thought I should pay a little more attention. And you know what? It paid off."

"What did you discover?" she asked, chewing on a corner of a biscuit.

"The zeppelin came because the Tao ship is sinking."

"Why? What's the connection?" Kavika asked.

"Not a hundred per cent sure, but there's been a lot of activity both with the Corpers and the Real People since it happened. The Real People spent considerable chits getting people to help save the Tao ship. It's as if it belongs to them."

"Or something on it belongs to them," Lopez-Larou said. "My guess is that the monkey-worshippers run a farm. Like the rice farm run by the slavers, except the Taos weren't harvesting rice."

"They were harvesting blood," Kavika said. "*My* blood."

"There's definitely a stronger connection between the two groups than I'd realised." Kaja turned to Ivanov. "I'm surprised that you weren't aware of this."

Ivanov waved the comment away. "I keep to my own business. As long as I have my missiles, everyone leaves me alone. So it's just me and my Vitamin Vs."

Kaja shook his head. "I think you know more than you let on."

Ivanov grinned like a beast. "I'll always know more than I let on. It's how you survive."

"So what's the zeppelin for?" Kavika asked.

"Isn't that the question? Where does it come from? How is it powered? Who's on it?" Kaja let the questions hang.

"It needs fuel," Ivanov said. "Unless it gets energy from the sun, it has to land to refuel sometime."

"What sort of fuel does a zeppelin use?" Lopez-Larou asked.

"Don't know and don't care," Ivanov grunted.

They sat for awhile, not talking, just eating. The winds were calm, but the gray slab of the sky promised rain. Finally it was Oke that broke the reverie, lowering himself to the deck and padding over. He whispered into Kaja's ear. The Pali leader's head shot up, and he looked at Kavika. The expression on his face was anything but happy. He put down his bowl of fish.

"Come on. We gotta go."

"What is it?" Kavika asked.

"Princess Kamala. She wants to meet you."

Kavika's eyes went wide. No one talked with the princess. As royalty in exile from Hawaii, she was beyond speaking to. In fact, he could count on two hands the number of times he'd seen her in person outside a procession.

"What does she want with me?"

"Don't know." Kaja stood and nodded to Ivanov. "But we need to go."

Kavika had planned to walk, but one look from the Pali leader made him reach out and grab the nearest rigging. Soon he was pulling his way towards the old ship the Hawaiians called home. It felt good to use his muscles, although he could feel his skin pulling at the wounds in his back and side. He had a little trouble with a net, and was forced to hang on with an elbow, lest he fall a hundred feet.

Mano, who was following close behind, probably to help him if he needed it, laughed at him and flashed a shaka as Kavika glanced around to see if anyone had seen. Hanging on with his elbow, Kavika shaka'd back. The sense of belonging that he'd lost when he'd been beaten from the sky had returned, and it filled him with warmth.

They alighted on the deck, and Kaja ran up the stairs to the bridge. Kavika had grown up looking at the black tinted windows his entire life. Never once had he set foot on the bridge, nor did he ever think he would.

An immense Samoan with arms the color of night, thanks to his many tattoos, stood at the top. He let Kaja through. Kavika tried not to look into the gargantuan's snarling face, but he couldn't help it. The guard looked adept at snapping necks and hurling Pali Boys to the deck feet below. But he let Kavika past.

A narrow deck led around the side, the window on the left and the railing on the right. The door onto the bridge stood around the corner. It opened from the inside; Kaja stepped through it and beckoned for Kavika to come in behind him. It took a moment for him to adjust to the relative darkness of the room, so he just followed Kaja's lead. When Kaja bowed, so did Kavika.

Then he saw her. She sat in a large wicker chair with a flared back. Another Samoan stood on her left and a thin elderly Hawaiian stood on her right. She wore her gray hair long. Seeing her was a shock; for some reason he'd always thought of her as young and vibrant, but the woman before him was anything but young. Of course, she couldn't be. Princess Kamala had been with them ever since the Cull. Maybe she'd been a girl then, but now... now she was a grandmother.

"Kaja, is this the one?"

"Yes, Princess." Kaja kept his head down, slightly bowed at the waist when he spoke to her.

Kavika noted that she was staring right at him and that he wasn't in the proper position. He corrected his stance and now stared at her toes, which were each painstakingly painted with a flower, each encircled by a gold or silver ring.

"And you say he was monkey-backed?"

"Yes, Princess."

"But he doesn't look like he was monkey-backed. He looks like any one of your Pali Boys."

"He was Kapono's son."

"That explains much... including his curiosity. How is he feeling now that he's been freed from the monkey?"

"Kavika," Kaja said, "Princess Kamala wants to know how you are feeling."

"Er, do I tell you or her?"

There was a pause as Kaja received direction.

"Tell me," Kaja said. Then to Kavika's unasked question added, "It's just the way it's done."

"Okay, then. I'm actually feeling fine. Maybe a little stiff."

Kavika waited for Kaja to repeat what he'd said, then realized that he wasn't going to when Princess Kamala asked another question.

"When is he going to stop being curious and get back to being a Pali Boy?"

Kavika was taken aback by the question. He turned to Kaja and saw his leader's face crease into a frown. They briefly made eye contact and Kavika saw the unhappiness in the other's eyes.

"I'm not sure I understand the question, Kaja," Kavika said carefully.

"This ship, our people, and this city live in a balance," Princess Kamala said. "Life here is like a surfboard. You know what that is, don't you, Kavika?"

"Yes, I do," he said to Kaja. "My father told me stories."

"So maybe you know that it's very easy to fall off a board by tipping your balance too far to either side or too close to the back or the front."

"Yes. I know this."

"Your curiosity has caused this to happen already. The Tao ship is going to sink."

"But I had nothing to do with that. *They* rescued *me*." Kavika glanced again at Kaja, who had his eyes closed. The princess must not have known that he'd helped.

"There are some who must be sacrificed for the good of the many."

Was she talking about him? Was she upset that he'd survived? But he knew the answer the moment he thought it. Of course she was. It messed up her precious balance. He'd been thrilled and excited to meet the princess, only to discover that she didn't measure up to the legend. That was probably why people hardly ever saw her and she kept herself hidden away on the bridge.

"You also caused us much trouble by attacking the Japanese. I know that Kaja helped you with this. We've already spoken to him about it. But you must not do anything more with them, Kavika. You are not allowed to interact with anyone outside our group."

Not allowed to interact with anyone? Did that mean Lopez-Larou and Spike as well? There was no way he could follow that directive.

"What about the blood rapes? What about the monkey-backing?"

"It's a necessary evil we have to endure if we're to find a cure for Minimata Disease," she said, as if each word weighed more than the last.

"Come on, Princess. We all know that there is no cure. We all know that the blood is for the Real People."

"Kavika," Kaja whispered sharply.

Kavika straightened and shook his head. "No, Kaja. Do you see what she's asking us to do?"

Kaja stood as well and turned to Kavika. "It's what we have to do to survive. Let's face it. There are more of them than there are of us. Don't you want us to survive? Your actions have put us at risk and will put us in greater danger yet."

"My actions?" Kavika scoffed. "What about Keoni and all the other Hawaiians who have been blood raped and monkey-backed? Are we going to sacrifice them for the good of the many, Princess? Are we going to give up our blood for the white people?"

"Do not speak directly to the Princess," commanded the thin Hawaiian on her right.

Kavika turned to the Pali Boy leader. "Kaja," he said, trying to control the indignation in his voice. "You can't possibly be in agreement. She wants us to forget her people, she wants—"

"Silence!" Princess Kamala stood. "Do not presume to know what I want, Pali Boy. I don't want to lose anyone. Each person we lose to this secret I've kept all this time wounds me and the people. When Keoni was monkey-backed, I felt it. When your sister got Minimata, I felt it. When you were monkey-backed, I felt it. I feel it all and it hurts me." She took a step forward, made a fist and held it to Kavika's face. But he stared past this to the tears in her deep brown eyes. "But it would be much worse if the Neo-Clergy came and attacked us. For all the high-flying, death-defying stunts my Pali Boys pull every day, it would be nothing in the face of their weapons. *Nothing.* Do you hear me? We'd all be killed."

She stumbled backwards, the effort to remain standing too much. The Samoan caught her and both he and the other man stared angrily at Kavika.

"And then where would we be?" she asked tiredly.

Her impassioned speech had captured him. He fell to his knees. "Princess, what do you mean, 'Neo-Clergy'? 'Weapons?'"

She was silent for a moment, as if considering something, then she regarded him.

"We are not alone in this world, Kavika. A lot of the people in the city think that this is all that's left of humanity, but let me tell you, we are only a speck in the middle of a great ocean. There are other floating cities and places on land where people still struggle to survive.

"Before the Great Plague, the white men were as plentiful as the fish in the ocean. The Cull was a leveler. It killed off most of them. But like cockroaches, they found a way to survive. They discovered a way to cheat this fate. This is the reality we live with."

"Why did the Japanese let this happen?" Kavika said.

Princess Kamala shook her head. "I've said too much already." She turned again to Kaja, who bowed his head. "Tell Kavika that we *must* remain in balance. Tell him that he does not have my support."

Kavika looked into the princess's face, but she averted her gaze. He got the message. He scooted back a few feet and stood. Kaja tapped him on the shoulder and gestured that it was time to leave. But as he was ushered out the door, he couldn't help but ask, "You knew my father, didn't you, Princess?"

"Yes, boy. And he didn't listen to me either."

Then they were out the door.

Kaja didn't wait for him. He took the stairs two at a time. When Kavika managed to join him halfway across the deck, Kaja game him a walleyed look. "You should have just shut up."

"I couldn't help it. Hey, what'd she mean when she said my father didn't listen to her either?"

"You work it out. I'm too busy right now."

"Busy doing what?"

"Trying to figure out how in the hell I'm going to save your ass when you go and tip the balance again."

"What?" Kavika asked, but he realized he was alone.

Kaja was already swinging away.

CHAPTER TWENTY-TWO

Two hours later he and Lopez-Larou stood beside the ship the Sky Winkers called home, the deck scattered with the viewing chambers that looked like immense smokestacks.

In the meantime, he'd filled her in on what the princess had told him.

"I think she expects you to do something."

"But she told me not to."

"That's not what she said." She'd tapped her finger to his forehead. "You need to listen with this, not just your ears. She said that your father didn't listen to her either, right?"

He'd nodded.

"Two things. How does she know that you aren't going to listen to her? You haven't done anything yet, but she's talking like it's a done deal."

Kavika had nodded again as the truth was laid out. "And the other?"

"That your father had been in a position just like you. Didn't you say he died?"

"Yes, diving the line."

"And were there any strange circumstances about his death?"

"Not that I heard. Do you think—"

She'd shrugged. "I'm not sure what to think, but the Princess seems to have her own ideas."

Now, standing before the Sky Winkers, Kavika tried to come to terms with the idea that something might have intentionally been done to his father.

They boarded the ship and walked towards the first door. It was locked, as were all the others except one. It was strange that the deck was so clear of people. This was probably the only place like that in the city.

They went through the door and found stairs going down into the hold. As they descended, they could see the entire cargo hold. Several large circles of light struck the floor beneath the smokestacks. Men and women huddled in the darkness at the edges of the circles.

They almost tripped over a man resting on the stairs.

"Have you seen Leb?" Kavika asked.

The man lifted a finger and pointed towards midway down the hold.

Kavika and Lopez-Larou made their way through the host of slumbering bodies, taking short-cuts through the middle of the light when they could because it was the only empty space. When they arrived at the right place, Kavika searched for Leb's face. When he saw it, he reached down and shook the man's shoulder.

Leb woke immediately, but at first he didn't recognize Kavika. He got to his feet. He was still wearing his *I Grok Science* shirt, although Kavika imagined it might have been washed at least once or twice since they'd last met.

"*El Gato*," he said. Then to Lopez-Larou, "I don't think that we've been properly introduced. I'm Doctor Timothy Lebbon. Friends call me Leb."

Lopez-Larou exchanged pleasantries, then she asked "What kind of doctor are you?"

"I'm the kind who likes to stare at the sky. It's why I am here."

"*El Gato*?" Kavika asked, interrupting. "Is that 'cat'? Are you calling me a cat?"

"Only because you must have nine lives. We heard about your escape. We were very happy for you, but we don't like what's happening because of it."

"Or like curiosity killed the cat?" Lopez-Larou glanced at Kavika. "Right. Where have you heard that before?"

"Neo-Clergy," said Kavika, simply.

"Ah. Right to it, aren't you?" Leb grabbed Kavika's elbow and pushed him to a place where no one else was near. "What do you want to know about them?"

"For starters... everything."

"Do you mean you've never heard of them?" Leb glanced back and forth to gauge their reactions. "Of course you haven't. What am I thinking? You all are townies. You live your life inside the city."

"And you don't?" Lopez-Larou countered.

"No, we do. But we try not to. Every waking hour we concentrate on communicating out of this place, especially to our satellites in space."

"Yeah. Okay." Lopez-Larou nudged Kavika.

He ignored her. "The Neo-Clergy?"

"Right," Leb said, getting back to it. "The Neo-Clergy goes back to the first days of the Cull. Their full name is the Apostolic Church of the Rediscovered Dawn, but they're commonly referred to as Neo-Clergy. It's a Christian group that relies equally on prayer and automatic weapons. They believe in their own God-given right to survive, and have let no one stand in their way."

"Are they violent?" Kavika asked.

Leb nodded vigorously. "Of the worst kind. Not only are they supremacists, but they take advantage of smaller secluded groups. They've been using Fiji and Guam as farms for more than a decade."

"Farms like they have here with the Mga Taos?" Kavika asked.

"*Had*. Stress the past tense. The monkey ship is going to sink. No doubt about it. The bombs your girl and the Vs used were enough to kill it."

"How'd you know?" Lopez-Larou asked.

"You call us 'Sky Winkers' and you think we're stupid, but we watch everything." He looked back at Kavika, "They use the blood to stay alive. Not all of them need it, mind you, but some of them require transfusions or they'll die. In the early days, they were a little weak on the science – from what we understand, they just took the blood from children – but they forced the surviving scientists at Los Alamitos to work on the problem. Since then, they've devised better ways of harvesting and delivering the Diego antigen to people from blood groups that should be dead."

Kavika shook his head. "Then why are the Japanese involved? Why help the white guys?"

"It's bigger than that now. At first, the Neo-Clergy concentrated on keeping their church members alive, but it's since spread. This city is a cooperative venture between the Japanese Ishihama International Corporation and the Neo-Clergy. The Japanese need the Diego antigen as much as anyone. In this day and age, it's the only chance to survive."

"Jesus," Lopez-Larou said. "It's such a waste. Instead of trying to keep some old men alive, why not concentrate on achieving a decent birthrate? As it stands now, a woman has half a dozen miscarriages before a fetus develops with the proper blood. Why not concentrate on the future instead of the past?"

"Don't kid yourself. That's what the Japanese are doing. Earth is past the point where people are merely trying to survive. Now it's a matter of who ends up on top—who has the highest concentrated population."

"Why does it matter?" Kavika asked. "Why can't we all just live in peace? My father talked about how there used to be world wars. I thought we were beyond that now."

"You would have thought that we were, but national identity survived the Cull. The Japanese want to be on top."

"And to hell with everyone else."

"But don't you see? You're doing the same thing, if less aggressively," Leb said. "You identify yourselves as Hawaiians. Who you are is based on what blood you have. That's what the Cull tried to stop." He put a hand on his own chest. "Take us, for instance. You call us the Sky Winkers. The term has nothing to do with blood. We come from all races. Our identity is based on a shared vision and a thirst for knowledge."

"But how else am I to identify myself?"

"How about as a Pali Boy? Sure, you define being a Pali Boy as being a Hawaiian warrior, but it doesn't have to be that way. If a Spanish or Chinese or Korean wanted to join the Pali Boys, would that be possible?"

"It would mean we'd have to change what a Pali Boy is."

"That's the point, isn't it?" Leb spread his hands wide. "That's the point of all of this. The Cull gave us the opportunity to reset. We don't have to operate under the same parameters. We can redefine ourselves however we want. It's our choice."

"I'm not sure we have the choice you think we do," Kavika said. "As long as the leaders have any say, I'm sure we don't. I can tell you right now that Princess Kamala wants us to remain Hawaiian. It's probably the same for every other group."

Leb grinned madly. "You'd be surprised. If this boat is any indication, we're on a decent track. Although people have aligned themselves by blood and heritage, we've also begun aligning ourselves by interests. Vitamin-Vs"—he gestured towards Lopez-Larou— "*Los Tiburones*. These groups have come together and presented a united front, not because of blood, but because of what they do or believe."

"Back to the Neo-Clergy," reminded Lopez-Larou. "What can we do about them?"

"You've done a hell of a lot already. Sinking the ship, however accidental, is a huge blow to their farming. My guess is that they'll be forced to start over, if not here, then somewhere else. Maybe some other floating city."

"You said that before. Are there other places like this?" Kavika asked.

"Of course there are," Leb nodded. "I mean, not with these dynamics, but there are other floating cities, yes."

"Is that what the zeppelin is for?" Lopez-Larou asked.

Leb touched his nose with his forefinger. "Bingo! But that's all I know about the machine. The Neo-Clergy knows about us and although we don't present any threat to them, they still manage to hide things from us. It's in their nature to be secretive."

Kavika turned to Lopez-Larou. "It'd be bad if the zeppelin brought in more Neo-Clergy." Then a idea dawned on him. "Wait—the Real People *are* Neo-Clergy, aren't they?"

Leb leaned in close. "Of course they are. I mean, what are the odds that so many white folks in one place have the Diego antigen?"

"I see a lot of white people here," Lopez-Larou. "How do we know that *you* don't require blood to survive?"

"Well and honestly put, young lady. Now, you're thinking. But I'm afraid all you have is our word. When the Cull happened, we were aboard the ship the Mga Taos are now using, the one that's sinking. It was a university ship. I was assistant professor of physics. Those you see here"—he spread his arms—"are the surviving faculty and students and their offspring. We lost more than ninety per cent when the Cull hit. A lot of bright minds perished." His face took on a somber expression. "Blood is blood, and it doesn't care if you're smart, stupid, black, white or pinstriped. We are what's left, plain and simple."

"What are we going to do?" Kavika asked, as much of Leb as of himself and Lopez-Larou.

Leb shook his head. "With the Neo-Clergy? I doubt there's much you *can* do."

"But there has to be something." Kavika punched his hand. "The thought that they can get away with this is driving me nuts."

"Outrage is a good fuel for revolutionary fire. Stoke it and see if it catches."

Kavika had no idea what Leb meant. "What?"

"Never mind." Leb waved his hand as if he were erasing the statement. "You just keep your heads down. It's no secret that the Corpers want your head." He patted Kavika's head. "Just make sure yours stays on your shoulders." He looked at Lopez-Larou. "And you, too. Now, off with the both of you. I need my sleep. It's going to be night in a few hours and that's when we get busy."

CHAPTER TWENTY-THREE

AN HOUR LATER they were back in *Los Tiburones* territory. The guards now carried an assortment of machine guns. Kavika had seen machine guns, rifles and pistols before, but only a few at a time; *Los Tiburones* had an arsenal and they weren't afraid to show it. More important was the reason why. Upon returning, Paco Braun sent for Lopez-Larou. Someone called Sanchez Kelly was there as well. He was tall and as lean as razor wire, and his eyes were hidden behind mirrored sunglasses.

"They brought men with guns and body armor," Braun said upon their arrival. There was no question who *they* were.

"We in any danger?" Lopez-Larou asked.

"We'll be ready for them, whatever they try and do." Braun shrugged. "We've pulled back in all the runners. We're closed for business until this is over."

Lopez-Larou narrowed her eyes. "You pulled mine back, too?"

"You weren't around," Braun said, "so I let them know."

"It's not like you had a lot," Kelly remarked.

"But they were mine. How did you know which ones were mine?"

"I could say that I looked for the ones that I rejected, but that would be mean," Braun said, grinning. "Suffice to say I keep track of such things."

"Without business, how am I expected to pay you back?" she asked.

"Good question." Kelly turned to Kavika. "She any good in the sack?"

"What?" Kavika rose on the balls of his feet as anger flared through his cheeks.

"Easy there, Don Ho," Braun laughed. To Kelly, he said, "He sure is a pretty thing when he's mad, isn't he?"

Lopez-Larou fumed, her arms crossed. "Leave it alone, Kavika. All he wants is to get a rise. Other people's misery keeps him from remembering how fat he is."

"Blam!" Kelly said. "A hit!"

Braun gave her a heavy-lidded stare.

"We're going to be on lockdown soon, so if your boyfriend wants to go back to his pack of circus clowns, he needs to get going."

"I'm not staying," she said. "I have something to do."

"You are staying. You're my responsibility and the ghost of your mother would haunt me if I was to let anything happen to you."

"I'm old enough to take care of myself, *Tio*."

"She's right, amigo," Kelly said.

"You just want her clients," Braun said.

"Best to get rid of the competition before they get too big. I didn't do it with you and now look at you. You're the biggest of us all." He smirked. "In business, too."

"Seriously, *Tio*. I'm not staying."

"Fine. Check out a pistol, though. If you're going to be locked out, I want you to have something other than this muscle-head backing you up."

They left Braun and Kelly. Lopez-Larou went to a container used as an armory and selected a 9mm pistol and four magazines.

"Why don't you stay here?" Kavika asked. "It'll be safer."

"Then who's going to take care of you?"

"I can take care of myself," he said, but she wasn't paying attention.

They went to her container, where she packed a bag. They were gone within minutes. Kavika didn't have a place of his own; as a Pali Boy, he slept wherever he wanted. But if there was one place where he knew she'd be safe, it was aboard the submarine. So that's where they headed.

Ivanov gave her a room. It was cramped and smelled like body odor, but then that could describe anywhere in the sub.

Kavika and Lopez-Larou discussed their plans. They needed to check out the People of the Sun for Spike. Although it seemed certain she was dead, Kavika wouldn't rest if there was any chance at all that she wasn't. And if she *was*, he wanted revenge. Mr. Pak, and Abe Lincoln, had set them up. Mr. Pak had had his neck wrung by Wu, but Abe was still alive. The idea that he was still out there, walking around, made Kavika's blood boil. But he and Lopez-Larou agreed that doing anything to Abe Lincoln might be too difficult, especially after Braun's announcement that the zeppelin had brought in more Neo-Clergy with weapons and body armor. How a Pali Boy could succeed in the face of those odds was beyond him.

An hour later they were on the leper ship. Lopez-Larou had several clients who preferred to smoke themselves to sleep, and with the closing of business, they'd be hard-pressed to get fixes. They traded a small bag of marijuana for two sets of clean leper robes. Made of patches from hundreds of different sources, the robes were surprisingly colorful, and they were a lot like the orange robes worn by the Mga Taos in that they could hide every inch of skin if that's what the wearer desired.

The two of them left the leper ship, shrouded in the robes. They ambled along an indirect path to the ships of the People of the Sun, eventually reaching the demarcation line of red-painted rails. They stepped past and continued unhindered, their hoods drawn completely over their heads. They walked hunched over to keep anyone from looking into their faces.

Halfway across the first ship, a man approached them. He

spoke first in Korean, then in rough English. They ignored him, knowing that he wouldn't touch them. He left, furious, but they didn't see any more of him.

Pak had lived on the third ship. Kavika remembered the maze he and Wu had gone through before they'd found Spike. It had been so terrible to see her strung up like that, wounded and helpless.

KAJA WATCHED FROM up high. He had Akani, Oke and Kai with him, just in case. The People of the Sun had made explicit demands that they not use their ships for any stunting, but now that their cannibalism was public, all bets were off.

He glanced over his shoulder at the zeppelin. Its presence meant trouble. Although Kaja couldn't read the future, he knew that something bad was coming, if it wasn't already here. He'd put the Pali Boys on alert and ordered them to travel in pairs. Several of the other groups had closed their doors, including *Los Tiburones*.

He thought of the girl. He'd had his shot when Kavika was monkey-backed; he wondered why he hadn't taken it. He liked the way she handled herself, and she was easy enough on the eyes. Watching them over the last couple of days, he knew that their relationship had changed. The fleeting touches, the stolen looks. Something had definitely happened and he could guess what.

But he was glad that he hadn't tried to get with her. Kavika was a good kid. Princess Kamala liked him, that was clear. Normally she'd command someone to her bidding, but she'd let Kavika have his say, and had then left the door open for him to make his own decision. Secretly, Kaja hoped Kavika would. He hated the status quo. There were problems enough with living aboard a floating city without having a group dedicated to the manipulation and eventual destruction of all the others. Publicly Kaja couldn't afford to do anything about it, but if there was any way he could help Kavika privately, he would.

He caught a movement out of the corner of his eye—Boxers. Kaja counted six of them, all armed with machetes. They were following Kavika and Lopez-Larou. Somehow they must have known the two weren't real lepers beneath the robes.

Kaja slipped back to his Pali Boys.

THEY'D BEEN CURSED at, yelled at, and even spit on. The People of the Sun needed a lesson in politeness. Kavika thought he had it figured out, though. As human-meat eaters, the very idea of a leper sickened them. Lepers were tainted meat. There was probably nothing they hated worse.

All the better. When the next person came toward them, instead of ignoring her like they'd planned, Kavika angled towards her and made retching noises. The young Korean girl's face twisted as she backed away, the idea of leper puke just a little too much for the pretty young cannibal.

They finally came to the door to Pak's container. Lopez-Larou knocked, but there was no answer. Kavika didn't wait; he jerked the curtain aside. It wasn't Pak, but another Korean. Kavika recognized him from the battle at about the same time the man recognized him. His eyes went wide.

There was no one behind him, so Kavika pushed him into the room and knocked him down.

The man tried to ward off Kavika's blows, but Kavika kicked his hands twice, hard. The man began to cry.

"Where is she, you cannibal fuck?" he demanded.

"Please—don't." Fear crumbled the man's face. He held up his hands. "I don't speak good English."

"I don't care, you shit. Who are you? Where is she?" Kavika reared back to kick again, but his target screamed.

"I'm Song. Please leave me alone. I do nothing." Then he raised his voice and screamed in Korean.

Kavika smacked him hard across the face "Help isn't going to get here in time to save you."

Kavika knelt on Song's chest and wrapped a length of rope around his neck. Then he stood, pulled his hood back over his face, jerked Song to his feet and pushed him out in front. To Lopez-Larou he said, "After you."

She shook her head. "No, after *you*."

He pushed back out through the curtain, then whispered in his prisoner's ear. "You are a dog on a leash. Get out of hand and I will pull you back. Understand?" He yanked back on the rope until Song nodded. "Now let's go to her."

Song refused to move.

Kavika punched the side of the man's head and yanked hard on the rope. "Let's go get her."

Song began to take them the same way he'd gone before.

A pair of Korean men turned the corner, saw the trio, and turned and ran.

Kavika glanced at Lopez-Larou. "This is going to be fun. You ready for this?"

"Oh, yeah."

They were once again led through a maze of containers. It was clearly constructed to prevent outsiders from seeing what was going on. The Pali Boys could have just looked inside, but the People of the Sun wouldn't allow transit across their ship and the Pali Boys had respected that desire.

When they turned the final corner, Kavika was ready to see Spike's body. But there was nothing there except for the bloody space on the wall and the pieces of metal that had been hammered through her hands to hold up her body.

"Where is she?" he hissed.

Song pointed to a door in the side wall, all but invisible except for the slightly imperfect seam of the door.

"Open it," Kavika commanded.

Song turned to look behind them, which made Kavika turn. There was nothing there, but Song had been looking for something, or someone. He hoped this wasn't a trap.

Kavika prodded Song, who opened the door. When he tried to step through, Kavika jerked him back. He held the rope tightly and made the Korean close it after the three of them had stepped through. The room was much larger than he'd expected, and it was cold. He glanced around at the shelves and the boxes and realized that this was a walk-in refrigerator.

"Where is she?"

Song pointed to the back corner.

Kavika passed the rope to Lopez-Larou. She grabbed it.

Kavika drew his knife and stepped carefully forward. The place was so vast and there were so many boxes that there was no telling if someone was hiding somewhere and ready to strike.

Long, thick pieces of meat were hanging from the ceiling along the right side wall. It only took a moment before Kavika realized that they were human legs. He felt his bile rise a little, but he held it down.

He turned at the end of an aisle towards the far corner where Song had pointed.

"Over here, Song? Is this where she is?" he asked, loudly enough to make himself heard across the cold, crowded space.

"He's saying yes," Lopez-Larou answered.

Several boxes were stacked on top of each other, as tall as a man. If this was where she was, then there was no hope that she was alive. His gut sank with the knowledge.

"Is she in one of the boxes?"

"He says look behind the boxes."

The space was cramped; he had to turn his body and slide himself past the boxes, almost knocking them over. When he was finally past them, he saw a shelf about waist high. There were a thousand things he'd seen in his life that he'd remember until he died, but the sight of the row of women's heads resting on the shelf was something he wished he'd never seen.

"Did you find her?" Lopez-Larou called.

Kavika opened his mouth, but his voice didn't work. The truth of her death sunk in. He'd known it in his heart for some time now, but had really hoped that he'd been wrong.

"She's here," he said, breathlessly.

"Is she...?" Lopez-Larou asked tightly. His silence answered her. "Oh."

He heard a blow, and a body hitting the floor. In another moment she had joined him, her body pressed into his in the cramped and horrible space.

"Oh, Kavika."

They stared at the face of the boy who'd spent his life trying to be a woman. In death, the muscles and flesh of the face had gone slack; her skin was gray with a hint of blue. All the heads had been shaven, although Spike had kept her head closely shaved anyway, so that her wig would fit snugly against her scalp. Her eyes were open and staring. A single gold earring still hung from her left ear.

Kavika found himself looking around for her wig. He wanted to put it on her head. She'd want to die a woman. But she'd been killed and decapitated somewhere else. It wasn't there. But then it came to him. Like the earring, the wig was nothing more than an affectation, an accoutrement. Spike— or Leilani, which was who she really was—had already achieved what she'd wanted. She *was* a woman, and even in death they couldn't take that away from her. The presence of her head beside those of the other women was an elegiac acknowledgment of a truth that Leilani had spent her last years trying to prove.

"What do we do with her?" Lopez-Larou asked.

"I can't leave her here," he said, his voice cracking.

"Hold on." She slipped back into the main room, then after some rustling, returned with Song's shirt. She tied the sleeves together and held out the material.

Kavika gulped as he reached over and grasped the sides of Leilani's head. Her skin felt strange, more like a piece of overripe fruit than a person. But touching it helped, because he knew now that there was nothing left of her inside. This was not Leilani. This was just a reminder of her, of the life she'd once had.

The refrigerator unit hummed low in the background.

He lifted the head from the shelf and placed it in the fabric, and watched in silence as Lopez-Larou buttoned the shirt and tied the arms together. When she was done, she tied the bundle to her belt underneath her leper's robe. "Now what?" she asked.

"What'd you do with Song? Is he..."

"No. But I should." She glanced at the shelf. "For what he did." She nodded at the heads. "For them."

"Then do it," Kavika murmured.

She looked at him sharply.

"I'm serious," he said. "Do it. Kill him."

"I..." she began to say something, then seemed to change her mind. "Fine." As she turned, she slid a knife from the sheath at her belt.

Kavika followed her and watched as she knelt and placed the point of the blade at the top of Song's spine. He began to scream, but didn't move under the point of the knife, as if he was afraid to get cut. Pressing her other hand against the hilt to steady the blade, she pressed quickly, sinking into the skin and parted the spine. Song screamed once more. There wasn't a twitch. His mouth was locked open.

Kavika felt nothing, standing in the cold container, holding his best friend's head as he watched the deliberate murder, although the lump that had formed in his chest slowly collapsed.

She wiped her blade on the gray hairs of his bare chest, then sheathed it as she stood. "Too good for him, if you ask me."

"Perhaps. But just like taking out the trash or squashing a bug, it had to be done." Then he drew his own knife. "Better keep yours handy," he said holding up blade. "By the way Song was looking, he was expecting company."

"I was afraid of that."

"My guess is that this was supposed to be a trap."

"But the robes?"

"I doubt they'd do us any good now, except get in our way." He removed his and tossed it on the floor.

She did the same. "Do we make a run for it?"

"I'm too damn angry to run, but if you feel you should, I'll make sure they don't come after you."

"But there might not be anyone there."

"There is," he said firmly. The lump in his chest threatened to return. He swallowed hard.

"I don't know how you can be so sure. Anyway, I'm not going. If you're going to stay and fight, then so am I."

"You don't need to."

"Leilani was my friend, too."

Kavika stared at her, remembering the night he'd found them laughing after they'd fought in the morgue ship. He'd just been beaten down and their combined good humor had saved him from doing something stupid. It was a good memory, one that he used now to fuel his anger.

He nodded. "Let me go first." He slipped by her and gripped the inside handle of the door. He was as angry as he had ever been, but there was something else, a detachment that was new. He was above himself, outside of himself. Not the detachment he'd known while monkey-backed, no; more of a combining to become something new. This was a recognition of his anger and his desire to do murder, while embracing a cold, calculating tactical understanding of the situation.

He held his knife in his left hand, low and loose. He jerked the door open, shot his head out, saw what he wanted to see, then pulled the door open all the way.

"There are five of them," he growled, then stepped outside.

Lopez-Larou followed close behind.

In the cul-de-sac, they placed their backs against the wall where Spike had been tortured. Five Boxers awaited them, dressed in their usual mufti, weapons ready. Neither a grin nor a scowl from any of them, just grim faces used to the business of death.

But Kavika wasn't about to let them think this was business as usual. Lopez-Larou was on his left; he feinted to the right to gauge their movements.

They held steady. He dodged left, causing the center Boxer to separate from the others, and ran at the wall to his right. Just before he hit it, he jumped and ran along the wall and swung at the surprised Boxer nearest him, carving a line from his left eye to his right ear. The Boxer fell, blood gushing from his face, smothering a scream.

All four of the Boxers turned toward Kavika, as he alighted on the deck, standing over the body of the fifth.

Lopez-Larou made her move, duplicating Kavika's tactics. She ran right at her target. He expected her to swerve back to the left, as did the Boxers opposite her, who held their ground. It wasn't going to work; he wanted to shout out for her to stop, but he had no time. Her eyes widened as she came to the point where she should change direction. Instead, she launched herself into the air, catching the middle boxer in the jaw. His eyes went blank as he fell to the deck. She turned as she landed, the knife in her hand impaling the forehead of the Boxer standing between her and Kavika.

In no time, they'd changed the odds from five to two to even.

Lopez-Larou staggered, and Kavika caught her. They armed themselves with the fallen Boxers' machetes and advanced together.

The last two Boxers fought desperately, but it was nothing compared to Kavika's and Lopez-Larou's pure outrage exhibited. It was only moments before the five Boxers lay dead or dying on the deck.

They wordlessly dispatched the living, stepped over the bodies, and wound their way back through the maze of false walls and cargo containers. When the maze opened onto the main deck area, they found more Boxers waiting for them.

Fifteen of them, this time.

These had heard the battle and were more reckless. Anger flashed from their eyes. They held their machetes tightly, white-knuckled grips eager to rend and hew.

"Fuck," Lopez-Larou whispered.

Kavika nodded. His thoughts exactly. "Well I guess we're going to have to—"

He never finished his sentence. Kaja appeared on the deck before him, gripping a bungee with one hand and a deck rivet with the other.

"Grab on, brother."

Another two Pali Boys appeared, grabbing onto Kavika and Lopez-Larou. Kaja grabbed Kavika as well, and all five of them sprung into the sky.

The Boxers screamed their frustration in Chinese.

They soared into the rigging, and Kavika reached out with the others and grabbed at the empty bird nets above the ships of the People of the Sun. He held on, then glanced over at Lopez-Larou to make sure she was okay. She was grinning, her anger gone, as was he. They were happy to be alive.

But they weren't done with their revenge just yet.

CHAPTER TWENTY-FOUR

AN HOUR LATER, they were at the morgue ship. Kaja and Ivanov stood by as Kavika presented the head of their dear friend to her brother. The head was still wrapped in Song's shirt. Respecting the somberness of the moment, everyone except for Chito had their heads lowered. Chito stood, straight-shouldered, angry tears trickling over his cheeks.

"Was this all you found?" he asked.

Kavika nodded. He swallowed, trying to find just the right words.

"What happened to her killer?" Chito asked.

"Dead," Lopez-Larou said.

Chito nodded. "Thank you for that."

He took Spike's head and held it to his chest, hands lovingly embracing it. Anguish clouded his eyes. Everyone gave him respectful quiet, each person experiencing the same loss in different degrees. Finally he spoke, his voice low and thick.

"We knew about them."

"What do you mean?" Kavika asked.

"He means that they knew about the cannibals," Ivanov said flatly. "They're Water Dogs. They had to have known."

Chito shook his head. "We don't stop people from doing things. There is so much evidence we find in the water of what other people do to each other. Too much. We... we don't judge people. We let them live."

His voice quavered with barely contained emotion. Kavika blinked away his own tears.

"I could tell you about the murderers and the molesters. We know about evil. Everything ends up in the ocean. Everything."

"Yet you don't do anything," Ivanov said.

"We don't. We never have. It's our contract with the city. Give us everything you have to give us and we'll ask no questions. We take it, remake it, and recycle it."

"And so people like them exist," Lopez-Larou said.

"It's not your fault," Kavika said, feeling the hollowness of the words even as they left his lips. Lopez-Larou gave him a look that told him that she felt the same way. Still, he let the words hang there, if only to comfort Chito.

"No. But it is our fault that they are allowed to continue doing what they are doing." He held the wrapped head to his chin and kissed the fabric. "And now I'm paying for it. Correction—*Spike* paid for it."

"Leilani," corrected Lopez-Larou.

Chito paused; then, as if it had cost him whatever self-control he had, he added, "Leilani." He broke into tears.

Kavika turned to the others. "We have the power to do something, you know?"

"The power to do what, exactly?" Ivanov asked.

"Everything. Anything we want. The Pali Boys own the air and the Water Dogs own the ocean. All that's in dispute is in-between, aboard the decks."

"That's a whole lotta space," Lopez-Larou said.

"Sure, but that's not where the battle needs be fought."

"What battle?" Ivanov seemed vexed. "What are you talking about, boy?"

"What's the greatest fear someone has aboard a ship?"

"Fire," Ivanov said immediately.

Kavika shook his head. "Fire is bad, but you can survive a fire. No—sinking. Sinking is everyone's greatest fear. And who has control of the water? Who is capable of bringing down any ship they desire?"

Lopez-Larou grinned and pointed at Chito. "The Water Dogs."

"You're crazy, boy." Ivanov shook his head.

"Am I? What about all those movies you like to watch? You told me all about *Kelly's Heroes* and how a bunch of misfits no one wanted were able to kill so many Nazis. What about *A Bridge Too Far*? Isn't that one of your favorite movies?"

"Those are just movies," scoffed Ivanov.

"That's not what you said before."

"There was some kind of rational thought behind the plan to save Kavika. Hell, had I known that he'd come back and want to destroy everything we've worked so hard to build, I might have had second thoughts."

"What are we destroying that doesn't deserve to be destroyed?" Kavika turned to address them all. "There's a conspiracy of blood rape and monkey-backing occurring on this ship, that are an affront to humanity. There are cannibals who've been eating our friends and loved ones for Pele knows how long. There are the Real People who have held us hostage in this city just so we can be their private farm animals. Which one of these is something you worked so hard to build? Which one of these things is something you don't want to see destroyed, Ivanov?"

All eyes turned to the Russian and pinned him to the spot. He stood uncomfortably, trying to gauge what support he might have among the others, but none was forthcoming. "I still think you all are trying to bite off more than you can chew. You mentioned *A Bridge Too Far*. Well, this just might be that bridge."

Kavika shrugged. "Then I suppose it is. I suppose we should lie down and take it, right? We should just give up right now. I mean, it isn't so bad, right?"

"What's a little blood rape between friends?" Lopez-Larou said, dryly.

"Yeah," Kavika continued. "What's a dozen people farmed to give blood to the old white folks, except for a way for us to show our appreciation for all they've done for us?"

"Hey Kavika, want to know what I'm looking forward to?" Lopez-Larou asked.

"What?"

"Being eaten, buffet style, by a bunch of nutritionally-challenged Koreans."

Ivanov held up his hands, shaking his head and frowning. "Enough, already. Jesus, but you kids have a black sense of humor."

Kavika gave the Russian a deathly stare. "Who says we're joking? Isn't this what you've worked so hard for? Isn't this what you're unwilling to fight against just because you might not succeed?"

Kaja laid a hand on Kavika's arm. "I think Ivanov agrees, Kavika. He's just cautious. It's probably something they taught him in Russian submarine school."

"Da." Ivanov nodded.

Kavika felt his heart hammering, and his face tingling. He knew his cheeks were red, but there was nothing he could do about it. He'd come a long way from the scared kid he'd been a few weeks ago. Being afraid of failure was no longer an option. There was work to be done, and they needed his energy to keep going.

"What's the plan?"

Kavika looked blankly at Lopez-Larou. He had no idea, but given time, he was sure they'd come up with a doozy.

FOUR HOURS LATER Victor Ivanov returned to his submarine. He was in such a hurry, he cracked both of his knees and an elbow into the piping as he slid into the ship and hurried to his quarters. He needed two things.

First, he needed a bottle. He found it beside the others, freshly distilled and placed in the bottom drawer of his desk. He spun the cap free with two fingers and upended it into his mouth. His throat burned, but it was a good burn. One that reminded him of the Siberian winds twisting on the Kamchatka Peninsula, back when Vladivostok used to be a city. He'd had to pull guard duty for so long in such bad weather that at times it was as if his voice had frozen.

Then he thought of the second thing. It was a wish, rather than a reality. Hell, it really wasn't even a wish. At this point there was nothing to be done about it. Kavika's idea had taken hold with the others. If it had only been the boy, maybe Victor would have done something about it. By now, too many people had been brought into the plan.

He slammed another length of bottle.

Had the status quo been that bad? Sure, there were the unfortunate few who were selected for monkey-backing. And he felt bad for them, he really did, most of the time. But not everyone was destined to make it. Some had to die. What did the Americans say? *You can't make an omelet without breaking a few eggs?*

The boy had come up with a good plan. The ringer for them all had been the zeppelin, but Kaja had devised a way to deal with that, too. There was a balance of power that had remained in the floating city for decades, a balance that had allowed Ivanov to survive despite himself. Now the balance was on the brink of being destroyed. All it needed was for someone to give it a nudge, and that someone looked like it was going to be Kavika.

Victor sat back, holding the bottle to his chest, and thought about everything, past and present. He'd lost his own sense of balance in the universe. His decisions had been formed by relationships and promises he'd been forced to make in order to survive.

Like father like son. Kapono had been the same way. He'd discovered that Victor had been working with the others and had threatened to tell everyone about it. On the outside, Victor had feigned indifference, but on the inside, he'd been worried about the Japanese needing to find someone else to deal with. And as long as they had the grain and potato that he needed to create his absolution, he needed to remain their trusted man.

Kapono was as trusting as his son. Both cut from the same

cloth, both wanting to believe the best of people. Didn't they know that people only showed what they wanted others to see—what they could afford to reveal?

Valeri opened the door and slid into the empty seat across from Victor. He had a cup of steaming coffee, smelling of burned seaweed.

"What are your orders?" he asked.

"Forty degree down bubble and then level off." Victor grinned at the idea of just leaving. He had enough power to go. Even though he had nowhere *to* go it just might be worth it, especially if he could rig some way to see the faces of the Nips when they realised that their secondary power source had disappeared.

Valeri smiled wanly. "If only we could leave. We wanted to years ago."

"We should have," Victor admitted.

"It's really too late for that, I think."

"Nothing's stopping us. We could close the hatch, vent the air, pressurize and dive. There's nothing that could stop us."

"Abe wouldn't appreciate that," Valeri said.

Victor stared at his second in command. "How long have you been—"

"A few years now." Valeri reached out and snatched the bottle of vodka. "None of us have a future here. We're just trying to hold onto what was."

"So you decided to find your own future."

Valeri smiled sadly.

"What happened to chain of command? What happened to following your captain?"

"Don't sound so hurt, Victor. We've ceased to be a ship for some time now."

Victor knew the truth when he heard it. "Why them? Why not the Nips?"

"The Japanese have limited scope. Besides this and another half dozen floating cities, their ability to hold other locations is tenuous at best."

"So The Real People?"

"Rediscovered Dawn. They've been around since The Cull.

They have their fingers in everything. There's nowhere where they don't have someone waiting."

"Waiting for what?" Victor eyed the closed door and noticed that it was locked. Valeri held the coffee in one hand, but his other was hidden beneath the table. "I've spoken to Abe at length, but he's never asked me to do anything on any scale."

"That's because he had me. What does he need with an alcoholic washed-up submarine captain?"

Victor snatched the bottle back from Valeri and took a swig, grimacing. He could feel the coming of the end; he was being out-maneuvered, running out of space.

"So what are *your* orders?" Victor asked.

"Find out what that rag-tag group of yours has decided, then have you foil their plans. The Rediscovered Dawn survive best when people don't know where they are. They are more powerful as an idea than as a reality."

"And you expect me to tell you?"

"Why, of course, Victor. Why wouldn't you?" Valeri smiled maliciously. "After all, we're shipmates."

"What if I was to tell you I am also in the employ of The Rediscovered Dawn?"

Valeri's smile faltered. "You're kidding, right?"

Victor shook his head.

"Then I'd have to ask to see your tattoo."

"Yours first," Victor said through clenched teeth. "Abe doesn't like it when people pretend to be one of us."

For the first time Valeri appeared to be unsure of himself. He placed the coffee on the table, then brought up the hand that had been in his lap. He peeled back the sleeve of his left arm to reveal the symbol of The Rediscovered Dawn. The scarlet semi-circle was vivid against Valeri's white skin.

Victor nodded. "Good. I'd figured he'd convinced you, too, but I couldn't be certain."

"Now you," Valeri said, carefully rolling his sleeve back into place.

Victor adjusted his grip on the bottle. "Hold this," he said.

Valeri leaned forward, reaching for it, but instead of handing the bottle over, Victor brought it around in a savage arc, smashing into the side of Valeri's head without breaking. Valeri slumped sideways on his seat, his head falling against the bulkhead.

Something metallic clattered to the floor. Victor set the bottle down and reached under the table; Valeri had been concealing a knife, the kind formerly worn by Russian marines.

Victor had always regretted doing the Corpers' dirty work and getting rid of Kapono. One of the main reasons he'd taken his boy under his wing was to try and make up for his disloyalty. But now things were coming to a head—he'd made too many deals with too many people, and now he was being asked to choose sides.

Who he'd end up with, he didn't know. He had to take things one at a time. His first order of business was to remove Valeri. Victor hefted the knife, then tested the edge with his thumb. It would do. He pulled Valeri off the chair and onto the floor, and straddled the other man. He had his knife ready, but first he needed to remove some clothing.

Something about dismemberment helped take the edge off.

CHAPTER TWENTY-FIVE

THEIR PLAN WAS equal parts insanity and genius. It required cooperation and trust, something that had been in short supply in the floating city. This was something the Japanese and the Real People had long capitalized on; if they were able to keep people at odds with each other, then they could remain relatively unnoticed as they went about their business. Until Leilani. Her life and death had galvanized the outrage of her friends and family alike, bringing them together in a way that had never occurred before.

Kavika and Lopez-Larou's first stop was the silver and black barge that Donnie Wu had taken him across. Lopez-Larou and Chito had known it was a slaver, but Kaja had had no idea.

"What's a slaver ship doing in the city? Some of our own are working there. I've seen them."

"Wu sort of explained it to me," Kavika said. "Those without family, those with no affiliation, those without living space were sent to the slaver barge, where they indentured themselves of their own free will. In exchange for making rice in the holds and other odd jobs, they were given a place to stay and sustenance. Anything they earned over and above that went to their home ship."

"I can't believe Princess Kamala would allow that," Kaja said.

"Do you really find it so hard to believe, Kaja? After everything she said to me?"

Kaja frowned. "I suppose not. It's just so damn depressing to think that we have to do this to our own people."

The evacuation took place under the cover of the deepest part of the night. Clouds shrouded the moon. Leb opened the doors to the Sky Winkers' ships to allow the evacuees a temporary place to stay. It was important that no one in the zeppelin or Freedom Ship had any idea that the slaver ship was empty; it would be needed later on.

The Water Dogs had their own preparations to make, as did *Los Tiburones*. Kavika didn't envy Lopez-Larou's job. She had to sell the plan to Paco Braun and Sanchez Kelly. Not only was it going to be a dramatic shift in their customer base, but the very nature of the chit would be redefined.

As a part-time Pali Boy, Kavika had never had any use for chits. All of his food, lodging and the everyday things he needed to survive were provided by the Princess and her staff, down to and including medicine for his sister. Sure, he was *aware* of chits, and what they meant to others aboard the floating city, but he'd never thought he'd be in a position to care beyond that.

It was Lopez-Larou who finally explained it to him. Pali Boys, Water Dogs, Sky Winkers and all the other groups had the potential to operate without chits, but *Los Tiburones* were utterly dependent on them. They could provide drugs, but they needed something of value in return. There was enough food to go around, and no-one tolerated hoarding. Drinking water was plentiful, provided by the Freedom Ship and the submarine, which had the means to desalinate seawater.

So *Los Tiburones* had created their own currency. They called them chits. The value of a single chit fluctuated greatly, but converting them was a standardized process. When a chit was cashed, the person who issued it was required to produce a good or service for the benefit of the holder. There was an acknowledgement that a chit could not be cashed if doing so would harm either party—it was too close to blackmail or extortion—but enough chits could indenture the purchaser for a long time. They could be traded from one person to another, but they remained tied to the person who'd issued them. So a chit from Sanchez Kelly, thanks to his notoriety and social status, was more valuable than a chit from someone working aboard a refinery ship and squeezing diesel fuel from oil.

To *Los Tiburones*, chits were everything. And Lopez-Larou had the almost impossible job of selling them an idea that had no worth.

So how was she going to sell it?

One possibility had been to count on the social consciousness of the two kingpins, but that was quickly determined to be a lost cause. Neither Sanchez Kelly nor Paco Braun *had* any social consciousness; there were as likely as not to sell their mothers for a few extra chits.

Another option had been to use their past respect for her father, but that, too, was dismissed. Their respect had been predicated on an understanding of her father's capacity for violence and revenge. Now that La Jolla was dead, the little respect remained was what allowed Lopez-Larou to survive as the proverbial thorn in their sides.

She'd finally settled on laying out the truth. She wasn't smart enough to determine what new form of currency could be used. Perhaps the chit system would survive, even if the value fell. But it was just as likely that something else would surface to replace it. She knew that one could never underestimate the need for people to medicate their lives through drugs, or doubt that desperation would kindle a mechanism for trade.

It was a given that there would be a great upheaval once the plan went into effect. Knowing in advance might enable the drug lords to prepare something. Regardless, their support was needed.

Kavika spent the evening with his mother and sister in their new cargo container. The fresh air and sun had done much to change his mother's demeanor. Color had returned to her skin, her hair shone, and her sad eyes, as she beheld her daughter trembling in the clutches of Minimata Disease, held a new purpose.

Kavika combed his sister's hair and sang to her like he'd done before the disease had attacked her. When he finished, his mother did the same to him. He was too old for such attention, but allowed it anyway, pretending for a few stolen moments that everything was as it used to be.

Near midnight, Kaja came and asked him to follow. Kavika went to ask what it was about, but the Pali Boy leader's stony face promised no response. When they reached the center of the ship, they climbed to the top of the containers. Nine stories up, they could see the lights from all the ships, twinkles of life in an otherwise dark and restless sea. But his attention was fixed on what was at hand. All the Pali Boys were arrayed before them. Never before had Kavika seen them all in one place. There were more than a hundred of them, and to Kavika's utter shock, all of their eyes were on him. For a moment he wanted to bolt and run; the memory of his beat-down from the sky was still fresh. But then he saw everyone's smiles. They seemed happy that he was among them.

"What is this?" he asked.

"A ceremony," Kaja said, motioning for him to come to the center. Lights ringed a man-sized space. An ancient man with ruined legs sat and smiled toothlessly, the tools of a tattooist around him.

"What kind of ceremony? Kaja, what's going on?"

"I've told you that you are now a full-time Pali Boy."

"Even though I haven't made the leap?"

Kaja gave Kavika a sly smile. "Given the chance now, I know you'd have no qualms about making the leap. You've done more than that. You've established your bravery in ways that no one else can compete with."

Kavika lowered his gaze. He felt pride, but he also felt embarrassment, especially now that all the eyes of the Pali Boys were upon him.

"We also want to honor you," Kaja said, his voice carrying

the authority of a leader and loud enough to be heard by all. "We have not always treated you as a brother. There were times when we felt you were living off the notoriety of your father rather than carving your own path through the waves. But that was then and this is now."

"That was then and this is now," said the others in unison.

"You once were beaten from the sky, but that was then and this is now."

The others chorused the phrase.

"You were once just a kid, but that was then and this is now."

"That was then and this is now."

"You are a Pali Boy and a member of a sacred brotherhood."

"Sacred brotherhood."

"Where you go, we will follow."

"We will follow."

"Where we go, you will follow."

"You will follow."

"We are family."

"We are family."

Everyone stared at Kavika as he stood amidst them. His hands were at his sides. His face was red. He tried to meet their gazes, but he found it hard.

"What do you think?" Kaja asked him quietly.

"I don't—I mean, thank you."

Kaja reached out and clasped Kavika's arm.

When they'd finished, Kavika glanced around and asked, "So is this all there is to it?"

Kaja laughed. "He wants to know if this is all there is."

The others laughed with him; some of them nudged each other conspiratorially.

"No, this is not all of it," Kaja told him. "We have a tattoo to provide you. Being a Pali Boy is blood deep, but there are times when seeing is believing."

Kaja guided Kavika to the tattooist. Kavika watched as he cleaned his right shoulder with alcohol, and felt the first needle pricks of the shark bone that was used to create the tattoo. It was simple, but it meant so much: a hand curled into a shaka, the back of a fist with the thumb and pinky finger extended. It was an image of belonging, of instant camaraderie.

When it was all done and his skin was buzzing with the pain, he was asked to stand. The Pali Boys approached him one by one, welcoming with a shaka and embracing him, now brothers forever.

Kaja came after Kavika had met and brothered every Pali Boy and embraced Kavika in the same way. Then he held Kaja at arm's length. "I'm glad that we've done this. It makes me happy and honors your father. He would be proud of you, Kavika."

Kavika felt that pride suffuse him, and a sense of belonging that he'd never known before. But seeing Kaja brought to him another idea, one that would bring him even closer to his father.

"What about that?" Kavika asked, pointing at the dark tattoo line bisecting Kaja's chest from neck to crotch.

"This? This comes from diving the line. Only myself, your father and a few others have done it."

Kavika leaned close to Kaja and whispered "169."

Kaja's face went rigid.

Kavika had thought for so long that he'd dreamed those numbers. He hadn't known what they'd meant until he'd had the chance to relive, over and over, the events that had separated him from the monkey. So much of it had been clothed in his nightmares; where reality ended and began had become an equation that needed to be solved. The numbers had always meant something, and it wasn't until he saw the representation of the anchor cable on Kaja's chest that he'd realized exactly what it was.

"I dove the line," Kavika said. "I dove the line and survived."

Kaja looked uncertain for a moment, glancing at the other Pali Boys. Only those closest had heard the exchange, but they were passing it back to the others. Soon the low rumbling of conversation surrounded them.

Kaja held up his hands.

"Kavika says that he dove the line," he said so everyone could hear.

"Does he have the number?" a Pali Boy asked.

"Yeah, does he have the number?"

"He does," Kaja affirmed.

The cry went up. Pali Boys cheered.

"I didn't know how much you'd remembered of the separation," Kaja said to Kavika.

"I didn't know how much I remembered either. So does this count?"

"You dove the line, didn't you?"

Kavika nodded.

"Then it counts."

This time they had Kavika lie down. The tattoo took hours, and was more painful than the shaka. But eventually a line as wide as a man's thumb began to appear from Kavika's neck all the way to his manhood. He burned with pain, but concentrated on the end state.

When the tattooist was done, Kavika got to his feet, a little wobbly. But when he saw the dark line cutting him in half, it was like he was a different person. He was a Pali Boy. He'd dived the line, one of only a few who'd done it.

But his happiness was short-lived.

The gathering was disturbed by a lean figure climbing atop the containers: Sanchez Kelly.

"They've killed Paco Braun," he announced breathlessly. "They've killed Paco and they've taken Lopez-Larou."

Kavika felt a sense of déjà vu. The last time a friend had been taken, he'd found only her head. This time had to be different.

It just had to be.

CHAPTER TWENTY-SIX

SANCHEZ KELLY LAID it out for them. After Lopez-Larou had come to them with the plan, there'd been much discussion. The drug lords weren't as heartless as one would expect, but they weren't exactly happy about losing their wealth either. Still, they'd been considering a change in their *modus operandi* anyway, something more concrete than the trade in favors. Their idea had been to deal in blood, and sell it to the Corpers for technology, something that was sorely lacking outside the Freedom Ship. In turn, the Corpers would receive a legitimate supply of blood, doing away with the festering resentment caused by the blood rapes.

So Braun and Lopez-Larou had gone to the Freedom Ship with the intention of selling this idea to the Corpers. If they could manage to do it before Kavika's plan went into effect, they'd have a firm commitment from which the Corpers would be hard-pressed to renegotiate.

That is, until the Rediscovered Dawn stuck its nose into the negotiations.

Kelly held out a small video playback device. He pressed a button and they watched as a Japanese man listened, nodding now and again.

"We retrieved it from Braun's body. They just threw him into the lagoon."

"Didn't they know he was recording?" Kaja asked.

"Oh, they knew. You'll see later. The sound went to crap with the water. No way to fix it in time. But it doesn't really matter what they said. You'll get the gist of it."

The camera's point of view looked down slightly on the Japanese man. The conversation went on for several minutes. Occasionally, the camera would turn to Lopez-Larou, on Braun's right. There was an occasional hiss of sound, but nothing recognizable.

Two more Japanese entered the room and began to talk animatedly. The conversation, which had previously been fairly calm, grew more frenetic as the camera turned back and forth to take in everyone present. Lopez-Larou looked worried, and a little frightened.

Then things changed dramatically. All the Japanese turned towards the door as it slammed open and three men strode in. They wore some sort of armor and carried pistols and machine guns of a sort that Kavika had never seen before. They all had blond hair and blue eyes. One of the Japanese men tried to say something, but was silenced by a backhand from one of the new arrivals.

The camera moved frantically for half a minute. No one could make anything out. When the picture finally stabilized, the camera lay on its side at floor level. Lopez-Larou could be seen struggling as she was taken out the door. Then six Boxers filed into the room, grabbed Braun and carried him through the halls to a viewing platform, atop which stood several more armored men. The image jerked as the camera was picked up and carried out behind him. One of the armored men sawed off Braun's head, brought the camera in close to look at him, said something and then threw the head and the camera into the lagoon. The picture tumbled for a moment, then flickered and went black.

Everyone stared at the screen. No one moved.

Kavika was the first to speak. "Son of a bitch," he said, drawing out the words slowly.

No one said anything else for a moment.

"This changes everything," a Pali Boy said.

Kaja shook his head. "No, it changes nothing."

"We can't still go in and take them down," another Pali Boy objected.

"Kavika? What do you think?" Kaja singled out the fresh minted Pali Boy.

"It really doesn't change much, other than we're going to have to save Lopez-Larou, now." Seeing the looks of some of his fellow Pali Boys, he added, "And she does matter. To me. And if she matters to me, then she should matter to you."

"She matters to all of us," Kaja said. "This is more than a matter of Pali Boys against the world. This is *all* of us against the damned Neo-Clergy. And if the Japs are with them, or whoever else, then it's us against them, too." He turned to the Pali Boys. "So where are we with the plan?"

"The slaver ship is clear," someone said.

"How about the Water Dogs? Have they done what they needed to do?"

"We don't know," someone finally said.

"Then find out. Kavika is right. We'll stick with the same plan, but we'll move up the timeline." He turned to Sanchez Kelly. "What's your part in all of this?"

"I was going to let the others do everything and kick back until it was time to take credit," Kelly replied. "But I think now I'd rather see what happens from the front. As much as I had problems with old Fatty Braun, we were friends. If anyone was going to kill him, I was hoping that it would be me. In fact, I'm pretty pissed off that it wasn't."

Kaja shook his head. "You are one strange customer. So what are you going to do?"

"Whatever Lopez-Larou was going to do, I'll do."

Kavika glanced at Kaja, then back to Kelly. "She was supposed to have already done it."

"What?"

"Spike the drinking supply of the Freedom Ship with MDMA."

"Ecstasy? She was going to spike the Corpers' water with love dust?" Kelly laughed. "I'd like to see that. Problem was, she didn't have near enough to make that work."

"She knew that," Kavika said. "She was going to steal yours and Braun's stashes."

Kelly stopped laughing. "I got hold of a bad batch. All I had in stock was dried psilocybin mushrooms."

"Psilo-what?"

"What's that do?" someone asked.

"About the same as LSD. If she managed to get my stash and add it to the MDMA, then it's hippy flipping we go."

"How do we know if she did her part?" Kaja asked.

"I can go back and see if she managed to liberate my drugs, but that wouldn't prove she made it. Isn't there anything else I can do?"

"Do you have any weapons?" Kavika asked.

"Does the pope have a pointy hat? Hell, yeah, I have weapons." Kelly pulled one pistol out of the small of his back and another from beneath his left arm. "I have a small armory back on the ship."

"Then it wouldn't hurt to go back, get the weapons, and arm as many of *Los Tiburones* as possible," Kaja said. "We're about to pick a fight with Neo-Clergy. We're going to need all the help we can get."

Kelly looked around at the sweating faces of the Pali Boys, then put his weapons away. "I'll do what I can." Then he left.

After Kelly had begun climbing down, Kaja turned to Mano. "Go tell Ivanov that the time-table has been moved up. Tell him we attack in an hour."

Mano took off, but instead of climbing down, he leaped out, hands outstretched for a bird net. He caught it, flipped himself on top of it, and was soon swinging away.

CHAPTER TWENTY-SEVEN

THE REAL PEOPLE.

Kavika should have realized, just by the name, that they already believed they were better than everyone else. It was right out in the open and no one even realized it. Or maybe everyone did, and they just didn't care.

And now here they were, standing at the edge of Real People territory. There'd been much talk about the initial strategy. The Water Dogs had wanted to make it a complete surprise attack. They'd argued against giving any advanced notice, claiming that Leilani's death gave them the right to dictate strategy.

But both Ivanov and Kaja had dissuaded them, after almost coming to blows. They reminded the Water Dogs that after the dust cleared, everyone who survived would have to live together once more. If the Water Dogs were known to sink vessels without fair warning, no one in their right mind would ever trust them again. They could never be sure if some imagined slight or minor fishing infraction might lead to the Water Dogs drilling holes in the bottom of their boat. They eventually saw reason.

Kaja was also concerned about losing Pali Boys. He had no doubts that when the proverbial seagull shit hit the fan that some of his boys would die in the ensuing battle, and he wanted to mitigate that as much as possible. Delivering the news that the Real People's chances of success were virtually nil was one of his strategies.

So here they were: Kaja, Kavika, and a dozen Pali Boys. All they were waiting on was Ivanov, who was bringing several of his own men. Together they'd confront the Real People with a unified front.

When Kavika had first met Abe Lincoln, it had been in a neutral location. This was Kavika's first time aboard the Real People's ships. They were comprised mostly of a fleet of fishing vessels, ending at a pair of oil tankers that now stood on their ends. They were rumored to have been placed there on purpose, welded onto the frames of nearby ships and reinforced with steel girders. The Water Dogs had informed them that the decks below the water line were free from water. The ships had also been rebuilt from the inside, constructed like the skyscrapers of old, with the floors running vertically; the Water Dogs didn't know which one held the Real People hierarchy, but there was more movement in the one on the left.

The minutes ticked by.

Finally, Mano came running. He skidded to a stop, out of breath. He didn't look happy.

"What is it?" Kaja asked. "Where is Ivanov?"

"The sub is locked up tight." He shook his head helplessly. "I don't know where he is. No one answers. I knocked for ten minutes."

Kaja and Kavika exchanged glances.

Kavika shook his head. "This can't be good."

"What do we do now?" Mano asked.

All eyes turned to Kaja. He looked worried for a moment, and then shrugged. "What else is there to do? We carry on. We have to." He turned to Kavika. "You ready?"

Kavika nodded.

"Then let's go," Kaja said, stepping over the line and into Real People terrain.

They were all armed with the same weapons. Sheathed knifes adorned their calves, and Escrima sticks jutted across their backs.

Kaja, Kavika and Mano walked on the deck. The other Pali Boys jumped and leaped, sometimes beside them, sometimes behind them. Where they could, they swung from netting, guide ropes or cables. Bungee cords were wrapped around their arms and chest, quickly deployable when needed.

They crossed one boat without any contact. But a solitary man was waiting for them on the second boat.

"You all need to stop here," he said. He stood as tall as Kavika, but was enormously fat. His arms, visible below the straps of a Harley-Davidson muscle shirt, had tattoos of motorcycles and naked women. Some of the tattoos were nothing but dark blotches, their shapes lost to time. A white beard hugged his cheeks, but like Abe Lincoln, he wore no mustache.

"We're here to talk to Abe."

"Abe don't want to talk to you." The man folded his arms.

"He doesn't know that. He doesn't even know what we want."

"What's your name?" Kavika asked.

"They call me Van Buren."

"Well, Van Buren, my uncle used to say you either could be part of the solution or part of the problem."

"What?"

"And I think you're part of the problem."

Kaja made a gesture to one of the Pali Boys, who tapped a companion on the shoulder. They dropped and wrapped bungees around the man's legs; when they rebounded, he came with them.

Kaja laughed. "That's one problem taken care of."

"If only they were all that easy," Kavika said, shaking his head.

They crossed the second ship, seeing movement in the wheel house. The Real People certainly knew they were there.

They finally reached a flat barge where even the wheel house had been removed, as long and as wide as the whole of what the Hawaiians owned. Beyond that stood the inverted ships, and beyond that was the great wide sea.

With nowhere to swing, the dozen Pali Boys came down to the decks. They spread out in a fan on either side of Kaja. Kavika stood on his right, and Mano on his left.

"What now?" Mano asked.

"We could go knock on the door," Kavika suggested.

What had once been the deck of the ship was now the face. Gone was every aspect of a ship, only to be replaced by a flat wall with windows, much like the concrete towers Kavika had seen in vids or in magazines.

Kaja gestured with his chin. "Looks like we won't have to. Look."

Kavika saw Abe Lincoln step out of a door on the left, wearing khaki pants and a yellow plaid shirt. Behind him followed a string of men, all in plaid as well, except for a single man wearing strange black armor.

The last time they'd met, Abe had reached out and offered his hand, but not this time. As they approached, the men with him fanned out, matching the front presented by the Pali Boys. Abe stood in the middle, with the man in black behind him.

Now that the man in black was closer, Kavika could make out armor plates on his arms, torso and thighs. His blonde head was unadorned, except for dark sunglasses and a headset. He held a large machine gun.

The other Real People were weaponless, but they were all tall and wide at the shoulders. Their hands appeared capable of snapping a neck with little effort.

"I thought I sent someone to meet you," Abe said.

"We left him hanging," Kavika said, which drew a few snickers.

Abe pointed imperiously at Kavika. "This one is a known murderer."

Kavika said. "You mean Song? If that's who you mean, then yes, I guess I am."

"He was a family man."

"He was a cannibal."

Abe stared hard at Kavika as if he'd heard that for the first time. Finally, he shook his head. "I don't believe that for a second."

"Believe it or don't," Kavika said. "It's true. I found my friend, or part of her, in his freezer."

Abe waved his hand. "That's hardly a reason to kill someone."

Kavika laughed at the astounding illogic of the conversation. "Eating someone is hardly a reason?"

"We all have to do what we have to do to survive."

"Is that how you justify taking all that blood?" Kaja asked.

Abe shrugged. "You have enough. We only take what we need."

"You don't even ask," Mano said.

"Would you have given it if we had?"

Mano shook his head. "Hell, no!"

"That's why we take it."

"You from the zeppelin?" Kaja asked, pointing to the man in black.

He got no response.

"Pretty big gun."

Still no response.

Then in one swift move, Kaja grabbed Abe and spun him around, putting him in a neck lock and pressing a knife against the Real Person's jugular.

"And this is a pretty big knife," Kaja added.

The man in black raised his machine gun and pointed it directly at Kaja.

All the Pali Boys drew their sticks.

The Real People took a step forward.

"We're all going to remain calm," Kaja said in a loud, even voice.

"Let me go." Abe brought a hand up, but lowered it when Kaja pressed his blade hard enough against his neck to draw blood.

"Not yet. Not until he puts down the gun."

"I'm not putting down the gun," said the man, his accent strange.

"Then I'm going to put an end to your leader."

The man grinned. "He isn't my leader. Go ahead. Kill him if you want."

Abe's eyes went wide. "He's not kidding—he'll kill me!"

Kaja tried not to show his uncertainty, but Kavika knew him too well. The Pali Boy leader hesitated a moment too long. And it seemed as if the strange man knew it too.

He stepped forward and placed the barrel of his machine gun in the center of Abe's forehead.

"So what is it you would like to tell us?" he asked calmly.

"Please, Jacques..."

The stranger cut Abe's plea off. "Please, nothing. These creatures should have been under your control. This confrontation is *not* what we'd planned."

"Did he just call us creatures?" Mano asked incredulously.

"He called *you* a creature," Kavika responded calmly, aware that any false move might start a gunfight. "I don't know what he called *me*."

"You are creature. You are *merde!* You are nothing."

"I hate to differ with you, Jack, but I'm more than nothing. I'm a Pali Boy."

"It's Jacques, *troudoc!*"

Kaja shook his head ever so slightly. "Enough, Kavika. Let's not antagonize the man with the gun, even if it is pressed against another asshole's head."

"Please, what is it you came to say?" Abe asked.

Kaja looked from one end of his men to the other, then into the gunman's face. "I came to tell you that you have one chance to give up. We have the ability to sink every one of your ships and remove the zeppelin from the sky. Your time assaulting our people and stealing our blood is over."

After he spoke, silence fell over everyone for a few moments. Then one of the Real People laughed. Then another. Finally all of them were laughing, even Abe. It was such an unexpected response that Kaja let up on the knife, and Abe slipped free. The stranger removed the barrel of the machine gun from Abe's forehead, and Abe scurried behind him.

When he'd finished laughing, Abe smiled wryly. "What are you going to do with us when we all surrender?"

"What?"

"We have over a hundred and fifty men. I was just wondering what you were going to do with all of us. Do you have a jail? Do you smack our wrists? Do you kill us? I mean, you've thought this through, right?"

"We'll send you on your way."

"How would you do that?"

"There's an unaffiliated ship. We'll untether it and set you adrift."

"I hear a *but* in there somewhere," Abe pressed.

"Well, we never expected you would actually surrender."

"Well, you were right, because we won't. In fact," the older man said as he lifted a hand above his head, "we'd like *you* to surrender instead."

"Us? I don't think—" Kaja stopped mid-sentence as the day was shattered by the sounds of gears grinding.

Great squares of decking on the left and right of them began to rise, revealing a host of other armed men in black, standing on a platform. When they'd reached man height, the men poured out and onto the deck, taking positions all around Kaja and his men. Now they were hopelessly outnumbered—and they had committed the cardinal sin: They'd brought sticks and knives to a gunfight.

Finally a tall figure emerged from the platform. When they saw him, the Pali Boys groaned.

Ivanov.

Although he didn't look happy, his stride was sure. He walked to join Jacques and Abe.

"Hello, Kaja."

"What the fuck, Ivanov?" Kavika demanded.

"I tried to warn you."

"The hell you did," Kaja said. He scowled and shook his head. "What now?"

"Now I do this." Jacques pressed the gun again at Abe's head.

Abe smiled confidently, and Jacques pulled the trigger.

The back of Abe's head exploded, showering Ivanov with blood and bone.

Everyone's jaw dropped... except for the men in black.

Jacques was the first to speak. "I told you. He was incompetent. We don't allow that sort of thing to go unpunished."

"Who the hell *are* you?" Kavika asked.

"I am Major Jacques Chiroc. I am commander of Team Three, Special Operations Group of The Apostolic Church of the Rediscovered Dawn."

Kavika barely heard the words. He was too stunned by the sudden turn and then re-turn of events. All he could do was stare at Ivanov and the blood he now wore like a mourner's cowl.

CHAPTER TWENTY-EIGHT

THEY WERE IN the shit. Fifteen of them were surrounded by about fifty Neo-Clergy, armed with machine guns. Their only hope was that Princess Kamala would come through.

The sun was setting beneath a cloudless sky. Spot lights speared the dusk above the barge, creating pools of light and shifting shadow. The Pali Boys' weapons had been taken and they'd been made to kneel. Kavika, Kaja and Mano were in the middle of the line.

Kavika thought about running, but he couldn't leave his brothers behind, or Lopez-Larou. He'd sworn that he wouldn't let happen to her what had happened to Leilani.

"Check them for the marks," Jacques commanded.

Two Neo-Clergy commandos stepped out of the ranks. One walked behind the first Pali Boy, while another shone a light on his chest. "No marks," said the commando in front.

They moved to the second Pali Boy with the same result.

On the next, the man with the torch called, "Mark here."

Jacques turned to them. "He's been tested and found

wanting. He's no good to us."

Before anyone could ask what that meant, the commando standing behind the Pali Boy – Lukini was his name – withdrew a stiletto and shoved it into the back of his skull.

Kavika watched in shock as they murdered his friend. It had happened so fast, he didn't know how to respond. For a long moment, no one did or said anything; then there was pandemonium.

Several Pali Boys leaped to their feet, only to be struck to the ground with the men's rifle butts. Kaja's eyes were wild; he struggled to stand, but Mano held him down, throwing his body over the Pali Boy leader.

"Can't do nothing now. Wait, Kaja. Just *wait*." It took a few moments, but Mano managed to keep Kaja from getting himself killed.

When everyone settled down, they began to look around at their own chests. They knew the score now. If they'd been tested and not monkey-backed, their blood wasn't useful to The Rediscovered Dawn. If they hadn't been tested, there was still a chance. At least they'd live a little longer. Several of those who'd been tested stared in horror at the blood rape holes in their chests, gingerly touching what was now a death mark.

The commandos came to Mano, Kaja and Kavika, but Jacques waved them off. "We'll save them for last."

They went past them to the end of the line and worked backward. Three more Pali Boys didn't have the mark, but the fourth, who'd become more and more agitated as the men came closer, had been tested. He wept openly, but didn't say a word as the commando standing behind him shoved his stiletto into his skull.

Before the commandos could move onto the next Pali Boy, the one on the other side of him, Liko, rolled to his feet and sprinted for the edge of the barge.

Jacques lazily raised his machine gun and put a three round burst into the Pali Boy's back at the last possible moment. He fell to the water far below, the cloud of blood from the exit wounds drifting after him.

The remaining Pali Boy bared his chest and beat his fists

against it, and in a fit of useless bravado, spit onto the shoes of the commando. The commando kicked him in the face for his effort.

"Now for you three."

Kavika glanced to the side and saw the misery in Mano's eyes; he knew what was coming next.

"You have not been tested," said Jacques to Kaja. "You shall join the rest of the cattle." Then he turned to Mano and Kavika. "But you two, on the other hand, have been tested and have been found wanting."

The commandos moved towards Kavika.

"Wait, Kavika was tested—he has the right kind of blood!" Kaja yelled.

The commandos were in position.

"You don't understand," cried Kaja. "He was monkey-backed. He escaped it."

Jacques shook his head. "There is no escape from it. Our scientists have perfected this filtering treatment. Once connected, there is no more hope for the human host."

"I was monkey-backed," Kavika said, speaking up. "Look at the holes where they had the tubes. See? Here, and here," he said, pointing to the scabbing wounds.

Jacques leaned in close. "We need to study this." He snapped his fingers and pointed at Kavika. "Take this one below." Two of the commandos marched over and grabbed him from behind.

"Wait!" he protested, struggling.

But they weren't listening. One placed his armor-plated forearm across Kavika's throat, wrenching his chin out of the way, and they escorted him across the deck. He didn't want to leave; his friends were there. Who was going to protect Mano?

He heard shouts from behind him. Then a shot. Then another shot.

He tried to get a look before he was dragged below. He managed to see Mano hitting the deck. He could also see Kaja, blood pouring from a wound in his shoulder. Then he was hustled so quickly down a set of metal stairs that he could barely keep his balance.

He passed several dozen Real People, none of them armed; they jumped out of the way of The Rediscovered Dawn commandos. Several of them averted their faces, as if they were afraid to be noticed.

They went down two more flights of stairs until Kavika was certain they had to be below the water level, then they turned and crossed from the barge to one of the skyscraper boats. Cold radiated from the connecting metal hall.

The demarcation between the two ships was stark. Where the barge was darkness and shadows, the new ship was all light and chrome. Kavika felt the thrum of generators beneath his feet; they'd need a lot of power to keep all the lights going. They went down one more set of stairs before they came to a door. The commandos beat against it. After a moment, it was opened by a young Real Person.

"Commander Chiroc wants this one held for later."

The Real Person made a face. "Just a Pali Boy." He shook his head and turned away. "I guess the frog has never seen one before."

Kavika was ushered into a room that opened into a long hallway with barred doors on either side—a jail.

"Never mind what he wants him for. Just make sure nothing happens to him."

They threw him into the first room, and he fell to his knees. The overhead light revealed a thin mattress on the floor and a bucket. He heard the cell door slam and lock behind him. He turned and sat, drawing his knees up and wrapping his arms around them. He felt the cold of the ocean. He felt the cold of his friend's deaths.

So much for his plan.

KAVIKA REALIZED THAT he'd been hearing an irregular tapping noise just below the threshold of hearing. He didn't know how long it had been going on, but now that he concentrated on it, he heard it clearly.

He stood and searched his cell. There was a mattress and pail, and nothing else. The back wall felt colder than the others, though; the ocean had to be on the other side. The cold seeped into his bones. He figured he was down about fifty feet.

He heard the tapping again, louder this time. No, he corrected himself, it wasn't louder, he was closer to the source of the sound. He pressed his ear to the wall and it was louder still.

Then he jerked his head back.

The sound was coming from outside.

It took a moment, but he realized that it could only be the Water Dogs. No-one else had access to the water like they did. Although the commandos were armed for war, he doubted if they'd brought any diving gear. But he reminded himself anything was possible.

He reached out and tapped in turn. Five taps, then four, then three, then two, then one.

The sequence was repeated back to him.

He repeated it back again, then counted to five.

Someone did the same.

"Hey!" Yelled the jailer. "Keep it down in there. No tapping."

Kavika tapped three more times, then stopped. The tapping was all fine, but where would it get him? It wasn't like whoever was on the other side would be able to free him. He started thinking about what had transpired. The deaths of his friends served to demonstrate how serious things were, but the biggest let-down was that Ivanov had turned traitor.

The temperature in the cell was rising, sharply. Sweat beaded on his brow. He could swear that the metal wall had taken on an orange tinge. Orange and now... red. And it was even hotter. Suddenly a rope of flame leaped at him, followed by a stream of sizzling sea water.

Kavika leaped to his feet and backed away. He almost called for help, but stopped himself. The Water Dogs had brought along a cutting torch. They'd somehow tracked him below decks.

Fear and elation coursed through him. He was going to be rescued—if he didn't drown first. He stepped to the side of the arc of light that ate angrily through the metal hull, well aware that when it went, he'd be in the path of a blast of water.

Kavika jumped when jailer came to the cell door.

"What the hell is that noise?" he asked. Then he saw the red-hued wall. "What is that? What have you done to my cell?" The man opened the door, locked it behind him and pocketed the key, then strode towards the wall.

"I don't know how you did this," he began, placing his hands over the red wall and the gushing water, "But—*aiieee!*" His flesh sizzled and burned. He leaped backwards, staring in shock at his blistering hands. Then the wall collapsed inward, sending a disc of metal squarely into his face.

The gushing water was almost impossible to navigate and the cell was filling quickly.

"Help!" came a cracked voice from down the hall.

Was that... "Lopez-Larou?"

"Help me—Kavika? Is that you?"

The jailer was wedged against the cell door. Kavika was already knee deep in water. He dove for the man's pants, latched his fingers around the key and jerked it free, then fumbled with the lock for a moment before opening it.

The water swept them both into the hall.

"Lopez-Larou!"

"Over here."

He had trouble pinpointing the direction. He tripped and flopped down the hall, the water surging past him. He screamed her name again, but there was no response. He peered into the cells; all were empty except the last one, where she was standing against the back wall. When he got inside, he saw she'd been badly beaten. Her lip was torn at one corner and her nose was a bloody pulp. "Come on. I'll get you out of here."

He turned and they fought their way back up the hall. Now the water was knee deep throughout the jail area and rising fast. By the time they got back into his own cell, it was up to his waist. But he was in no hurry. They would have to wait until the entire room filled before they could swim out.

Lopez-Larou opened her eyes and managed a weak smile. "I was hoping you'd save me."

I was hoping I would too, he thought to himself.

He took a deep breath, and before he could tell her to do the same, the water was over their heads.

CHAPTER TWENTY-NINE

KAVIKA PUSHED LOPEZ-LAROU through the gap in the hull first, then followed after her. As soon as they were outside, strong hands grabbed them, and the Water Dogs propelled them forward at great speed using their powerful flippers.

Kavika could feel the pressure building in his lungs. A light grew, ahead of them in the water, until in a hollow rush, he was brought into a diving bell. Two Water Dogs joined him, one holding a Cousteau tube, the other lugging Lopez-Larou.

The distance between the surface of the water and the top of the bell was about five feet. A hose stretched from the top of the bell to the surface somewhere, allowing those inside the chance to catch a breath and depressurize if necessary.

"Get her," he said, his voice echoing in the metal bell as he realized that Lopez-Larou wasn't breathing.

The Water Dogs worked as a team. One supported Lopez-Larou above the water line while the other compressed her chest and pumped air into her lungs.

But there was no response to their efforts. He saw them

glancing at him out of the corners of their eyes.

"Don't stop!" he urged. "Keep trying."

They did as he asked, but it was clear that the more they administered to her, the less chance they thought she had of survival. Maybe she'd been too badly beaten. Maybe she had something broken on the inside. Maybe it had all been too much for her.

They tried to stop again, but Kavika was maniacal about saving her. The inside of the diving bell rang as he screamed at them to resuscitate her.

Then finally she coughed. They turned her head so she could expel the sea water. She brought up gouts of phlegm-laced ocean.

Kavika blazed with relief as he pulled himself over to her. He took her from them and cradled her head against his shoulder.

"Hey... hey, there. Everything's going to be all right now."

Her coughing slowed. Tears bubbled from the corners of her eyes. Finally she said, "They hurt me, Kavika. They hurt me bad." She pulled her shirt down, revealing nine tiny wounds that Kavika knew well.

Rage shot through him. Rage at the pain they'd caused Lopez-Larou. Rage at the murders of his Pali Boys. And rage at the traitorousness of Ivanov.

"They said I could be their donor," she coughed. "They were going to take me back with them. They were going to use me." She coughed again, this time bringing up water.

"That's okay," he whispered. "We'll get them." He shivered with the cold, or anger, or both. "We are going to get them." He held her until she was able to use her legs to support herself in the water, then he turned to the Water Dogs. "Where's Chito? What's the plan?"

The one nearest him had a mole where his nose met his left cheek. "There is no more plan. We're to take you to safety."

So everything had gone to shit. That was just great.

The Water Dogs waited until they were ready, then they propelled them through the water between a series of bells. Twice Kavika thought the distance between them was so far he wouldn't make it, but make it he did. All he had to do was fight against the cold.

Eventually they came to the last bell. This one was made of glass or plastic. Outside, Kavika could see what could only be Ivanov's submarine.

He turned to the Water Dogs. What were they doing? Why had they brought him here?

"Wait," said one.

The other caught his breath, dove and swam to the submarine. He knocked several times against the hull with a piece of metal he pulled from his belt. The effect was immediate. Bubbles shot from the side of the submarine as a torpedo tube opened.

The remaining Water Dog gestured for Lopez-Larou to go inside, but Kavika wasn't having any of it.

"What are you doing? Don't you know that Ivanov turned traitor?"

The Water Dog shook his head. "It's not that way."

Kavika's eyes shot wide. "The hell it isn't! I was standing on the barge when he stood by and watched my friends get stabbed in the brain."

The Water Dog kept shaking his head and acted as if he hadn't heard Kavika. "It is not that way."

"I heard you the first time. Saying it twice doesn't make it true. Where's Chito?" He raised his voice. "I want to talk to Chito."

"He's inside there," said the Water Dog, pointing.

"He's in the sub?" Kavika asked, incredulously.

The Water Dog nodded.

The other Water Dog returned to catch his breath. He gave his compatriot a look, who in turn turned to Kavika.

Kavika's eyes narrowed. "How do I know that you aren't leading us into a trap?"

"Would we free you from the Real People's ship to take you into a trap?"

Kavika felt his concern falter at the logic. Still, he had to be sure. He glanced at Lopez-Larou, who was suffering but stable. "I'm going first," he said, then took a breath and let himself down into the water.

Once under, he swam into the opening of the torpedo tube. This was the second time he'd been in one; he'd been told about the first time, but only remembered flashes of it. Once inside, he waited for something to happen. The tube was large enough to hold two of him if necessary. What were they waiting for? His air was going fast. He felt a buzzing in his brain, taking over all coherent thought. He hammered at the metal door. Then, with a hollow *click* and a *snap,* the water gushed out and the chamber filled with air. In a matter of seconds, the door opened and he was pulled into the torpedo room of the submarine, gasping.

Hands hooked him under his arms and lifted him. It was the muscle-bound Anatoli who helped him to his feet. Chito was there, as was Kirill, the short mechanic who kept the ship running. The yellow light in the room brought out the man's scars, said to have come from an old engine room fire.

"Ivanov sends his regards," Kirill said, tripping slightly over the English consonants.

Behind him, Anatoli and Chito closed the door. Anatoli pressed a button and Kavika'could hear the gush of water as it refilled the tube.

"What do you mean, he sends his regards?"

"He knew you'd be angry. Better let him explain. Just know that he is on your side, not theirs."

Kavika's head spun with the information. How long ago had he made a deal with the Corpers, or The Rediscovered Dawn, or whomever? Whose side was he on, besides his own? "Chito, what's going on?"

The Water Dog smiled grimly. "We knew for a long time that Ivanov was in the employ of the Corpers. We approached him a few years ago. Given the chance, he joined us. We've had a secret cooperative against the Corpers and the Real People ever since."

"And you didn't let me know?"

"Donnie Wu knew. But the information died with him."

"Were you going to tell any of us?"

"We were, but Ivanov felt that you wouldn't understand. He wanted to explain it to you himself. He still takes the death of your father seriously. He blames himself for that."

The tube gurgled behind him, seeming to take an eternity.

Then Kirill pressed a button to clear the water, and in short order they had Lopez-Larou on her feet.

Chito took one look at her. "Let's get her to the med unit."

Kavika carried her down the hall, escorted by the others. When they got there, one bed was already full. Liko lay ensconced in bandages. The last time Kavika had seen him, Jacques had shot him in the back. The Water Dogs must have rescued him and brought him here. His heartbeat, on the monitor by his bed, was slow but steady.

They put Lopez-Larou on another bed. Oleg, the ship's medic, came from behind a curtain and began to work on her. Kavika recognized him as the one who had taken care of him after the monkey had been removed. Oleg pushed Kavika out of the way, working with the brusque efficiency of midwives and nurses.

Kavika watched for a few minutes as they patched her wounds and put salve on her bruises. So much had happened in the last few hours; too much. His thoughts went to Kaja. He couldn't help but wonder what was happening, to him and the surviving Pali Boys. There was nothing else to be done. He had to find a way to rescue them.

Grisha walked into the room, tall and lean, his skin the color of dried fish. "Come with me."

Kavika raised his eyebrows. "What is it?"

"I must introduce you to Dragonov."

Kavika thought he'd met everyone aboard the submarine, and didn't remember anyone called Dragonov.

"Please. You follow. Ivanov has planned this to be."

Kavika thought about all the war movies the old Russian liked to watch, and wondered exactly how long he'd planned for the events of the last twenty-four hours. Finally, he gave in and followed.

They climbed to the top of the conning tower. Petr and Sasha, two deckhands he'd met before, stood staring across the floating city. Petr wore a headset, and Sasha was holding binoculars to his face. Between them was an immense rifle with an angular stock.

"I introduce you," Grisha said proudly, pointing at it. "Dragonov."

"What is it?" Kavika asked.

"It's like the finger of God," Sasha said, without removing his glasses. "It's a sniper rifle from back when we ruled the world."

"We used to rule the world?" Petr asked.

"Yes. At least all the important parts. We gave the throwaways to the Americans."

"That was nice of us to give them so much, *nyet?*" Petr raised his hand. He seemed to be listening for some moments. When he was done, he turned to Kavika. "That was Ivanov. Your friends are still alive. Some. Of the fifteen that went to the ship, six are still alive."

Kavika gulped. "Is that including me, or does that make seven?"

"I'm afraid that's including you."

Kavika let the news sink in. The Hawaiian contingent aboard the Floating City was one of the smallest of them all. *Every* loss was significant. As far as they knew they were the last Hawaiians on the planet.

"What's going on? Where are they?" he asked softly.

"Here," Sasha said, offering the glasses. "Take a look."

Kavika accepted the glasses. It took several tries before he was able to get the full benefit of binocular view. He let Sasha adjust the angle and direction of his view until he focused on the image of his fellow Pali Boys. What he saw made him whistle softly.

They were hanging from chains affixed to a crane on one of the skyscraper ships, a hundred feet above the flat deck of the barge. He focused and brought them in to sharp clarity. In fact, the chains from the crane held up a long metal crossbeam, from which the Pali Boys hung by metal manacles. Kavika named each one of them until he came to Kaja. The leader had been beaten. His lips were like mangled tuna sushi, and both eyes were swollen shut. If it wasn't for the blood that bubbled at the corner of his mouth, Kavika would have thought he was dead.

"What's Ivanov doing now?" he asked.

"Nothing. He's not in a position to do anything other than relay information."

"What do you mean?"

"He's wired. I can hear whatever is going on around him."

"You mean you can hear everything? You can hear Jacques?"

"Yes. That's exactly—wait." Sasha adjusted a knob on the radio attachment on his chest. He acknowledged, then listened for a moment. "Good. Wait for the signal," he said. Then he switched the knob back to where it was. "That was Mr. Kelly. He is ready with Ivanov's part of the original plan."

"The whalers?" Kavika asked, a slow smile beginning to displace his frown.

"Yes. Out of the six, he found four still working, and eleven harpoons. He doesn't think that two of them are close enough to be effective, but there is one that is virtually under the zeppelin."

Kavika swung the binoculars to the Zeppelin, then looked directly below it. He recognized several *Tiburones* moving aboard the ship, their movements slow, never once looking up at the Zeppelin. They knew what they were doing.

He lowered the glasses and handed them back to Sasha. For the first time in a long time, he felt like there was some hope after all. "When's everything set to go?"

"We're waiting for Ivanov to get the commandos into a clear area. Grisha here is an expert at the Dragonov."

"I shoot seals in the arctic." The narrow man rubbed his stomach. "They taste best."

"Do I have time to get my boys ready?" Kavika asked.

Sasha and Petr exchanged glances. "We can't be sure. It all depends."

Kavika grabbed the rail at the top of the conning tower. "Then I need to hurry." He pulled himself up.

"Wait!" Petr shouted. "What are you going to do?"

"Save my Pali Boys. Try not to shoot them when this all starts."

"Here," Petr said, handing him a length of red pipe. "It's a flare. Remove that end, place it on the other, and hammer it against something so that the top is pointed towards the sky. I'll try and hold everything off for as long as I can. You fire this when you're in place and ready."

Kavika took the flare and stashed it in the sheath where his knife should have been. "Give my love to Lopez-Larou," he said.

Then he was over and gone.

CHAPTER THIRTY

ONE AFTER THE other they dove into the oil at the bottom of the barge. It had been on the ship as long as the oldest of them. This was Hawaiian oil, and by Pele and Lono, it would protect them against the commandos of The Rediscovered Dawn.

The Pali Boys were sixty-seven strong. Every full-time and part-time Pali Boy had come. Kavika had stood on top of a cargo container and told them what had happened. He talked about the death of Lukini and the others, as well as Liko's jump and how he was now recuperating in the submarine. At the mention of the deaths, everyone murmured. But at the mention of Liko's dash for freedom, they all cheered. Then Kavika told them about the six left and how they were hanging high above the barge. Many of them had seen this already. Finally, Kavika told them of what the Corpers and the Real People had been doing to them. He told them about the lies and about what the blood rapes were really for and how they could harvest a special plasma of O-Neg blood from those who had been monkey-backed. He told them of the vats of what he believed to be blood he'd seen aboard the Freedom Ship. Then he told them that he knew of a way to save Kaja and the other Pali Boys, and in order to do that, everyone would have to come and join them.

And they came.

Now, as each of them covered himself in oil and marched back up the steps to the deck of the tanker, Kavika couldn't help but stare at the spot where he and his mother had been told to live after the death of his father. He'd come so far, so fast. Part of him felt dishonest, as though he hadn't changed at all, whatever Kaja had said. But another part, a more honest part, felt different in the way that only comes from surviving.

He was the last. He dove into the oil, then he exited. He pulled on his sharkskin foot and hand pads, then joined the rest of the Pali Boys on the deck. The very last thing was securing the flare from where he'd put it before the oil. It rested in the sheath, ready to be used.

Mr. Nakihama got another glass of water from the dispenser. He was more thirsty than he'd been in a long time, as if he'd gone to sleep after two or three bottles of Sake and had just awoken. He stepped into the hall, then leaped back into his doorway.

Mr. Tagahashi skipped down the hall after his secretary.

"How much fun!" Nakihama said.

He stared at the two until they were out of sight. Only then did he notice the colors on the walls. He was pretty sure they used to be white, but now they were striped like a rainbow. The hues were incredible. He especially adored the sea-foam greens and the crème colors. They reminded him of the Fiat 500 he'd had before the Cull. In fact, if they ever returned to Tokyo, it was waiting for him in the parking lot.

Then the air rippled. It was a small ripple, but it was a ripple nonetheless. The ripple disturbed him. He knew that Mr. Tagahashi didn't want any ripples aboard ship. Ripples were not regulation.

Nakihama straightened his tie, as he always did when he thought of his boss, the corporate head and spiritual father of them all. He turned the opposite way and skipped—two steps left, two steps right, two steps left.

"Oh, yes." Skipping was definitely authorized. It felt so good to skip. It felt just right.

LOPEZ-LAROU ROLLED ONTO her side and puked on the floor.

Oleg came to her and wiped her brow with a cold cloth.

"How are you feeling?"

"What? Where am I?" she asked.

"Aboard the submarine. You got beat up."

Beat up. Those two words didn't do it justice. Flashes of the commandos kicking her in the head, chest and gut flashed through her brain until she puked again, the memory too much for her.

"Where's Kavika?"

"The runt Pali Boy?" Oleg shrugged. "Don't know. He went up the hatch to the conning tower and talked to Kirill. Probably going to come back so I can fix him like I fix you."

She rolled back onto her back and watched the ceiling swim for awhile.

Oleg cleaned up her mess, then had her lean forward so he could give her water with electrolytes. After he made sure that she and the wounded Pali Boy were okay, she got out of bed.

Or rather, she fell out of bed. Her feet weren't working so well. It took awhile for her to convince them to work together, but finally she managed a standing position. With the help of every available surface she began the trek to the conning tower. With any luck, she should make it there by Christmas of next year.

IT ALL CAME down to this, and Sanchez Kelly didn't know how he had become the spearhead for this plan. He hadn't even planned on participating, and now he was the man who would strike the first blow.

How the hell had that happened?

Drug dealers do better in the dark. Standing out front was

for soldiers, or liveried policemen. Of course, they were fresh out of soldiers and their number of liveried policemen were at an all time low.

Don't volunteer, his dad had said to him. Volunteering will get you killed, he'd said. Then he'd gone off and joined the IRA and had died in Belfast. Talk about making a point.

Of course, Kelly hadn't really volunteered, this time. He was just asked to do something and he acquiesced. Without even a by-your-fucking-leave, he let them talk him into being the vanguard of a misguided suicide mission.

Kelly did what he always did when he felt a little overwhelmed. He rolled a joint. He took his time. Knowing that the zeppelin was directly above him, he forced himself not to look... which was much harder than it seemed. Like telling someone not to think of a white elephant and now all they think about is a white elephant. Or like saying, don't look at me, and you have to look at that person, even if it was going to get you in trouble. But he'd figured out a way to beat it. He'd poured a glass of water onto the deck near the harpoon gun. The lights of the zeppelin reflected mirror perfect in the puddle, giving him a cheat.

Now rolled, he brought the joint to his lips and lit it. Three short puffs to stoke it, then a deep draft. *Hold it. Hold it. Hold it. Ahhhh.*

He turned to look at the city. He had a chance to be the Head Drug Mama Jama. In fact, if he wanted to, he could probably walk away from the harpoon gun, slink back into his cargo container, safe in *Los Tiburones* territory, and resume business as usual with whoever survived the onslaught. Part of him wanted to do just that.

The light flashed three times, then went dark, then three more times. Everyone was in place.

He walked to the bow of the boat and took off his cowboy hat. He wiped his forehead, then waved the hat three times.

"Yep. That should do it," he said to no one in particular.

Then he turned and walked back to the harpoon. It was covered by a tarp. Leb from the Sky Winkers had ensured him that it was ready to fire. All he had to do was point and shoot.

He heard gunshots in the distance.

It had started.

He took another drag and removed the cover from the harpoon gun.

More gunshots, and now popping noises.

With his left hand, he caressed the gun. According to Leb, this boat had once been a Japanese whaler. The Winker wanker had told a story about small boats like this one chasing whales across the sea and shooting them so that a chosen few could eat some of the meat. Kelly had seen vids of whales. They were like the amiable fat guy who bothered no one. Why someone would want to eat them was beyond him.

The shots were coming fast and furious now. Louder deeper sounds told him that the commandos and Real People were returning fire.

He took another drag on his joint, then placed it behind his ear like a pencil.

That there were people who had hunted the whales into oblivion was a crime worse than any narco-terroristic-murder he'd ever committed. The kind of people he killed were the kind who deserved it. They were bad people who had bad things coming to them. Like those fuckers in the zeppelin.

He swung the harpoon so that it was pointing almost straight up, checked the mechanism, took aim, then pulled the trigger. The harpoon shot true, dragging a cable as it rose, and pierced the body of the zeppelin. An alarm sounded immediately and lights snapped on.

He took the joint out from behind his ear and put it in the corner of his mouth. Puffing softly, he grabbed the cable spool with both hands—it was heavier than he thought; he hoped his stomach wouldn't rupture—lugged it none-too-prettily to the side of the boat, and then dropped it into the sea.

A light from above speared him.

Don't think of a white elephant!

Don't look at me!

He looked at the zeppelin.

The bullet took him through the chest and knocked him back against the gun.

He took another drag on his joint, made a gun with the finger and thumb of his left hand and shot the zeppelin out of the sky.

FIRECRACKERS WERE GOING off!

Hooray! He loved firecrackers!

Mr. Nakihama ran to the window, unlatched it and stuck his head outside. He heard them, but he couldn't see them. Where were they?

Suddenly his vision was filled with what he'd expected—explosions of pink and blue and yellow, showering the Floating City with flowers.

He clapped his hands with glee.

How marvelous that Ishihama International would bring a celebration to this terrible place.

He reached his hand out and brushed one of the explosions. They were so close. If he could only reach farther...

He removed his head from the window and ran into the next room, where he was able to open the door to his deck. He hurried outside and leaped onto the railing, balancing precariously as he cheered the celebration. It was going to be a new day. Perhaps this was the day they were going to return to Tokyo. Perhaps this was their final day amidst the ghetto of the sea peoples.

A brilliant chartreuse pagoda blossomed in the air. He screamed in jubilation as he leaped out and grabbed it. He'd never felt so warm and so good. He loved this pagoda. It was his pagoda and he'd live in it for all time.

GRISHA WATCHED THROUGH the scope of his Dragunov SVD sniper rifle as the Jap leaped to his death, falling atop the mast of a nearby ship. With all that water in the lagoon, it was a mystery how he'd missed it. An even greater mystery was that this was the twentieth person he'd seen jump from the ship.

Grisha chuckled.

There must be one hell of a party going on in there. He

remembered once when he was drinking in Greece, he'd had so much Ouzo he'd woken in a car five kilometers away from their barracks. There had been two dead chickens in the backseat. When he'd finally returned and told Anatoli, the damned Cossack wouldn't let him live it down. People got to calling him *Kooritsa* Grisha, "Chicken Grisha." Grisha guessed he'd gotten hungry from the booze and needed some food. The car lighter had been in his hand when he'd awoken; maybe he'd tried to cook the chickens with that. Regardless, it was a tale of what happened when too much alcohol got into you.

He had to stop watching the ship, however. His job was the commandos. The Draganov had a maximum effective range of 1300 meters—the distance of thirteen football pitches—at which he could knock the center out of a coin with a 7.62 mm round. The commandos were fanned out across the barge surface only 700 meters away. They'd never know what hit them. It would be like the finger of God had come down and tapped them in the head. Not God, though, but rather *Kooritsa* Grisha.

He swung his aiming point around, then counted and prioritized his targets. He let his finger rest against the smooth steel of the trigger and waited.

THE SMALL ARMS fire was becoming a pain in the ass. Worse, the zeppelin had taken a hit. Even as Jacques watched, it lurched and rolled on its axis. Now full, with three years worth of serum from the vats on the ship, it was the only way for them to return to his headquarters in Las Vegas. The loss of the air machine would become a great problem.

When the firing had started, his men had immediately responded, hitting the decks and rolling into combat firing positions. They'd aimed alternately high and low, each assigned an angle and direction, but held their fire until a target presented itself.

Jacques had knelt as well, searching for the source of the firing. It was small arms fire and didn't present much of a problem to their body armor, but they needed to make sure whomever was firing wasn't able to get a lucky headshot.

Pot-shotting.

He'd had the same problem in Denver and in Phoenix. Uppity locals with no sense of their position in the hierarchy, falsely believing that they could attack The Rediscovered Dawn, lawful inheritors of the planet. He'd disabused them of the notion on both occasions, penalizing them by exterminating entire families. It was important that people knew their place in life.

Like the denizens of this ghetto of a floating city. Did they really think that this was their only option? Did they really not know that California lay less than a hundred miles to the east, and offered a much better lifestyle?

As much as he hated the Japanese *troudocs*, Jacque had to give them props. They'd introduced an hegemony in this backwater, making of their ship a nautical Mount Olympus... considering, of course, that the potential for worship was just now blooming in the minds of the subservient populace. Given enough time for two to three generations to pass, the Japanese would become mythological characters in stories and be worshipped by those struggling to survive aboard the surrounding ships.

He'd seen it in Needles, California, where the inhabitants worshipped *The Man Who Walked Between the Rocks*.

He'd seen it in Carefree, Arizona, where the residents of a nursing home were treated as gods—food, gifts and virgins lavished upon them for their goodwill.

He'd seen it in Bombay Beach along the Godforsaken Salton Sea where, much like this place, a family had lived in a houseboat in the middle of the water and were treated like royalty.

He never underestimated a population's requirement to be ruled. He never underestimated their desire to attribute earthly events to the sublime. The more remote and the more removed the people were, the greater their ability to allow themselves to become subjugated by a belief or an ideal.

Yes, the Japs deserved props for what they'd done, especially for establishing a string of serum factories along the coast.

Although the treaty with The Rediscovered Dawn wasn't worth the paper it was written on, they honored it because the Japanese, and Ishihama International in particular, had a product that was in dire need.

A round rang off the deck a few meters from him.

He switched his frequency to the zeppelin. "Find the source of that fire and remove it," he commanded. *Pot-shotters. Merde!*

He had a dozen commandos in the zeppelin. They'd been there to supervise the transfer of serum and guard it, but had found themselves further engaged protecting it from assault from the city. They'd taken out the man who'd fired the harpoon and were tracking the pot-shotters where they could. Intelligence from the ship indicated that the only armed assembly, other than the Russians, were a missmatched group calling themselves *Los Tiburones*—The Sharks. Interesting that drug runners should work together and form a collective. If he had more time, Jacques would have loved to study them.

Where once he'd been an associate professor of anthropology at the University of Montreal, now he was a commander of The Rediscovered Dawn.

Where once he'd been studying the effects of external stimuli on a culture or a society, now he was doing everything he could to exploit and kill them.

Ah, how times had changed.

CHAPTER THIRTY-ONE

THE MOON HAD been eaten by the sky, hiding their figures.
Thanks be to Mother Kapo.

The wind whistled through the rigging, hiding their noise.
Thanks be to Pele.

He whispered prayers to Great Ku, God of War. The word
itself meant *to stand up*, which was what they were doing.
These commandos had been brought in to support the Real
People, all of whom strived to push them down. Ku appeared
in many forms. Sometimes he was an old man weary from war.
Sometimes he was a young man, eager for battle. But tonight
he was Ku-ka-ili-moku. He was the Seizer of Land and the
Protector of King Kamehameha. Ku demanded sacrifices. He
demanded blood. And tonight he would get all these things.

Kavika had climbed the highest of all of them. With his oiled
skin against the blackness of the night and the darkness of
the crane, he was virtually invisible. He moved incrementally,
squinting so to hide the sheen from his eyes.

He could feel Bane, Kai and Mikana behind him. Behind

them climbed two more.

They were carrying *Hoe Leiomano* swords scabbarded across their backs. The blades were two-foot lengths of deadly-sharp steel, and the rubber basket hilts were encrusted with shark teeth, dipped in Takifugu venom, harvested by the Water Dogs. The Takifugu had enough poison to kill thirty men if need be.

Oceanside, thirty Pali Boys climbed the hulls of the inverted ships, armed with bungees and blowguns. Their slender steel darts had flights made from seagull tail feathers and carried Lion Fish spines. The venom of the Lion Fish wasn't like that of the Takifugu: it didn't kill except in massive amounts, but it was the very essence of pain.

He'd reached the spot where he'd be forced to climb along the thin arm of the crane. Looking down, he saw the tops of the heads of the commandos. Ku could have reached out and squeezed their heads. He tried that, but nothing happened.

Two more harpoons struck the zeppelin. Gunfire erupted from the commandos, bullets smashing into the harpoon boats. Splinters of woods danced in the ship lights, but not before the cable reels could be tossed overboard. Just in time too, as the occupants of the zeppelin managed to dislodge the first harpoon. The Water Dogs needed to hurry.

Kavika closed his eyes and shimmied outwards, prayers to Ku and Pele mixing into an improvised mantra. He opened his eyes again halfway along; he'd passed several of his Pali Boys and was nearing where they'd hung Kaja. He reached it and let his body drift off the arm of the crane; when his feet felt the chain, he lowered himself ever-so-slowly so that his movement wouldn't cause a rattle.

He had two bungee cords wrapped around him. He unwrapped one end of one and attached it to the crossbar, tugging on the clip to make sure it was in place, and then tied the other end under Kaja's arms. He unwrapped the other bungee cord and attached it to the crossbar as well, but this one he left attached to his waist.

Once that was done, he paused to check the others. Everyone had made it to their assigned man. It was almost time to use the flare. All that was left was to wait until the rest of the Pali Boys were in place.

"Kavika," came a tired, pain-filled voice.

"Easy now," he whispered. "We'll get you down in a moment."

"Don't get them killed," Kaja said.

"If we die, we die," he whispered. "Remember, Kaja—live large. Now keep it down, or the commandos'll hear us gabbing."

Kavika settled in for a wait, but it turned out he didn't have long. Within minutes he saw the first light flash from the left ship, then a second flash from the right.

It was time.

Just as he was pulling the flare from the knife sheath on his calf, Chito sunk the slaver ship. The grind and squeal of the old barge slipping from its moorings was impossibly loud. It startled him, and he lost his grip on the flare and watched as it fell.

It struck the back of the commando beneath him, who immediately looked up. The man was about to shout something when his attention was caught by the events transpiring on the zeppelin.

Two cables attaching the slaver ship to the Zeppelin snapped taut. The commandos aboard the zeppelin opened fire with all they had, but there was nothing they could do, no matter how many rounds found the ship. Chito, brother of Leilani, was bringing them down.

Two more harpoons fired. One missed its target but wrapped around the tail of the zeppelin, and the other hit it amidships, right where the commandos had been firing. The cables were attached to the ships belonging to the People of the Sun.

The Water Dogs had opened holes in their hulls that were too wide to repair, and the sea was pulling all three ships underwater.

And with them came the zeppelin, drawn inexorably down. Commandos leaped out as it fell, small black specks plummeting to the sea and to the decks of nearby ships. The airship crashed into an old whaler beneath it, the one from which Sanchez Kelly had struck the first blow. The fiberglass vessel splintered and coughed gouts of flame that ate at the canopy of the airship, igniting the hydrogen spilling free from the harpoon-made holes. As it struck the ocean, the zeppelin exploded, sending flames and shards of metal flying in all directions.

A round sizzled by Kavika. He'd temporarily forgotten about the man he'd hit with the flare.

His attention snapped back to the man below him, who was steadying his aim as he prepared to fire another round. Then the commando's head exploded.

Yes—Grisha had come through!

Kavika reached over to the manacles. Just as Sasha had promised, they were designed to be locked, but had just been closed. He glanced at his compatriots. They were ready.

He drew the *Hoe Leiomano* and held it in his right hand; the bungee cord attached to his waist was held loosely in his other hand. With a warrior cry, he pushed himself out and away from Kaja. He had to time it right. The bungee strained to stop him, and at his lowest point, he was still a few feet from the deck. Just as he started to rise, he used the blade of the *Hoe Leiomano* to cut the bungee cord.

Now he was among the commandos.

They were already being shot at by Grisha and his Draganov. Most of their fire was concentrated toward the Russian, although the conning tower of the submarine was really too far away for their rifles.

Los Tiburones had also moved closer. Led by an old friend of Lopez-Larou's, one of her father's old Campesinos named George Ibarra, they were firing from behind metal ship rails. The shots were mostly blind, but they were enough to keep the commandos off balance and a nuisance they couldn't completely ignore. Even though they wore armor, a lucky shot to the head would end them.

On the deck he rolled to his left and brought the *Hoe Leiomano* to bear against the closest commando. The blade slipped harmlessly off the armor of the man's chest, but Kavika followed up with a smash of the shark teeth to his unprotected face. The man's eyes shot wide as the detrodotoxin tore into his bloodstream.

Kavika left him twitching on the deck.

He was taking a step towards his next opponent when a shot took him down.

He heard a scream from far away.

He hoped it wasn't his own.

LOPEZ-LAROU SCREAMED.

Egor had come into the conning tower with a tray of food. But instead of giving anyone anything, he'd jabbed a fork into Sasha's ear, shoved a knife into Petr's back, and had begun beating Grisha over the head with the metal tray.

One minute the big man with the snake tattooed on his bald head had been polite and cordial, then next he'd become a homicidal maniac.

Sasha lay dead, while Petr writhed on the floor, trying to remove the knife from the center of his back.

Egor had ignored her, taking her for the beaten med patient she really was. That had been his mistake. Her scream had been out of surprise, but what she did next came from the heart.

She pulled the knife from Petr's back; it was stuck deep and she was still weak, so it took two pulls. When it came free, she raised it and plunged it into Egor's back. He stiffened and stopped beating on Grisha, who fell to the floor, his face a bloody mess. The metal tray gripped in Egor's right hand was unrecognizable. But instead of going down, he turned slowly to face her.

She backed against the hatch, but it had closed behind her. She didn't have the time or strength to open it. She was weaponless as he came at her.

Petr reached out and grabbed Egor's foot, and the man fell into her, driving all the air out of her stomach. Breathless and ready to vomit from the pain, she couldn't help but go down with him.

She brought her right arm up to ward him off—her left arm trapped along her side—but he was too heavy. His face was mere inches from hers. She did the only thing she could do, opening her mouth and biting into his cheek, gnashing her teeth together as hard as she could.

He roared like a wounded bull and jerked his head upwards. The movement tore his skin and she came away with an oval of meat. She spat it out right before he brought his head down onto hers, creating a galaxy of shooting stars in her head.

He raised and lowered his head again.

Gone were the stars, replaced by a storm of dark, murky pain.

She felt something pressing into her left hand. It was slick and metallic. It took her a moment to figure out what it was.

"You fucking bitch. Stab me, will you?"

So blinded by the pain was she that his words were like liquid, moving with a tide of hurt that seemed to grow and grow and grow.

"I'll teach you to fuck with me."

She felt her clothes ripping.

She wanted to shout, to tell him to stop. But her brain couldn't find her mouth.

Suddenly her left hand found enough space to move. She pulled and it came free. Hardly knowing what she was doing, she rammed it into the first piece of flesh she found. The body on her stiffened, then went slack.

Soon she realized that she was the only one breathing.

When her vision returned, the face of the monster was mere inches from her own. Protruding from his eye was the fork Petr had passed her. The monster's other eye was open, mad, and dead.

She tried to move, but his weight was impossible. She pushed against him. She tried to pry him off with her hands. She tried to move her legs. There was nothing she could do. He was just... too... heavy.

Tears of frustration fell onto her face as she began to beat against his back with her fists.

His left leg burned from the trail of the bullet. It had stitched a line across the side of his left thigh. He was lucky it hadn't hit the bone; as it was, the impact had spun him and knocked him to the deck.

Kavika rolled several feet to his left, then checked the direction the bullet had come from. He watched as Bane buried the blade of his *Hoe Leiomano* into the side of a commando's neck. They locked eyes a moment, then a string of bullets stitched across Bane's front, crimson blotches marring the oil-slicked surface of his skin. He danced backwards and fell to the deck.

Kavika counted seven commandos and three Pali Boys left on their feet, if he included himself, and Ivanov. The Russian was sticking close to Jacques. At first the odds didn't look in their favor, but it was becoming clear that the commandos were running out of ammunition, as they began to toss away their weapons. The Pali Boys had caught a break, thanks to Ku for his intervention. Now the interlopers would have to fight the old fashioned way.

Even as he got to his feet, the seven commandos were gathering into a protective pocket on one end of the barge, dragging a pair of wounded Pali Boys with them.

Kavika called out to his remaining two Pali Boys. "Kai! Keoki! Left and right. Look for an opening."

The two men swung out. Kavika flexed his fingers on the *Hoe Leiomano* and strode down the middle of the barge.

"Jacques Chiroc!" he challenged. "Come and fight me."

He could see the commando leader in the center of his men. By all appearances, he had no intention of coming out. Instead, one of his men separated from the group and took up a fighting stance.

Kavika approached him and said, "One chance. Run now or die."

The commando had a stiletto in one hand, and by the way he held it, it was clear he knew how to use it. "I should give you the same choice." The commando's accent was similar to Jacques. He cut an intricate pattern through the air, raising his other hand to defend himself.

Kavika recognized him as the one who had killed the Pali Boys who'd been previously marked. It was his knife that had gone into the necks of Mano and the others.

When they were separated by ten feet, Kavika took three quick steps, feinted and watched as the other's armor-plated forearm came up to block the blade. But Kavika let the blade slide past and instead grazed the unprotected hand with the shark teeth. Then he backed away.

"Is that all?" the commando asked. "You barely—" His eyes rolled into the back of his head and he fell backward to the deck. His legs rattled for a moment, then stilled.

There were now six commandos left.

"You're going to have to do better than that, Jacques!"

"GET YOUR ASSES out here and help us," Jacques screamed into his headset. He listened for a moment as he watched his man go down, then added, "And bring every fucking gun you have."

"You better ask them to hurry. Kavika looks pissed," Ivanov said, standing behind Jacques.

"You're going to have to do better than that, Jacques!"

The Pali Boy was death incarnate. The intelligence provided about these Hawaiian stuntmen had been severally lacking. Likewise, the information about the group that lived below the water had been almost non-existent. He now regretted killing Abe so quickly. He should have kept the incompetent leader alive so he could see what a tremendous failure he had wrought, including the loss of one of the Monsignor's zeppelins, which was akin to the loss of a national treasure.

"Come out and fight me," chided the Pali Boy.

"They have something on those weapons," the man next to him said.

"Don't you think I realize that? Just don't let them touch you and you'll be okay. Now get out there and hurt the boy."

The commando looked at him with horror-filled eyes. It was a sad thing when his men lost their courage. He'd never seen it happen to his own men before, but he'd witnessed it in his enemies often enough.

He pushed the commando. "I said get out there, soldier!"

The commando reluctantly marched out of the protective circle, which closed behind him. Although it was clear by his features that he didn't want to get anywhere near the Pali Boy, he was too professional not to obey an order.

It was over just as quickly. It looked as if the Pali Boy just walked up, kicked the commando on the top of one knee, then raked his weapon across the back of the commando's neck, causing him to fall down and die.

"You want me to fight you, then put down that weapon of yours."

"This old thing?" Kavika said. "We call it a *Hoe Leiomano*. It's a weapon we've been using for a thousand years."

"What's on it?"

"The poison from a Takifugu."

"And what is a Takifugu?"

"It's a type of pufferfish. Very deadly. Nasty spines."

"Don't you think that's a little unfair?"

"You weren't saying that when your machine guns had bullets."

"*Touché.*" He glanced at the Pali Boys he'd brought with him. One had already died, but the other was still alive, if barely. "Do you want your comrade? There's one still alive here."

"I do. Let him come to me and I promise not to kill you with the *Hoe Leiomano*."

"I'm not thinking that's the best deal I can have."

"Trust me," the Pali Boy said. "It's the *only* deal you are going to get."

Jacques earpiece crackled. He listened for a moment, then smiled. It looked like the Real People had finally found their balls and were coming out to fight.

"You should have offered me a better deal," Jacques said.

IVANOV SUDDENLY MADE his move. "Run, Kavika!" He snapped a garrote over Jaques' head and snapped it tight around his neck. The commando leader's hands shot to his throat, clawing at the garrote, but he couldn't get his fingers under it.

"You killed my friends. You made me help you. Fucking frog."

He wrenched backwards. He'd done something terrible partnering with the Real People, but maybe this would make up for a little of it.

275

His smile vanished as pain exploded in his stomach, opening a hole as wide and deep as the whole wide ocean. He glanced down. Jacques had stabbed him, his hand still on the blade. Ivanov felt his hands weakening.

Jacques pulled free of the garrote and coughed. He turned to face Ivanov, who'd begun to stagger. "For that, I will kill every last man of yours and sink your fucking submarine to the bottom of the sea." He pulled out the stiletto, then shoved it under the Russian's sternum. Life left Ivanov's dull gray eyes.

He watched the old submarine commander fall.

THE DECK OF the barge opened once more, this time releasing a host of Real People. They wore their usual flannel shirts and jeans, and carried rifles, gaff hooks, and clubs. The cavalry had finally arrived.

Kavika shouted for the other two Pali Boys to watch themselves before hitting the deck.

No sooner had the Real People filled the space, than war-cries sounded from behind them. They turned towards the noise.

Like spiders descending on silken strands, the rest of the Pali Boys leaped off the tops of the skyscraper ships. The sight was magical, sixty of them flying with arms outstretched, gripping blow guns in their fists. The bungee cords began to draw tight, slowing them until they were hardly moving, when they brought their blowguns to their mouths and fired the darts dipped in Lion Fish toxin.

The Real People screamed and slapped at the needles as they struck, dropping to the deck, writhing in agony.

About half of the Real People went down in the first attack. The Pali Boys were jerked back upwards. They reloaded when they were at the top of their trip, then fell back down again to finish their enemy off.

"Who the fuck are you?" Jacques whispered hoarsely.

"Pali Boys—do you even know what that stands for, you murdering ass?" Kavika yelled. He glimpsed the flare lying on the deck several feet away. He ran over and grabbed it, removed the lid and fixed it to the base, then aimed it at Jacques. "Now let my boy go."

Jacques's eyes flashed wide and crazy mad. "You'll not have him." He pulled the stiletto free from Ivanov's chest, then plunged it into the Pali Boy at his feet.

Kavika's jaw dropped. "Why did you do that? You can't survive—we've won!"

"It won't be sweet victory," Jacques said with miserable intensity.

Kavika shook his head. Spite—he'd never understood it. It certainly wasn't the Hawaiian way.

He hammered the end of the flare with the blade of his *Hoe Leiomano*. A red star cluster shot free and exploded into the faces of Jacques and his men, and the oil-slicked Pali Boys caught fire beneath them. Those who could ran and fell off the side of the barge; those who couldn't, including Jacques, became pillars of fire, screaming their rage even as the fire ravaged their lungs.

After that, the battle was over. The Real People had no heart to carry one. They threw down their weapons.

The Pali Boys on the bungees cheered.

Los Tiburones cheered.

The Corpers carried on throwing themselves into the lagoon in their happy, trippy night.

And Kavika gave a prayer to Ku. He gave a prayer to Mother Kapo. He gave a prayer to Pele. Then he prayed for the dead Pali Boys.

Kai ran to him. "We did it!"

Kavika nodded. They had.

"What about Kaja and the others?"

"Why don't you get them down? I think they've been up there long enough."

CHAPTER THIRTY-TWO

THE DAYS AFTER The Uprising, as it came to be called, were filled with cleanup, burials and recriminations.

Those that were left of the Real People found sanctuary aboard the Freedom Ship. Their holdings were forfeit. After much debate from the leaders of all the factions, it was decided that the Hawaiians would be given one of the skyscraper ships, while the other went to the surviving Koreans, who'd been plucked from the water after the sinking of their own ship, swearing that only a few of their people had been cannibals.

The flat barge in front of the tall ships would be used as a community meeting place. The floating city had never had one before, which had gone a long way to keeping the groups fractured and isolated. It was agreed that there would be a market there, for selling and trading. In short order, a barter system started to displace the old chit system. More than a few citizens were more than a little relieved.

The Water Dogs resumed their domination of the sea, although citizens were once again allowed to fish directly from their own vessels.

Lopez-Larou became leader of *Los Tiburones*. In the aftermath of The Uprising, it was her people's medical knowledge, and that of the remaining Russians, that had kept many from dying of infection and their wounds. As such, she promised to provide weekly medical assistance at the central market on the barge.

The Vitamin Vs ceased to be known as such. Petr survived Egor's attack and took on the mantle of leadership. He asked that they simply be called Russians, which he felt was a more respectful term, honoring their ancestry. He had a box for Kavika that Victor had left. It was signed Uncle Evil and simply held an old media stick.

Those Mga Taos who survived the sinking of their ship were assimilated into the city. The surviving monkeys took to the heights and began a life of running and jumping and stealing food. The Taos still worshipped the creatures, but in a very different way from before.

The Corpers and the Boxers kept to their ship. What *Los Tiburones* had done to their water supply had shaken them to their core. It could just have easily been poison instead of the *trippy hippy juice*. And their partnership and affiliation with the Real People and the Rediscovered Dawn, and their promotion of blood rapes and monkey-backing, was something the citizens weren't going to forget. They'd asked to be part of the initial meetings, but were told not to show up. For now, the Freedom Ship was a reminder of how things used to be, and a place that if seen, was quickly unseen as citizens went about the daily business of surviving.

The Pali Boys themselves enjoyed a certain notoriety. Where before many of the groups and ships saw them as nothing more than a nuisance, a bunch of boys with nothing to do but cause havoc, now they called them heroes. Wherever they went, they were hailed as such. They knew it wouldn't last, so they enjoyed it while they could.

Kaja had been shot twice during the battle, one bullet shattering his left hip. It would take him months to heal. When he finally did, his chances of ever high flying again were virtually non-existent. Kavika was unilaterally asked to take on the mantel his father had once had, but he declined. The idea of a great wide world had been growing within him. The floating city, which had once been the beginning and end of his universe, now seemed so small.

He waited a month for the city to recover before he decided to go. He asked Lopez-Larou to join him. While she thought about it, he was asked to present himself before Princess Kamala. The distaste he felt for her was palpable, but like it or not, she was their queen, and he felt inclined to obey.

Her retinue acted as if nothing had happened. They were stuck in time. The old man was still there, along with the Samoan. Kavika still found that he was fascinated by her individually painted and ringed toes.

"You defied me," she said.

Kavika noted that she was now speaking directly to him. "I did," he said simply.

"And you think this is good."

"Of course I do. How could it not be good? We were being oppressed and now we aren't. We were being killed and used, and now we aren't."

"I hated every moment of that existence. Whenever one of you was blood raped or monkey-backed, my heart ached."

"Yet you did nothing."

"I did do something. I angered you. You were my hand. You had your own uprising and did what you thought was against my wishes. Had you failed, I could have negotiated with the winners and saved our people."

"You wanted this all along?"

"Of course I did. But I have to admit, I didn't think my Pali Boys would survive. It seems that Wu's and Kapono's plan to create warriors really worked."

At mention of his father, Kavika met the old woman's eyes. "Sometimes being a Pali Boy makes you forget you are a warrior."

She nodded and gathered him in with her eyes. "That's how it is supposed to be. The gamesmanship made you all free spirits. It is how we are, it is what we needed. You've seen the alternative."

She meant the Neo-Clergy commandos. They'd been hardcore opponents and fierce warriors. But at the end, when Jacques had gathered his men around him, they'd been no better prepared for it, and no more loyal.

"Why so complicated, Princess? Why didn't you just tell us what you wanted in the first place?"

"You saw what the world can bring to our city. You saw the dangers. Everything I do means I have to consider these things." She paused to let the words sink in. Then she said, "It's good you are leaving us."

Kavika smiled. "Is that a compliment, or an insult?"

The Princess stood, her painted toes spreading as she put her weight on them and held out her hand.

Kavika accepted it.

"It's a compliment, my Pali Boy. You have become too big for this place. We need you out there."

"Are there more of us out there?"

"There are. We used to be in contact with some of the other cities. It's been awhile, though."

"Maybe I can find them. Maybe I can organize them."

"Your father tried to spread the Pali Boy idea. I don't know if any of it took, but you could see for yourself."

CHAPTER THIRTY-THREE

A WEEK LATER Kavika was ready to go. He'd made sure that his mother and sister would be taken care of forever, and had said his goodbyes. All that was left was to convince Lopez-Larou to come with him, which was proving harder than he'd anticipated.

Finally, standing by a small boat filled with water, dried fish and his weapons, she laid down the reality of the situation. "I can't leave, Kavika. This is what I know. I wouldn't be any good anywhere else." She stared at the water.

"We can find a place. We can figure out what to do when we get wherever we're going."

She shook her head slowly. "But that's you. It's how you approach the world. You're not afraid to go somewhere you've never been and start a new life."

"And you are?"

"Definitely! That you aren't is the mystery to me." She puffed out her cheeks, and blew out. "Normal people don't like change. They want things to remain the same for as long as possible."

"I don't think that's normal at all."

"Your normal and my normal are different." She hugged herself and rocked back on her heels. "Oh, Kavika, I wish you could stay."

He looked long and hard at her. "I can if you want me to."

"I'd love to say that I do, but you wouldn't be happy. I can see it in the way you look at things. You aren't looking at the city anymore; you're looking at the horizon. You want to know what's on the other side."

He smiled wanly. "I can't help it. For so long I was happy not knowing. I didn't know the truth about blood rape. I didn't know about the Neo-Clergy. I didn't know that there's an entire world out there. Now that I do, I can't unknow. Now that I know, I have to know more."

"Where are you going?"

"Anywhere, for now, but eventually I'd like to go to Hawaii."

"You want to visit the *Arizona*, don't you?"

"Yeah," he said, drawing the word out. "I want to see what my father saw in that oil. I want to see the ghosts of who we were."

Lopez-Larou stared at the gray sea.

Kavika stared with her.

"Leb was wrong, you know," she said, eventually. "It *is* about blood. We can't get away from it. Sure, you can join some other group and be some other thing, but who you are, is who you are." She pointed to her jugular. "It's in here. You're Hawaiian by birth and you're your father's son. You'd do anything to remain that way. Wherever you go and whatever you do, you're always going to be a Pali Boy."

He'd been nodding slowly as she spoke. "It doesn't seem like such a bad thing."

"I suppose it isn't. It's a matter of what you do with it."

He turned towards her. "Isn't that always the case?"

She turned to him and smiled weakly. She stared at her feet.

"So I guess this is goodbye then," he said.

She nodded as tears sprung into her eyes, and walked to him, hugging herself.

He embraced her, put his chin on top of her head and

held her to him. Finally, he tilted up her chin and kissed her tear-sodden lips.

"Why don't you put your arms around me?" he asked softly.

"Because if I do, I won't let you go," she said, gripping herself even more tightly.

Kavika nodded. They kissed deeply; she sobbed once or twice.

Finally Kavika stepped away. "I've got to go," he choked.

"I know." She wiped her cheeks with one hand, still hugging herself with the other.

Kavika turned to get into the boat.

"Wait!"

He turned back.

She ran and threw her arms around him.

They hugged for a long while this time. They didn't kiss. They didn't cry. They just stood there, two people being one. Eventually it was time to go, and they parted wordlessly.

He climbed into the boat and began to paddle, heading east. Somewhere at the water's end, California waited. He'd been told about Los Angeles, San Francisco and San Diego. He wondered what sort of people he'd find there. Maybe he'd be like his father and start a new group. Perhaps the Pali Boys of Los Angeles. He'd open it up to all races, although he'd always have a special place for Hawaiians.

Daddy?

What is it, son?

What does it take to be a man?

Willingness to go it alone, to carve your own wave.

It'd been a long time since he'd remembered one of his conversations with his father. He felt now that it would be far longer until he remembered another one, if at all. The media stick that Victor had given him had two things on it. One was a recording of his father's stunts from when his father had been about his own age. The other was an apology from Uncle Evil. Both of them affected Kavika in different ways. He watched them once. He didn't know if he'd ever have the strength to watch them again.

Lopez-Larou called out to Kavika, but her words were lost

to the wind. He dared not turn around. Instead, he offered her a shaka. He held it there for a good long while before he dropped it.

Then he gripped the paddle and set about carving the waves.

THE END

ABOUT THE AUTHOR

WESTON OCHSE is the Bram Stoker Award-winning author of various short stories and novels, including the critically acclaimed *Scarecrow Gods*.

He is much in demand as a speaker at genre conventions and has been chosen as a guest of honour on numerous occasions. As well as writing many novels, Weston has written for comic books, professional writing guides, magazines and anthologies.

Weston lives in Southern Arizona with his wife, the author Yvonne Navarro, and their menagerie of animals. *Blood Ocean* is his second novel for Abaddon Books.

www.westonochse.com